Expelled from the Moon

SCOTT BLAKELY

Published by Philosophers Press

Visit us at Philosophersweb.com

Copyright © 2014 Scott Blakely

All rights reserved.

ISBN-13:9780615986876

DEDICATION

This book is dedicated to my children, Jessica, Jacob, and Jenna, who represent the future.

CONTENTS

ACKNOWLEDGMENTS

I would like to thank my loving wife, Darlene, who has encouraged and most importantly believed in me. She has been my partner in raising our children, and now with her support I have achieved the goal of completing my first novel.

ADHD

"This school is a prison," murmured T.J.

The junior high school was engineered with the most high-tech teaching tools. The walls were a perfect, glowing ivory, without a single window. The ceiling consisted of solid windows that would tint for the sun and only showed clouds or the occasional bird for sensory relief. Comfortable seating and uniforms completed the boredom. The heart of the room was the raised teaching platform where the show was performed, complete with a high definition display that encompassed the entire back wall. This expensive technology was only possible because the institution was also being used as a college during the evenings.

"What was that?" intoned Ms. Wick, the English teacher.

"Nothing," replied T.J., surprised he had said it out loud. Ms. Wick continued with her soliloquy, pointing to the display that burst with definitions as the other children feverishly took notes.

T.J.'s mind wandered as he considered how a college kid's butt might fit into his chair. Did they swap the chairs out at night? How could they accomplish such an effort every day? Where did they store them? He was in eighth grade and this was his second year in the new school. He had explored every inch of it. He had never seen a supply of adult seating, but he could not get past the ridiculous impression of a grown-up butt in his snug seat. Someday, he would figure this riddle out. The lecture droned on while T.J. decided how he would map out the entire school.

With a chime and a pop, English class ended. The doorway appeared and slid open. The class herded out into a hallway that's ambience was an exact opposite of the school's classrooms. It was like walking into a garden, where flowers and trees sprung up randomly along the pathway. Once again, T.J. was struck by the fact that it would take an incredible effort to move all of those chairs through such a hallway. This type of meandering path would not accommodate heavy equipment. T.J. hurried through a doorway, excited for his next class. As the door closed flush to seal them in, he moved to the back of the classroom.

T.J. enjoyed Introduction to Chemistry. While some of the concepts took effort to follow, the teacher, Mr. Troy, always backed them up with incredible lab experiments. Some of the experiments appeared to be magic, such as transforming clear liquids into varying colors when combined. The best ones were when Mr. Troy demonstrated the raw power of science as he had promised to do this day.

"Does anyone know what dry ice is?" began Mr. Troy.

In the front row, Megan raised her hand. "Sure. It's what you put in a cooler to keep it cold."

"Correct, but *what is* dry ice?" responded Mr. Troy. Nobody moved. "Does anyone know what carbon dioxide is?"

This time T.J. raised his hand and answered, "It's what we breathe out."

"Correct, but it is also what is generated whenever something is combusted or burned. Does anyone want to venture a guess at what dry ice is?" There still were no takers. "Well, dry ice is carbon dioxide."

"But carbon dioxide is a gas!" debated T.J.

"Correct! It is typically a gas," agreed Mr. Troy. "Water is a liquid, but it can also take the form of a solid or even a gas. That is what today's lesson is about. Water is the molecule H_2O and is incredibly important to us in its liquid form. It can also become a solid in the form of ice, which can be important if you want to keep your drink cold. If you want an example of how a gas can transform into a liquid, just imagine how rain precipitates from water vapor in clouds."

With gloved hands Mr. Troy held up a steaming block of white ice and placed it on his desk. "Today we will learn about the carbon dioxide molecule.

Its gas form is an essential ingredient for plants to grow through photosynthesis. Plants take carbon dioxide and water, add a little bit of energy from the sun, and make sugars and starch, along with the byproduct oxygen. Without carbon dioxide and photosynthesis, we would not have the basic food source from plants nor the essential oxygen we breathe. So photosynthesis turns carbon dioxide and water into food and oxygen. Who knows what you get when you burn food?"

T.J. blurted out, "You breathe out carbon dioxide."

"Correct. Now what would the reaction be when you burn plants, such as wood?"

Todd raised his hand and replied, "You get carbon dioxide."

"Yes. Plant matter can be burned in oxygen to give off energy plus carbon dioxide and water. Basically, photosynthesis stores energy in the form of plant matter that we can use by burning it; therefore, the ingredients carbon dioxide, oxygen, and water are essential to the energy equation for living organisms. Can someone tell me what Global Warming is?"

Todd raised his hand again and answered. "It is from burning fossil fuels."

"Fossil fuels are burned for their stored energy, and the byproducts are carbon dioxide and water. As an excessive amount of carbon dioxide is added to our air, it can have the effect of raising global temperatures."

"But that carbon dioxide in front of you is cold!" interjected Megan. "If carbon dioxide is cold, then why would there be global warming with more carbon dioxide?"

"Yes. This carbon dioxide in the solid form is very cold, as you will see in the very cool part of our lesson. However, gaseous carbon dioxide can cause the Earth to absorb more of the sun's heat and warm it. Now, let's get to the experiment!

"Carbon dioxide in the gaseous form is an essential component for building life. If gaseous carbon dioxide is compressed and refrigerated, it takes on a liquid form. When compressed liquid is unpressurized, some vaporizes back to gas, rapidly lowering the temperature of the rest of the liquid and turning it to a snow-like form which is compressed into solid dry ice." Mr. Troy motioned for the students to gather around his desk.

3

"Another interesting thing about dry ice is that it sublimates directly from its solid form back to a gaseous form. That is what you see with the dry ice appearing to smoke," Mr. Troy explained.

He broke off a piece of the dry ice and dropped it into the water. Where it hit the water, violent bubbles erupted and a fog appeared to roll onto the desk. "Now what do you see?"

"It's making the water boil," answered Megan.

"It is boiling that you see," agreed Mr. Troy, "but while it looks as if the water is boiling, it is actually the very cold dry ice that is boiling. It sublimates to its gaseous form faster in the relative warmth of the water.

"I should also mention that carbon dioxide in its gaseous form is invisible. Otherwise, why wouldn't you see this fog coming out of my mouth? Can you think of a time when you might experience fog coming out of your mouths?"

Todd raised his hand and answered, "It does on a cold day when we breathe out."

"Correct," applauded Mr. Troy, "but in both cases the carbon dioxide is *still* an invisible gas. What other molecule might comprise this fog then?"

Nobody answered until Mr. Troy added, "It might be right here in front of you."

T.J. volunteered, "Is it water?"

"It is!" exclaimed Mr. Troy. "The cold but invisible vapors of carbon dioxide given off from the dry ice condense water vapor in the air making a cool fog effect." As Mr. Troy dropped more pieces of dry ice into the water, the boiling intensified and a fog covered his whole desk and the experiment.

"Now we come to the best part of the experiment. I will make a dry ice bomb." Mr. Troy adamantly asked the students to return to the safety of their seats. "Keep your heads down, but also watch closely!"

T.J. was enthralled with this experiment. Was he really going to make a bomb?

Mr. Troy held up a plastic water bottle that appeared to contain a small amount of water. He dropped in a few small pieces of dry ice and the water instantly started to boil violently and the bottle billowed fog. He quickly sealed the bottle and dropped it into his garbage can.

Mr. Troy stood their smiling at the expectant students. T.J. called out, "Nothing happened!"

BANG! Water sprayed to the ceiling, soaking Mr. Troy. All of the students jumped or cried out. Then there was an explosion of laughter and calls for him to do it again. "One experiment at a time," responded Mr. Troy. "An important thing for you to know is that humans and plants are organic beings. That means we are made up of carbon molecules. Remember that carbon is introduced into our organic way of life as carbon dioxide which is transformed by photosynthesis."

T.J. missed the summation point about carbon while daydreaming about where he could lay his hands on some dry ice.

*****

Ethan Dire had done all that he could have done. He had hoped that the exertion of his daily, ten kilometer run through the early morning desert would have been enough to keep his stress level down. Today would prove to be another milestone in his career as either a success or failure. At least today's test flight would not be risking the life of a pilot. Now he waited for the fly over to see if the results of this past year would pay off.

At the age of forty, he had already accomplished quite a lot. Some of his previous innovations had earned him the nickname *Golden Boy* at the base. They had brought the attention of the top Air Force brass, who gave him the role of Lead Aeronautical Engineer for the *B-2 Spirit*, the *Stealth Bomber*. His decisions gained him the glory of the successes. They also tagged him with the heartbreak of failure, which could mean the loss of a pilot's life. He was grateful that they had been able to sufficiently improve the B-2's aerodynamics such that only one pilot had been lost in active operations to date. However, his personal accomplishments would never be known to the outside world as this was Area 51.

He shook his head at the thought and continued to scan the sky. The computer monitor still showed nothing inbound. A group of dignitaries, including two Generals, stood nearby. Even with letters of commendations from those Generals, he had not been able to transition from his current role. It was not that he disliked the quiet solitude of this desert fortress; he just needed a new challenge. Hoping to avert a midlife crisis, he had even applied to be an astronaut with NASA.

Luckily, he had gotten another opportunity with the wars in the Middle East. For the first time, the Stealth Bomber was thought of as less than stealthy. It had not even been higher technology that had brought this about. Daytime missions in the clear blue desert sky had allowed opposition ground forces to telephone sightings before the bombers could reach their targets. The missions were being defeated, not by radar which could not see the bomber, but by visual sightings from the ground. Of course, night missions and cloud cover would alleviate this situation, but the reputation of this invisible technology had been drastically damaged. While there were only twenty *B-2s* in service, it had become apparent that no more were ever going to be built.

Upon hearing the initial complaint about his bird, an obvious solution had come to him. He explained the concept to the area commander, who looked torn between disbelief and astonishment at its simplicity. The project had been given the immediate go ahead and every resource to accomplish it quickly.

The screen before Ethan beeped, returning his focus to the present. The B-*2* was in the air. Its transponder beacon on the screen showed it fast approaching. Three other screens, representing U.S., Russian and Chinese radar systems, would soon have their opportunity to locate the target. Ethan looked up at the sky and back down at the displays.

"It approaches," he announced.

The transponder screen had concentric rings showing distances, and the flashing light indicated that the bomber was passing directly over them. The other three radar displays were pleasingly silent. Ethan scanned the sky with his own eyes, as did the assembled dignitaries. Nothing could be seen except a few puffy clouds on a brilliant blue background. Looking back down, Ethan saw that the bomber had already passed. He could still see no sign of it.

Suddenly, applause broke out among the bystanders. His concept seemed to have passed the peer review of the brass. Minutes later the transponder screen again showed the B-2 approaching. This time the B-2 landed on the runway and taxied over to the group. From this vantage, it appeared a typical Stealth Bomber, if any Stealth Bomber could be called typical.

They crowded around the B-2. At the suggestion of General Kaylor, everyone got down on their hands and knees and crawled beneath the bomber. Then they rolled over and lay looking up at the bottom of it. They found themselves looking at liquid crystal displays, thousands of miniature televisions.

"We call it a *Chameleon Cover*," announced Ethan. "There are forty-eight hundred three inch LCD displays. Each receives its image from a computer representation created from cameras on the top of the bird. From the ground, an observer would only be able to see the sky, regardless of weather conditions. The only times of detection would be if located directly in front of the sun or while dropping a payload of bombs."

The group continued to marvel at this new technology as General Kaylor approached Ethan.

"Great job, on time and under budget!" he said while shaking Ethan's hand. "I am going to miss you."

"Sir?" responded Ethan.

"Your orders have come in. You are to report to the Cape Canaveral Air Force Base early next week."

*****

United States President Stephen Ryan thanked the G20 leaders and disconnected from the video conference. He turned to his National Science Advisor, Dr. Kevin Scott, who was quietly standing off camera. "What do you think?"

"It's official. They think you're crazy," replied Kevin.

Stephen stood up and walked around to sit on the front corner of his oval office desk. "So you think they bought it?"

"I think China wants to know how this will prevent a move on Taiwan, and Russia wants to know what your thoughts are about their intentions toward Ukraine. They think you must be foolishly distracted by the environment. You could have been an actor. They believed you."

"That is how I got into politics," conceded Stephen, "because I always consider myself a scientist first with the skills of an actor."

"But you're the President of the United States!" refuted Kevin.

"I know, and that is why we have been able to do what we have done. Back when I was on the Subcommittee on Higher Education, Lifelong Learning and Competitiveness, you were the one that hatched this crazy scheme into my every waking thought."

"Well, you asked for a plan to improve education. I was just thinking outside the box. That is what a scientist is supposed to do. It was your position as Speaker of the House that allowed all of the ground work to be laid. I can't believe that you actually took all of those gambles on the assumption that you would someday be able to pull the trigger as the President."

"At the time, I just wanted everything in place to convince a future President. I never considered the possibility that I would be that President. This is happening much faster than I could have anticipated."

Kevin laughed and added, "That was my original premise. You were inspired! First, you placed yourself on all the essential committees. Next, you actually accomplished the feat of getting them to think outside the box and pulled original ideas from them. You won public opinion as you slammed those bills through Congress. People loved your stance on education, spending billions on high tech schools and mandating science curricula at all grade levels. As a Republican Speaker of the House, when you finally teamed up with Al Gore to solve global warming, you became a shoo-in for President."

"I don't even believe in the Global Warming theory!" exclaimed Stephen.

"And yet here you are, the first President to sign a bill that you yourself had originally authored in the House. Your carbon capture bill has allowed us to work on stage three of our plan."

"You really think the G20 will eventually believe that the U.S. is so environmentally conscious that we will shoot the captured carbon dioxide into outer space?" asked Stephen.

"When you signed Al Gore on as your Deputy National Science Advisor, it was a master stroke to show the world how serious you were about the environment. During the video conference, I think Hatch of the EU wanted to speak out against the expense of a carbon capture program but decided to leave you to your foolishness."

"As long as they don't know what we are really up to," said Stephen as he walked back to his chair to contemplate the upcoming mission.

*****

"Well, was I right?" asked T.J. as he sat with his back against a tree opposite his friend, Billy.

"I don't know if I would call you right," responded Billy. "I didn't find any chairs, but that does not mean that you're right. Maybe they actually use our chairs at night."

"They are extremely comfortable chairs. They fit us eighth graders perfectly, but can you see Mr. Troy squeezing into one? Don't be so naive. There is only one explanation." T.J. studied a large parchment on which he had drawn a rough map of the school. "I have walked down every hallway of the school. I have looked into and documented every classroom and office. I did not see a single adult size chair, other than for the teachers. I walked the whole perimeter and found only the main entryways located along solid cement walls. I could not find the chairs."

"And that proves you are right?" asked Billy.

"Of course!" exclaimed T.J. as he stood up and started toward his next class. He called back over his shoulder, "It proves the obvious. There must be secret passages."

His next class was Astronomy. It was his favorite class, as he felt most comfortable in its teaching environment. It was all about using imagination with science, exploration of space, and adventure through the universe. The class welcomed his daydreaming, and he excelled in the lessons. As he entered the classroom followed by Mr. Morrows, T.J. let his eyes roam the walls and floor.

"Today's lesson explores a challenge that has been posed to scientists for the past 40 years," began Mr. Morrows. "How do we create a permanent settlement in outer space?"

"But we already have astronauts living in outer space on the space station," responded Charlie, an astute red headed boy who always sat in the front row and attempted to answer every question.

"The International Space Station is far from a permanent settlement. The longest any single astronaut has spent on it is less than a year. Supplies need to be continually replenished. My question is how do we create a self-sufficient settlement away from the Earth? I will give you some of the major challenges. Let's consider terraforming Mars." The display behind him lit with the image of a red planet.

"First, we need air. There is no breathable oxygen on Mars. It has a very thin atmosphere with only trace levels of oxygen. Would we have to bring oxygen and replenish it like on the space station?" Numerous images of the word OXYGEN with a circle around and line drawn through appear on the display.

"Second, we would need water. So far we have only found trace amounts of ice at the poles of Mars. We either have to find and extract it or bring it along. It is estimated to cost approximately $10,000 to transport one pound of water to Mars. That is one expensive bottle of water!" WATER with a circle around and line drawn through also appears on the display.

"We would need to bring food. None currently exists on Mars. You would need to bring it or grow it. Would farming be possible on Mars? Bringing food would also cost about ten thousand dollars per pound. Does anybody want to go halves on a quarter pound burger for twelve hundred fifty each?" A murmur of laughter spread throughout the room. The image of FOOD with a circle around and line drawn through added onto the display.

"How do we overcome the energy issue? Mars is a very cold place. We would need to heat it. We might also want power for lights, cooking, television, and computers. How could we maintain power?" ENERGY with a circle around and line drawn through appeared on the display.

"These are some of the major obstacles. I will call them the primary ones. Without oxygen, water, food, and energy, humans cannot live away from the Earth. There are other secondary obstacles such as solar radiation, the low gravity effects, and the cost of transport. Your project will be to pick one of the obstacles to setting up a space settlement. You will research potential solutions to overcome the problem. I want an in-depth analysis of the pros and cons of your ideas. In two weeks you will present me with a ten page report and give the class a five minute presentation on your real solution to riddles that have been puzzling scientists for decades."

"Why Mars?" asked T.J. "Wouldn't it be easier to place a settlement on the Moon?"

"Maybe it would and maybe it would not," answered Mr. Morrows. "While the Moon is closer and would cut transportation costs and travel time, it also has a lower gravity than Mars. If you wish, you may research your hypothesis for either Mars or the Moon. Both places are very likely to be supporting future societies. If you take this project seriously, you might be credited with discovering the means to allow man to live away from Earth! Gather into small groups and discuss the project for the remainder of class."

T.J. and the rest of the class scribbled down the assignment and then got into groups. Charlie came over and sat down beside T.J. He seemed to gravitate to T.J. whenever there were group discussions in astronomy. A girl named Ann also joined them.

"I think the whole concept is dumb," said Ann. "Why would we want to expend all of the energy to go to such a barren and dangerous place? I think of space as a place to send our garbage."

"At ten thousand dollars a pound?" rejoined T.J. "That would be crazy."

"It wouldn't cost that much just to fire it into outer space. We could at least send the dangerous stuff like nuclear waste," defended Ann.

Charlie looked interested. "I think we should look into sending criminals to the Moon. If we send all convicts, then they would have to build the new world to survive."

"Well, I guess you could at least make them go," added Ann. "Why would anybody freely leave their home on Earth for an impossible existence?"

"For the adventure!" declared T.J. "It would be incredible to explore the solar system and discover new ways to live. Doesn't that sound exciting to you?"

"No," replied Ann.

T.J. loved the project but was torn over which challenge he would attack. As the class period ended, he decided to research all four primary obstacles and present the one that appeared the most promising.

*****

"Gentlemen, please be seated," requested Dr. Kevin Scott. "I would like to welcome you to your home for the next year." The three men took measure of each other as they sat down at a table in the empty outdoor café.

Ethan Dire looked around at the cruise ships docked at the Port Canaveral quay across the water. Overhead, seagulls screamed for attention. While he was used to sand, the salt breeze and crowds of tourists in the distance disturbed him.

"I have reserved this restaurant for the next few hours. We are here alone, other than an Air Force staff sergeant here to serve us some refreshments. We can talk freely as you both have clearance. I am Dr. Kevin Scott, the National Science Advisor to President Ryan. I have asked you here to detail the job that is being requested of you. Why don't you introduce yourselves?" The staff sergeant delivered a tray containing three glasses and a sweating pitcher of lemonade and then moved away.

The older, barrel-chested naval officer poured himself a glass and took a long drink before responding. "I am Lieutenant Commander Warren Poet. I have been an engineer working for the Navy since 1972. I built and maintained a fleet of fast attack submarines and was stationed out of Newport News, Delaware. In 1998, I was asked to head up the Navy's Submarine Recycle Program at the Puget Sound Naval Shipyard in Washington. I have spent my career building nuclear powered submarines. Ironically, in the twilight of my career, they have me dismantling the babies I put together. I only have a few more years before I hit mandatory retirement, so I appreciate the opportunity to build this top secret submarine here in Florida. When I am done, my wife and I plan on settling here anyway."

Submarines! Ethan couldn't get his mind around the concept. He wiped sweat from his brow. "I am First Lieutenant Ethan Dire and for the past 20 years, I have been working for the Air Force on ATB black projects in the middle of the desert at a place commonly known as Area 51. The B-2 is one of my responsibilities. While I have no idea what you could want me to do for the Navy here in Port Canaveral, I am appreciating the change in scenery."

Dr. Kevin Scott refilled Warren's glass and filled the two remaining glasses. "You will both be working on an extremely sensitive project. In truth, budgeting for the project is off the books. Ethan, I am sure you can appreciate that coming from Area 51. What you will be doing will come out of the Submarine Recycle Program budget. Warren, this is where you come in. We are accelerating your program, while moving it to Florida. In the next 12 months, you will recycle four Los Angeles Class nuclear fast attack submarines."

Ethan stirred in his chair. "Excuse me, but why do you need an Air Force aeronautical engineer to destroy some Navy subs?"

Dr. Kevin Scott chuckled, leaned back in his chair and looked up to the blue sky. "I did not say we were destroying them. I said we were recycling them."

*****

T.J. scanned the faces of those sitting at his table near the base of one of the largest trees in the atrium. The glass roof was open and the day was beautiful. Some children were playing catch off in the distance. They had finished eating their lunches, and it was time for them to share what they had found.

"Are we in agreement?" asked T.J. "Do you all believe that there is a secret passage in this school?"

Billy looked amused. "Do you think we would be wandering all around the school wasting our time if we weren't intrigued with the possibility?"

Todd and Lisa, who had been brought in on the theory during a discussion with T.J. in the library, nodded agreement. Todd added, "The classroom seats are made for middle school butts. There is no way that our teachers' butts, no less the average adults' butts, fit into those seats. In the library, you had pointed out that those seats are adult size and wanted to know why they would be different."

T.J. nodded. "Yes. It had to be due to the difficulty in making the change of chairs in the library's garden setting. Look at the lunch area. The lunch atrium contains only benches. Good for both kids and adults. In the library, the combination of bookshelves, paths, and plants make it too difficult to swap chairs, so they went with the one size fits all, large adult chairs. That means only the classroom chairs would need to be swapped."

"Thus, your secret passageway theory," added Billy. "I have confirmed your mapping of the school. No storage area for chairs was found. Your secret passage appears to be real."

"What if there is a simpler explanation?" piped in Lisa. "Todd and I came up with an alternate theory. The atrium and library contain earthen floors. The classrooms do not."

"So you think that the passageway is underground?" questioned Billy.

"Not necessarily," stated Todd. "This is a high tech school. Why not have chairs that rotate out of the floor. Maybe at night, our chairs go under and an adult chairs rotate up."

"Did you check it out?" asked T.J.

Mary meekly nodded. "The chairs aren't attached to the floor. Our rotating theory fell apart, but we still like the idea of an underground passage. We have been bouncing some hard balls on the floor trying to find a hollow section, but we haven't had any luck yet."

"Keep trying," said T.J. "Although I think it would be difficult to move the chairs up from underground, it has to be somewhere."

*****

T.J. arrived early to chemistry class and took the far seat in the first row. He did not notice the look of surprise on his teacher's face. T.J. was too busy studying the outside wall.

"Welcome to the front of the class," Mr. Troy said to T.J. "This class will be worth your trouble." The screen behind him displayed the towering word THERMODYNAMICS. He launched into his lecture about the energy equation of chemical reactions. The display showed the definitions of endothermic and exothermic reactions. Various chemical reaction equations appeared as he discussed them. It was a lot of information for the students to follow, but T.J. was entertained by the passion with which Mr. Troy taught.

"How is thermodynamics important to mankind?" he continued. "It starts with the energy from the sun. Plants capture that energy in the reaction that we previously went over. Anyone remember what it is called?"

"Photosynthesis," responded Cory who sat just to the right of T.J.

"Correct. Plants use the sun's energy to combine the simple molecules of carbon dioxide and water to form complex molecules. Does anyone know why these complex molecules are important to us?"

While looking around at the classroom, T.J. raised his hand. "It's because we eat them?"

"Yes. The complex molecules contain the sun's energy in their molecular bonds. When the bonds are broken, thermodynamics requires the energy to be given back, as energy is neither created nor destroyed. It is just borrowed. Anybody care to guess which of the two types of reactions listed behind me describe the breaking of a complex molecule?"

From the other side of the room, Paul called out, "Endothermic."

"With a fifty percent chance, good try," said Mr. Troy. "No. Endothermic reactions absorb or require the addition of energy. While breaking the bonds of a complex molecule typically requires some small amount of energy to actually do the breaking, the breaking reaction gives off a great deal more energy, making it an exothermic reaction."

The display changed to show the words COMBUSTION and EXOTHERMIC REACTIONS. "Combustion is a term to describe the typical exothermic reaction, where a complex organic molecule is broken up and recombined with oxygen. Before you get too distracted by the term *organic*, it does not always mean grown without pesticides and artificial fertilizers."

The words ORGANIC and HYDROCARBONS also appeared on the

display. "Hydrocarbons are molecules that contain combinations of carbon and hydrogen. This carbon-hydrogen bond contains energy. Organic refers to the type of carbon-hydrogen complex molecules that plants make. Combustion breaks up the carbon and hydrogen bonds in an exothermic reaction when combined with oxygen. Why do you guess this is important to us?"

Cory raised her hand and answered, "That is how we get energy from our food."

"Exactly. Plants capture the sun's energy in organic, complex molecules. Animals will combust complex molecules to obtain their energy. Humans also have the propensity to combust complex molecules to obtain energy. Care to venture how?"

"We burn wood," stated Paul.

"We burn lots of things," agreed Mr. Troy. "Burning woods is a great example of combusting organic matter. Also, as dead organic matter breaks down, it can turn into a very useful hydrocarbon, petroleum. As we burn petroleum in the presence of oxygen, the exothermic reaction gives us the energy we need to run our machines. We have found cheap energy, but the cost is the addition of carbon dioxide and global warming which we discussed previously. President Ryan is pushing through legislation to capture the carbon dioxide. That is a good start, but it could be expensive."

"Now we get to the fun part." Mr. Troy dimmed the lights, causing the ceiling to darken. He started to prepare for his experiment. "T.J., please stay in your seat. This could be dangerous."

T.J. had taken the opportunity of the lights being off to more closely study the room's exterior wall. He should not have been so bold as to search the wall right next to the teacher, but at least it had been mistaken as an attempt to get a better look at what the teacher was doing. The mention of danger got most of his attention back to the experiment.

"I have a small bowl of soapy water and a tank of hydrogen. Hydrogen is the most abundant atom in the universe. Two hydrogen atoms combine to form a hydrogen gas molecule. I have a small tank of hydrogen, which I will bubble into the soapy water." A large soap bubble formed and started floating. Mr. Troy lit a candle at the end of a long stick, held it aloft, and poked it at the soapy, hydrogen gas bubble. A large orange flame burst from the bubble and consumed it to the awe of the classroom. "Hydrogen is very flammable. I add a little energy with the candle to break the hydrogen-hydrogen bond, and I get more energy." He repeated the pyrotechnics a few times more to the continued amazement of the class.

"Now to the best part of the experiment!" said Mr. Troy as he took out a second small tank of gas. "This is oxygen." Bubbling both the hydrogen and oxygen into the soapy water, this time he only made a small collection of bubbles. He also stood further away to lite his candle and allowed the bubbles to rise.

T.J. had found the secret passageway! After being returned to his seat, he had enjoyed the spectacle of the six foot burning bubbles. Watching it twice, he had once again taken advantage of the darkness between flames and returned to his search. He reached the back corner of the room. Firmly pressing on the corner of the room caused a whole section of the wall to rotate inward. He was about to make his escape.

K A B O O M!

The room shook. Everyone cried out and jumped out of their seats. More than a few girls screamed. T.J. closed the passage and rushed back to his seat, unsure of what had just taken place. The lights came back on and the ceiling again allowed sunlight into the room. The class found Mr. Troy sitting at his desk smiling triumphantly.

"Now that was a good example of an exothermic reaction!" he exclaimed. "We combined hydrogen gas and oxygen gas into the smallest of bubbles, added a little energy, and got a ton of energy back! Hydrogen combined with oxygen and the end product was just a miniscule droplet of water. Now that is clean energy! If we burn that in cars, the only emissions will be water."

"Then why wouldn't we?" asked T.J, having quickly returned to his seat. He was still kicking himself for missing his chance to get into the passageway.

"It would take energy to turn water into hydrogen and oxygen molecules. Petroleum is still much too cheap and abundant to weigh this as a viable alternative, unless you consider the other costs such as pollution and global warming."

*****

17

Ethan Dire was a lead engineer for the project, but even he was baffled by what they were doing. He shook his head in amusement at the sight of the four monstrosities that were sitting in dry docks in their newly constructed secret hangar. They had him working on submarines!

Ethan understood the sensitive nature of the things that he built. For years, people had been sure that they had been storing some type of alien technology at Area 51 instead of the truly revolutionary B-2 aircraft. Now he was working at a site that he deemed just as secretive. The code name for the location was Phoenix.

He could not believe that this top secret operation was right next to the highly visited tourist sites of Port Canaveral, Cape Canaveral, and the Kennedy Space Center. He was not used to this amount of human activity so close to his workplace. He had dined out alone several times at fancy restaurants catering to vacationers waiting to catch their cruise ship out of Port Canaveral. This was an epicenter of tourism, and they had him here engineering top secret weapons. But submarines!

Nobody would even be able to detect that their operation was here. The only entrance to the site was through an Air Force gate and down a service road. A small hangar was actually the entrance to their underground facility. That reminded him of Area 51. However, that was where the similarity ended. Just beyond the false airplane hangar, location Phoenix could be described as the world's only underground naval base. It was actually more of a lair, as it was above sea level but had what appeared to be a large sand dune placed on top of it. Water access was up the Banana River going through secure lagoons. Nobody without clearance could see it or would ever even know about it. It did not exist.

Ethan shook his head in disbelief at the site of the *Atlanta, Olympia, Houston,* and *Phoenix* sitting before him. All were Los Angeles class, nuclear, fast attack submarines. Regardless of being an Air Force aeronautical engineer, Ethan understood why they had selected him. Once he was given a set of engineering requirements, he was the best at finding solutions and building the final product.

The nearby Kennedy Space Center had donated several cranes to accomplish their work. The *Phoenix lair*, as he considered it, had been built around the gigantic vehicles, and there appeared to be no way for them to ever leave. Ethan and Warren had been given their first set of instructions. They were going to disassemble the subs, but not completely.

Warren was to lead the team in the dismantling of the four nuclear reactors. It was a sensitive job for which he had a lot of experience. He knew exactly how to safely dismantle the reactors and remove their radioactive cores.

Ethan had been given a different role. In a private meeting with Dr. Kevin Scott, he had been given implicit instructions. "Surgically remove each of the identified components of the submarines as instructed by Warren. Warren is to lead the team with his knowledge and experience. Your job is to complement him by planning the deconstruction in a manner that is efficient and completely preserves the integrity of the essential components."

"What do you deem as essential?" inquired Ethan.

"You and Warren will get a complete list of essential components. The rest of the submarines will be scrapped. So if you are instructed that a screw in the tail section is required to be preserved, cut the tail off and get it. Don't spare the nonessentials, which is everything not on the essential list. Cut out the process components, itemize and document everything for reconstruction, and crate them."

Ethan had just nodded to the orders. He knew why he was here. While he had demonstrated skill in aeronautical engineering, he had been more renowned for his ability to get projects completed ahead of schedule and under budget.

"Learn how the submarine processes work, dismantle them, and make sure you can reassemble them in the future," were Dr. Kevin Scott's final words.

*****

T.J. ran his hand over the plush moss on which he sat. He could feel the rough bark of the bald cypress through the back of his shirt. This was his favorite spot in the library, among the small clutch of cypress. From the size of the trunks, they had to be old trees. He had pondered how they must have constructed the library right around them, just pruning off the tops of the trees to make them fit into the glass enclosure. Most of the other trees were various forms of citrus punctuated by bright yellow lemons. He was glad to have the vibrant green, feathery cypress leaves back after a long winter, even though that appeared to have greatly increased students competing for this area as their oasis.

T.J. could see Mary and Todd approaching over the top of his book. They sat down on an ideally placed rock across from him.

Mary asked, "Are you here with your astronomy class?"

"Yeah. I am doing the research for my terraforming project," answered T.J.

Todd nodded and pulled open his book bag. "Mr. Morrows is pretty cool, but his projects are tough. I decided to work on the problem of acquiring water for a settlement on Mars."

"What's your solution?" asked T.J.

Todd removed his glasses and cleaned them on his shirt as he replied, "Water is too expensive to bring, but they have found traces of ice at the poles. I plan on presenting a large scale strip mining operation on Mars. They will convey truckloads of Martian soil through a super-hot room. Any water will boil off to be collected. I hope Mr. Morrows gives me credit for originality. I have worked in some math to give estimates on potential production. It's all fuzzy math, based on assumptions of the polar region that I found online."

"Good idea," congratulated T.J. "I am working on terraforming the Moon and could not come up with a solution for water. The Moon is apparently bone dry. The only apparent way would be to bring it. That is expensive and would be a boring project, although I heard that's just what Cory is doing."

"Figures," injected Mary. "She would pick a topic to prove we could never go to the Moon."

"I decided to try the energy issue," continued T.J. "Have you seen Mr. Troy's H_2O experiment?"

"You mean the hydrogen and oxygen explosion?" Todd responded enthusiastically.

"Mr. Troy really knows how to get our attention," added Mary. "I nearly wet my pants with the explosion. I don't know how he could stand so nonchalantly while lighting it."

"Well that gave me my idea for the energy problem," said T.J. "There is no petroleum on the Moon. No oil, gas, or coal to be found. It would be way too expensive to transport them, so maybe they could burn hydrogen and oxygen as a fuel supply. They could use solar or nuclear power to convert water into hydrogen and oxygen. Since pollution would be unthinkable in a lunar settlement, it would be the perfect solution. The end product is water!"

Mary laughed and asked, "But how would you get the water to the Moon in the first place?"

T.J. turned red. "That is why I worked so hard to resolve the water issue."

Todd added, "You could always do your idea on Mars."

"I could," responded T.J. "But there is the fact that it is a renewable resource. Once you get the water there, the total amount of water for the reaction is constant. That is the angle that I am working on. You somehow get the water there, convert it to hydrogen and oxygen, and get water back when you burn it."

Mary changed the subject by asking T.J., "Have you figured out how to get into the passage?"

"No. The classrooms are only open when the teacher is present. The doors seal as the teachers leave. During class they run too tight a ship. You are never allowed out of your seat in English, math, or history. Astronomy class has a lot more freedom with group discussions and all, but most of the time that takes place here on a library trip. I still can't believe that I missed the perfect opportunity during chemistry, but that explosion scared me half to death."

"Well, at least you solved the riddle," said Todd.

"No I didn't. I still don't know what's in the passage."

Mary patted T.J. on the back and said, "Chairs."

*****

The National Security Council was meeting in the War Room. The White House Situation Room, as it was formally called, was in the basement of the West Wing. Today, the President had summoned them to the War Room and they were there to discuss war!

President Stephen Ryan had been briefed shortly before dawn and called together the council. They were finally gathered just before eight. Today was going to be another long day.

"Good morning, Sara" he greeted, shaking hands with the matronly woman entering last. He could tell from her handshake that his Secretary of Education was nervous. As she started to take a seat at the very end of the long table, he stopped her. "Please, Sara, join us toward the center of the table. This is not a normal Cabinet meeting, and there are only ten of us attending with one more joining later."

"Of course, Mr. President," acquiesced Sara.

He turned to Paul Wiggin, his Chief of Staff and said, "Seal us in Paul, but have them inform me when our last guest arrives." He then turned to the Chairman of the Joint Chiefs of Staff. "General McKnabb, I believe you should fill us in."

"The Chinese have made a decisive move," he began.

"Against Taiwan?" stammered Mr. Fields, the Secretary of Treasury, jumping up and waving his arms excitedly. "They attacked even though we have such a presence there? We made it clear to them that it was in all of our interests not to escalate."

"No," replied the General. He calmly waited for Fields to return to his seat before continuing. "The Chinese military have invaded South America."

Stephen could see the astounded looks on everyone's faces. Sara's eyes widened like saucers. He could tell that she wanted to ask to be excused. Fields appeared to shrink in his seat.

General McKnabb stood and walked toward a screen that now showed a map of South America. "They hit in a location sometimes called *The End of the World.* It is the southernmost city in South America. It was not a surgical strike. They went in there quickly, in large numbers, and decisively took control of the capital of the Argentinean province. Initial estimates are five thousand dead in the city of Ushuaia."

"Ushuaia? South America? What can they be thinking?" asked the Vice President angrily from across the table.

"I'll take the question," said the National Security Advisor, rising to his own display which showed a detailed map of Argentina in the southern half of South America. "Argentina and Venezuela have had a hot and cold relationship for the past few years. Venezuela had been trying to align with Argentina using oil as leverage. Their relationship became stronger as they discovered some smaller oil fields in the Argentinean north. Recently, Venezuelan geologists found a vast oil field in the south, at the *End of the World,* as you have heard it termed."

The display zoomed into the very southern tip of South America. "This is the southern province of Argentina, Tierra del Fuego. This archipelago is actually split between Argentina and Chile. The northern half contains Chile's only known oil field, which pipelines oil into central Chile. The southern half of the main island belongs to Argentina. The capital of this province is the internationally known city of Ushuaia."

"Known?" asked the Vice President derisively.

"You would know of it if you ever took a cruise ship to Antarctica. Sixty thousand people reside there. They have an international airport, railway, and hospital. This morning their hospital has seen much more than it can handle."

The screen zoomed to a view of a burning metropolitan area. "When oil was discovered in the southern part of Tierra del Fuego, things started to move quickly. The simplest solution was to extend the pipeline to the north and put the oil into Chile. Strong relationships and agreements were made. We believe that Ushuaia was moving to secede from Argentina and join with Chile. Argentina would not want to allow this, but the island has quite a bit of natural protection. Oil and revenue were at stake. General."

General McKnabb's screen also became a view of the burning metropolis. "The Chinese must have made an agreement for the oil. Shortly after midnight, a fleet of container ships dropped off its cargo of what we estimate as five thousand troops. They did not worry too much about civilians and soon crushed the city and moved out across the island."

"Do they plan on keeping it?" asked the Secretary of Defense.

"There is no way to tell. They are currently securing the area. At minimum,

I would guess that they will be setting up a military base here in the Western Hemisphere."

The President leaned back in his chair. Invading Taiwan would have been very bad. This was much worse. "OK. We know what has occurred. Let's go around and get your thoughts."

Peter Owens, the Secretary of State spoke first. "We will put diplomatic pressure on them to go home. Maybe since Ushuaia is ready to raise the white flag, we can assure Argentina of their sovereignty over the region. We can then go in as negotiators and finalize the deal between Argentina and China. That would assure China that we respect their claim to buy the oil, as long as they agree to leave. But will China still be willing to buy it, now that they control the area?"

The Director of National Intelligence responded, "We think it is all about the oil. If we assure them that they will get the oil, I believe the issue will be resolved."

The General stated, "I don't think we could bring a carrier group to the area in less than three days."

Secretary of Defense added, "I am not even sure we would want to, for it would certainly escalate the situation."

"They will not be allowed to have a foothold in the West!" exclaimed the Vice President. "Cajole them, buy them off, or scare them away. We have barely kept Russia out of Venezuela, and now the Chinese join the dance."

The National Security Advisor agreed, "If we leave this door open, they will end up sending over millions of citizens."

The President looked to Sara. Her cheeks reddened. "Mr. President, this is beyond my expertise. I really don't think I should contribute."

Stephen nodded. "I have additional things to discuss today, so hopefully we can reserve your services for them. Treasury is also here mostly for informational purposes. Listen up, folks. We need to contain the Chinese within their borders. They are always looking for a way to expand and we must not let them get the opening."

Paul Wiggin, who was standing just behind the President, leaned in and whispered, "The final attendee has arrived."

The door opened and Dr. Kevin Scott entered. He stood waiting for the President to finish. "Each of you will exert all of your energies on this. State will negotiate for peace and make assurances for the oil. The Navy will bring as many carrier groups as they can to within one day's sailing of the region. I will call the Chinese President directly, as there must be no misunderstanding of what our intentions and expectations are."

"I am sure you are all familiar with my Science Advisor, Dr. Kevin Scott. Please, Kevin, have a seat. Just to get you up to speed on our crisis in the briefest way possible, China has attacked and occupied Ushuaia."

"Oh, no!" interjected Kevin. "They are in South America?"

"You are familiar with Ushuaia?"

"Of course, I took a Princess cruise from the city to Antarctica a few years ago," replied Kevin.

"Small world," responded the Vice President.

"Too small," stated the President, exchanging a look with Kevin. "If you don't mind, could you start from our beginning?"

"Absolutely, Mr. President," replied Kevin. "I am not sure that many know this, but the President is a very accomplished chess player. Back when he was a Professor at the University of Florida, his department's research fell under my oversight in the space-grant program. I was Deputy Director of NASA and took the opportunity to visit the prestigious Professor Ryan on a weekly basis. We always found enough time for a game of chess. I am sure that you are all aware of his skills in strategy, but you probably do not know its true depth."

Stephen noted that both General McKnabb and the Secretary of Defense looked about to challenge him to a game when he added, "Kevin won as many as he lost."

"I have been asked to fill you all in on the masterful game that the President is currently playing. Is anybody aware of the chess move called the *King's Gambit?*" asked Kevin.

The General answered, "It is the opening sequence of moves, where a pawn is sacrificed in order for rapid development of the game. In order for your opponent to keep his one pawn advantage, he must make moves that can seriously weaken his other positions."

The President remarked, "I can schedule you in for a match on Thursday." He got a nod back from the General.

Kevin continued, "Our King's Gambit was the promise to save the environment with the carbon capture program." Moans ensued from the Secretaries of State and Treasury.

Fields injected, "It has a cost that puts us at a disadvantage to other economies. I have been trying to talk the President out of his commitment to it for the past six months."

"And no matter how much you make me push," added the Secretary of State, "the other members of the G20 will not sign any type of treaty committing their nations to the same costs. China and Russia are especially two-faced, as they both ardently support our attempt at carbon capture but would never actually commit to the same. They are just pressing the economic advantage of the U.S. wasting capital on a program that everyone sees as overkill."

Kevin agreed, "It is a bad move, unless you are playing the *King's Gambit* in a major chess match. Fortunately, our opponents don't know that it is a strategic move in a bigger game. They know we are constantly trading moves with them, but not which game we truly play. In all fairness, this was just the first transparent move that they could see. Just about everything that you have seen the President do in the last four years as Speaker of the House has been part of the same strategy."

The Vice President asked, "So this is about global warming and energy? I am not Al Gore. I am not in agreement with the *Gore Philosophy* as the President seems to be."

The President laughed. "You forget that I was a scientist. If you want to stick to the chess analogy, I was just trying to convince my opponent that I was a novice player of the political game. When they see me playing the *King's Gambit*, they don't see anything more than an easy opponent and respond as I plan."

"We are dealing with dangerous adversaries," continued Kevin. "Our overall strategy is to play the match as a *Pawn Endgame*. That is where the only pieces left are the Kings and pawns. Truly the best scenario would be for us to play with only Kings and Pawns." He turned to the General. "What happens if you throw your most powerful tool, the Queen, directly at your opponent without regard to the consequences? Let us say that you decide to nuke the forces in Ushuaia. We would take the Chinese out of play in South America, but at what cost to the overall strategy?"

The Secretary of Defense sourly stated, "That would not have a plausible outcome."

"That is exactly why the game's participants don't know what we are doing. We are setting up a *Pawn Endgame*, where all anybody sees is a bunch of pawn moves."

The Vice President anxiously asked, "So you have told us it is not about global warming or energy. We know the adversaries are the rest of the world. What is the goal of this game?"

The President smiled as he leaned forward. "You want me to cut to the chase. Sara, I think you will be pleasantly surprised that all of our pawn moves, which we will explain shortly, have been to create a new paradigm for education."

The meeting continued for hours longer. The President and his Science Advisor took turns explaining the many smaller projects that they had undertaken in the past four years and their relevance to the final goal.

*****

"How soon before you think it will truly sink in?" asked Dr. Kevin Scott. He and the President had finally adjourned to the oval office. Stephen sat at his desk, while Kevin paced the floor, even after such a long day.

"They were given the timetable," responded Stephen. "Until now, the project has been opaque to all but our select group. As I float out more pieces of the puzzle, the stakes will rise."

"I think they were all taken aback by how much had already been accomplished. Fields kept trying to interject the improbably high costs of our project, but you kept him in check with your assurances that they were all approved and within budget. He finally just seemed too overwhelmed to keep up his objections. I think it was too much information after learning that the Chinese had invaded South America."

"Between General McKnabb and the State Department, we will come to an understanding with the Chinese." Stephen took a drink of coffee, set the mug back down, and rubbed at his eyes. "Kevin, you have had a long day. How quickly do you really think the projects are moving?"

"About as fast as the F-18 you sent to pick me up this morning," responded Kevin. "The Phoenix Project team executes each instruction seamlessly. Poet and Dire work so efficient that I feel we need to give them the full scope of their project. Those two are masterful engineers."

"Do it. But I'm even more concerned with the rovers. Are you sure they will be able to rendezvous with the resources, acquire them, and get them to where we need them? I wish we could have sent more to raise the probability for success."

Kevin took a seat and wished he could lean back and put his feet up on the desk. "As you stated to Fields, all assets are approved and budgeted for. We make work what we have. This is my part of the project, and everything is *predicted* to work out fine. It is your job to make sure that the new players that were included today do their parts."

"I believe they all bought into my vision of why this is important to our country's future."

Kevin disagreed, "Maybe the politicians. As you saw with the Secretary of Treasury, the General and the Secretary of Education also had a hard time believing this was really happening."

Taking the challenge, Stephen answered, "Fields had all of his arguments met, and I have not needed him yet. I have scheduled a chess match with General McKnabb, during which I will point out the strategic need for defensive measures for the project, thus challenging him into the project. As for Sara, I specifically selected her to be my Secretary of Education. She may find it hard to believe what we are intending to do, but when we deliver, she will know what to do with it."

"You gave her one week to get the tests approved and issued. I am not so sure she appreciated the timetable thrust on her. "

"Trust in her. I chose her because she is the best at teaching through inspirational paradigm. What better paradigm to inspire her."

*****

T.J. sat in the chair and awaited the upcoming full day of torture. It was not that he was bad at testing; it was the fact that he was scheduled to have a completely uneventful full day of tests. He actually preferred the regular day containing English, history, and math, as long as he had the possibility of an eventful science class. Today's National Standardized Testing was sure to be an absolute bore.

He was scheduled to spend the entire day in his English classroom with Ms. Wick. He wished for a power failure and solar eclipse, which would give him the chance to slip through the elusive secret passage. It was hard to believe that he had not seen a single opportunity to investigate the passage over the past few weeks. The teachers were always present in the classroom. Even now, Ms. Wick was observing each of them prior to having them start the first test section.

When he finally was told to turn the test over and begin, he was surprised by the first question.

You find yourself alone on a sandy beach next to a boat which is floating in placid waters. In the distance you see a pleasure yacht moving away from you and hear what sounds like a party aboard. Behind you, through some trees, you see a dark cave opening with what appears to be the image of skull and crossbones etched into the rocks adjacent. In the boat, you find a flare gun, flashlight, and a fishing pole with tackle. What is the first thing that you do?

    a)   Row out to the yacht

    b)   Fire the flare gun and wait for help

    c)   Use the flashlight to explore the cave

    d)   Fish from the boat as you row out to the yacht

T.J. laughed out loud, which earned him a reproving look from his teacher. They must have been reading his mind because he wanted to escape this stuffy classroom into the thrills of an adventure. He chose the option of exploring the cave.

He was disappointed when the next question asked him to solve for the value of x in the equation $2x + 5 = x + 10$. What he had initially thought might be a fun section turned into a math section filled with algebra, fractions, and geometry.

About halfway through the period, he came to another intriguing question.

You find yourself inside an ancient tower, dimly lit by flame filled lamps. A wizard in an arcane blue robe stands before what appears to be a shimmering mirror, but which does not reflect. The wizard informs you that it is a portal to an alternate plane of incredible knowledge, but you should follow him through only at great peril to your very being. The wizard steps forward, goes through the portal, and dissipates into the shimmering lights. What do you do next?

   a)   Follow the wizard to the alternate plane of knowledge

   b)   Steal the wizard's book of magic from the table and run from the tower

   c)   Run from the tower

   d)   Now that the wizard is gone you search the tower for magical artifacts

Once again T.J. felt the need to laugh but restrained himself. He would definitely follow the wizard to the plane of knowledge and get the answers to this test!

T.J. continued, only to discover that he was once again working through more math problems. He found himself actually enjoying this test. He was very good at math, as he liked the challenge of problem solving, but with the additional questions mixed in he found himself pressing through the work in hopes of another riddle to ponder. He was rewarded with another intriguing question.

You have been on a long, arduous quest to find the Hermit that Knows All Things. You finally find him after a dangerous climb to the top of a mountain. He sits before you serenely and states that you can ask him one question. You ask:

    a)   What is the meaning of life?

    b)   Does God exist?

    c)   What is mankind's place in the universe?

    d)   What is true love?

T.J. lunged right for the answer about mankind's place in the universe. He turned the paper over only to disappointedly discover that there were no more questions in this section.

*****

The next few sections also contained the exceptional questions scattered throughout. During the history section, he chose to take a time machine back to see dinosaurs. Mixed in with vocabulary questions, he risked a mummy's curse to find out how a pyramid was built. He also searched for treasure in a dragon's lair.

As he went through the final science section of the testing, he was pleased to have had such good teachers on the subject. He knew all the facts, performed the calculations, and worked through the logic questions. When he came to the last question, he was not sure if it was another one of the open, multiple-choice questions that had been conspicuously missing from this section.

Should mankind expend enormous resources and face exceptional dangers to leave Earth and explore the Universe?

    a)   Yes

    b)   No

There were only two available answers for this one, but in T.J.'s mind, "yes" was the only correct response.

*****

T.J. was back to his normal class schedule, but was currently enjoying the respite of sitting under his bald cypress in the library. He was putting the final touches on his Moon terraforming project. Pleased with his solutions and conclusions about the energy required to settle the Moon, now he had to work on the presentation he would give tomorrow. He wished his presentation could include some of the fantastic displays of science that he had witnessed in chemistry class, but he would have to settle for a poster board display and maybe some video clips burned from the internet. He was starting to look forward to chemistry, which was coming up shortly. Mr. Troy had promised an interesting experiment.

When the period ended, T.J. meandered along the garden pathways. The atrium was extremely bright today and he appreciated the way the path wound under trees and reflected the dappled light. Arriving at the chemistry classroom, he was glad to see Mr. Troy busily setting up. He was placing a large fire extinguisher behind his desk which contained numerous reagent bottles. T.J. could only imagine what was about to take place.

With a chime and a pop, the door sealed and class began. The wall behind Mr. Troy changed to display the word *Sodium* just before he dramatically spun around and said, "Today, we will be discussing sodium. Who knows what sodium is?"

From the back of the classroom, someone called out, "It's table salt."

The teacher typed on his keyboard and the display added *NaCl = Sodium Chloride.* "Table salt is actually sodium chloride, which is a chemical compound of the two elements. On Earth, that is the form that sodium is present in the greatest quantities. Anyone want to venture a guess where the largest amount of sodium chloride can be found?"

Megan replied from the seat next to T.J. "Would it be Salt Lake City?"

Mr. Troy was taken off guard by this answer and laughed aloud. "When I

32

asked where, I had not anticipated you responding with a specific place. Salt Lake City is named for its very salty lake. I was seeking the more general answer that salt is found in great quantities in the oceans. Sodium is one of the essential minerals required to support human biochemical processes. It is essential in the animal diet, but interestingly enough is not required by plants."

"Sodium is an element. It is a silvery, white metal. Yes, I said metal. But, while it is known as an alkali metal, it is so soft that you could cut it with a knife. In nature, it is never found in its elemental form because it is so reactive and readily oxidizes to a more stable form, such as salt. Today, we will experiment with its highly reactive, metallic form." The display added a picture of a few chunks of silvery, white metal.

"On the display, you can see what pure, unoxidized sodium metal would look like. Unfortunately, oxygen and moisture readily change its appearance and form." The display cleared and the word *Oxidation* appeared.

"What is oxidation you ask? Oxidation is the process where oxygen is combined with another substance. In our previous experiment where we burned hydrogen in the presence of oxygen, that was an example of combining hydrogen with oxygen." The display showed the chemical reaction $2H_2 + O_2 = 2H_2O$. "Two hydrogen molecules combine with an oxygen molecule to form two water molecules. When we burn natural gas, it is the methane recombining with oxygen to form carbon dioxide and water."

"The corrosion of metal is a form of oxidation." The display added the word *Rust*. "In simplified terms, rust is the form that iron takes in the presence of oxygen. It becomes iron oxide." The display cleared and once more the word *Oxidation* appeared along with *is a reaction where atoms in an element lose electrons.*

Mr. Troy sat down at his desk as the display returned to *Sodium* and its corresponding picture. "I have to show this picture of an actual pure Sodium specimen in its silvery form. When it is exposed to oxygen it readily oxidizes into a dull, tarnished state." The display added $2Na + O_2 = 2NaO$. "Now I am going to show you the violent reaction of sodium with water." Display added $2Na + 2H_2O = 2NaOH + H_2$ *Exothermic Reaction.* "Recall that an exothermic reaction is a reaction that gives off energy in the form of heat."

T.J. really perked up at the words exothermic and energy. He could feel himself breathing more slowly in anticipation. If Mr. Troy turned off the lights that would give him his chance to escape through the passageway.

But the lights did not turn off. Mr. Troy took a small white tablet from a reagent bottle with tweezers. "This is a piece of sodium."

"It looks like a Tic-Tac," stated Megan.

"That is because it is protected by a gel capsule. More correctly, we are protected from it by the gel capsule. As I said, sodium reacts violently with water." He placed a glass bowl of water on his desk and dropped the sodium capsule into it. Nothing happened at first, but then the gel coating dissolved. The sodium pellet started to move and appeared to boil over the water's surface leaving a pink trail behind. "I added some indicator to the water showing that NaOH is being formed in the water. That is the pink trail." Suddenly the sodium began to burn with an intense white light.

Mr. Troy paced before the front row of students. "The hydrogen being given off by the reaction is ignited by the incredible heat of this exothermic reaction. The sodium is burning in water, so I highly recommend not trying to put out a sodium fire with water!" He turned back toward the still burning sodium and exclaimed, "Mr. Gillooley, please get back in your seat."

T.J. was standing directly behind Mr. Troy at the desk watching the experiment. He glumly returned to his seat with a quietly muttered "Sorry" as he passed.

"Luckily, due to its reactive nature, sodium does not occur naturally in its elemental metallic state. It is typically found as a sodium salt."

The lecture continued on about the abundance and importance of sodium, but T.J. was lost in thought. He was busy incorporating what he had just learned into his terraforming project for astronomy class.

*****

General McKnabb made his first move with his white pawn forward to e4. President Stephen Ryan countered with his black pawn at e5. The General followed this with a second pawn moved to f4, which the President greedily accepted with his pawn.

"I see that you have questions, as you dare open with the King's Gambit," said Stephen. "It is good to see that the Chairman of the Joint Chiefs of Staff knows a little chess strategy."

"To be honest, I believe much of my climb through the officer ranks can be attributed to my competency in chess. Late evenings at Army Central Command often included the chess challenge. I won more often than not. One of the risks I took was in beating the commanding generals. I probably owe my reputation as a clever strategist to chess, so I will apologize now for beating you."

"We will see," rejoined Stephen. "So is this your typical opening or were you asking a question?"

"Mr. President, I have grave concerns about the Phoenix project. I believe that once it goes active, either the Chinese or Russians will move to take out the assets."

"That is why I challenged you to this match, General. I need your ideas for assuring that will not happen. Once the final mission has been initiated, there will be no turning back. All options will be on the table to assure success. As I explained, this will ultimately reduce the potential for aggressions with China and Russia. It will also catapult us far into the lead as the world's true superpower."

General McKnabb moved his knight to f3. "I am concerned that once they figure out what we are up to they will not allow us to get that far."

"That is why I am playing the King's gambit with them. They won't feel threatened or be able to know what we are planning far enough in advance to stop us."

Stephen made his move and continued, "What are you current thoughts on the Chinese in Ushuaia?"

"They have secured their position. It is sufficiently protected by the geography of the area, so pushing them off the continent from land would be difficult. They haven't brought in a surface navy, but our intelligence believes there is a considerable sub presence in the region. I believe they plan to just bring oil tankers in and out with the limited submarine protection and leave the ball in our court. Apparently, with your environmental persona, they are willing to see if you would dare risk a major incident with a tanker, even that far south. I believe they are there to stay."

Stephen nodded agreement. "So says the State Department. The Chinese claim it cannot be classified as an international incident since Argentina requested their assistance. Argentina has no option but to legitimize the action by agreeing to the fairly generous trade deal that China is offering considering they hold all the cards. Nothing State can do. It will be difficult keeping them at the tip of South America. Have any suggestions?"

The General made his move which was followed by a quick retaliation from Stephen.

"We need a strong presence in South America," replied the General.

"Then we might after all consider this a fortuitous event. Unfortunately, we don't have a lot of friends in South America. Columbia has been an ally in the area. This morning, we just signed a comprehensive trade agreement with Ecuador. This was a very aggressive deal, enough to actually break them out of OPEC. They have become full economic allies to the United States. You will be very interested in an additional provision slipped into the deal."

The General took the piece the President had just moved.

"Fast game. Are you sure you can keep this up?" asked Stephen as he captured the General's piece in kind. "We get to put military bases into Ecuador."

General McKnabb looked up from the board, suddenly distracted. "Nice move. I think it would be a good start to move the carrier fleet there to remind China not to look to the north."

"I also have some additional plans for Ecuador concerning the mission, but I like how you are thinking. What else can you suggest?"

General McKnabb folded his hands together and supported his chin on them. "I fear for the safety of the Phoenix project. I would arm our assets to the teeth."

They continued the match to an unsurprising draw.

*****

T.J. listened as Ann finished summarizing her terraforming report. "Just as Australia came to be inhabited by Europeans, so might Mars get its first settlement comprised of convicts from Earth." As she took her seat next to T.J., he wiped his sweaty palms across his pants.

Mr. Morrows asked, "T.J., are you ready to go?"

T.J. stood up and carried a box containing his presentation materials. He set it on Mr. Morrows' desk and started to organize the contents. First, he unrolled a poster and hung it over the front of the desk. It displayed the Moon overlooking the earth. He set out a glass baking dish and filled it with water from a bottle. After he put the disk that he had prepared into the computer controlling the room's display wall, a video of a rocket blasting off appeared behind him.

"My presentation covers the problem of getting usable energy for a settlement on the Moon. I first list all of the possible energy sources." He pressed a key and the display showed his list. "I then disqualified petroleum as an option due to problems associated with pollution in an enclosed environment. Bringing it to the Moon would also take much more fuel to transport it there than would be received on the Moon. It is also not renewable, so it would be too inefficient." He pressed a key and the display removed the word *Petroleum*.

"I next looked at the clean renewable energy sources. Wind won't work for obvious reasons." *Wind* disappeared from the display. "Solar appeared to be the best option until I discovered that night on the Moon is 14 days long and you would need a lot of batteries." *Solar* disappeared from the display.

"Nuclear power is my solution. While it is not renewable, it is at least a long term solution. The electricity it creates is extremely clean." The display cleared to show only the word *Nuclear*, soon followed by the words *Hydrogen* and *Oxygen*.

"Another energy solution would be to utilize the chemical reaction of combining oxygen with hydrogen. The solution of burning hydrogen in the presence of oxygen gives off a large amount of usable energy that would allow the user to escape the energy grid. Lunar vehicles could be run by this means. There would be no pollution as the byproduct would be a small amount of water that could potentially be captured and recycled. Where would the hydrogen and oxygen come from? The settlement would need to start out with a supply of water. I believe that Cory will soon be telling us how to get it there. Once the water is there, we use the electricity produced by nuclear power to split the water into hydrogen and oxygen. At that point, the energy captured can be taken off the grid to wherever you can transport the hydrogen and oxygen and recapture the water when you burn them." The display went to a video clip of a vehicle driving across the lunar surface. T.J. urgently rubbed the palms of his hands against his pants.

"That brings me to a little experiment that I have included to demonstrate that you can harness energy from a chemical reaction." He moved the baking dish to the front of the desk and poured what appeared to be a bottle full of white tablets into its water. He went back to his seat as the classroom watched. Nothing appeared to be happening.

Suddenly, there appeared to be a little movement to the water. Then, there was a tremendous explosion as white-hot sparks and orange flames leapt all the way to the ceiling! The classroom erupted with cries of fright. With a secondary explosion, Mr. Morrows fell backwards over one of the student's chairs, got up, and ran for the doorway to pull the fire alarm. Over the screams of the alarm, he ordered the children to evacuate the building. The doorway automatically opened. The flames were still loudly popping like a sparkler. Mr. Morrows quickly scanned the room to locate T.J. As he witnessed the last student file into the hallway already filled with students rushing every which way, Mr. Morrows realized that T.J. had somehow disappeared!

*****

T.J. made it back to his seat just as the water started to boil. At that point, he chose to move closer to the back corner of the room and the entrance to the secret passage. He got there just in time to witness the conflagration he had set in motion. Once again, he stood in shock as an explosion took his mind off his need to enter the passage.

With quick realization, he pushed at the spot in the wall where the passageway should have been located. Nothing happened. He continued to push, prod, and search the wall for any hint of an opening. He couldn't find it. Maybe he was in the wrong area of the wall. A secondary explosion rocked the room. T.J., in desperation, slammed into the corner with all his might and was flung into darkness. He quickly sealed the doorway behind him and pulled out a penlight that he had brought in case he found the nerve to pull off the distraction. He had done it. Now there was no turning back!

T.J. waved the penlight around and made a quick scan of the area that the small beam crossed. Sure enough, he had solved the riddle. He saw chairs. He was standing in what appeared to be a long passageway filled with chairs, at least in the short distance that the light beam covered.

"There had better be more to it than this," he said to himself. "I had better not have destroyed that classroom and probably my future, all to discover where they put the chairs." Shaking his head at the sad humor of it, he set off to explore.

The alarm sounds were almost deafening. As his ears adjusted, his eyes also adjusted. The alarms spaced along the ceiling actually had flashing lights. T.J. realized that he could see dimly without his penlight, so he put it away. As he traveled down the passageway, he found chairs in groupings every thirty feet. There must have been a set outside each classroom. He also found that the entryways to the classrooms were closed with latches. That must have been why he had not been able to push the entry open until he had slammed into it and jarred the latch free.

He came upon a lit computer desk with some chairs. It appeared to be an office, although it was located in a corridor. It was probably the janitor's. Realizing that if not for the alarm he might be encountering people, he hurried on. There would be time enough to pay the price for his curiosity later.

T.J. arrived at the end of the hallway. It opened into a large room that was quite dark. Retrieving his penlight, he found it to be a large dock or garage. This must be the freight entryway, which meant that his *secret* passageway was nothing more than the janitors' freight passage.

At the far end of the room was a corrugated metal wall that he thought must actually be a garage door. He wondered why he had not seen it from the outside and continued on to investigate. He opened a side doorway and stepped out into bright sunlight, only to discover a legion of fire trucks surrounding the school. Off in the distance, he saw teeming groups of students waiting to see some action. Deciding his consequences should be postponed until later, T.J. headed off in the opposite direction and took the extremely long way home.

*****

Two police cars were parked in front of his house when he arrived home. He had tried to figure out a plausible story for the whole incident during his round about trip home, but ultimately decided on telling the truth. He was going to leave out the part about the passageway, though.

"Hi, Mom, I'm home," he yelled as he entered the front door.

"T.J., come back here," called his father.

T.J. was not surprised to find his father home from work at this hour. It was time to pay the fiddler.

"What did you do?" his father accused as T.J. entered the kitchen.

"I was just doing my science presentation when the experiment kind of got away from me," T.J. pleaded.

One of the two police officers seated at the table opened his notebook and started writing. The other asked, "How did you start that fire?" He pulled out a chair from the table and gestured for T.J. to sit.

"I was explaining how energy can be obtained from chemical reactions. I dumped some sodium pellets into a dish of water. Instead of burning like I had seen them do before, they sort of exploded."

"Well, you are extremely lucky that the room had a glass ceiling. It just shattered and melted, but nothing actually caught fire. That was quite a disturbance you caused at the school. Where did you disappear to during the fire?"

T.J. gave his best version of the truth. "As soon as the fire started, I ran from the room. When I saw all of the fire trucks, I got scared."

He buried his face in his arms on the table which earned him his mother's comment, "At least you weren't hurt."

He continued to keep his face buried and was additionally rewarded by

40

the note taking officer who stated, "I recommend that you get him some counseling. He has gone through quite a traumatic experience."

His father walked him up to his room and left him to contemplate his day. T.J. just shook his head. He had found chairs!

*****

The next morning, T.J. and both of his parents had to undergo extensive questioning by the school's dean. Upon conclusion of the meeting, T.J. was informed that he would have to serve a 10 day suspension while the circumstances were reviewed.

The following day, his mother had to leave him in the care of the school psychologist, Ms. Maher. She once again had him recount his story, but she was much more probing. The questioning always seemed to steer toward why he had done something a certain way, rather than how he had done it. It wasn't until they got to the point of the fire that he realized how much she actually knew.

"After you poured the Sodium into the water, did you stay at the front of the room?" she asked.

"I believe that I returned to my seat."

"Why would you go back to your seat before the big finale?"

"I guess that I was done talking."

"It was from the back corner of the room that you disappeared when your presentation almost burned down the school. Do you want to tell me how you managed to disappear with your teacher actively looking for you?"

T.J. swallowed. They either had deduced where he had gone, or another student had seen his escape and told them. "I went through the passageway I found in the back corner of the room."

After he had given up that last piece of information which she had apparently been looking for, the whole process seemed to flow very quickly. Ms. Maher and T.J. both sat in comfortable chairs closely facing one another, and the interview proceeded again from the very beginning. This time he started from his resolution to find where the school kept the missing chairs. She went step by step through what he had been thinking and feeling as he recounted his story. He finally came to admit needing the diversion, but not expecting the intensity of the reaction. The meeting culminated with T.J. telling of his distress at seeing the school surrounded by firemen.

The following Monday, T.J. and his parents were called in to the school for another meeting. This time, they were led to a bigger room where a small group of people were waiting. They were greeted by Ms. Maher and led to some seats. Introductions were made. The meeting would be led by Ms. Maher, but it was also attended by the Dean, his teacher Mr. Morrows, and another teacher who was from the Special Education department.

"Unfortunately, this meeting can turn out in only one of two ways," began Ms. Maher. "Due to the severity of the circumstances, and the fact that the story has gotten media attention from the fly over by the news helicopter, T.J. may very well leave this meeting expelled."

"But it is not like he actually burned the school down!" exclaimed his mother. "There ended up only being some broken windows."

The Dean countered, "He created a very dangerous situation at the school. That cannot be overlooked."

"Please," his father responded. "T.J. has a very good school record. He has great grades. This will take away his future."

Mr. Morrows spoke up. "I agree. Other than this stunt in my classroom, I found him to be an extremely curious student and a pleasure to teach."

"It is this curiosity, combined with his impulsiveness, and constant classroom disruptions, that is leading us toward the other option."

Mr. Morrows threw his arms into the air. "Yes, they count asking questions as classroom disruptions!" It appeared that Mr. Morrows was on T.J.'s side.

"What is the other option you spoke of?" asked his father.

Ms. Maher regained control of the meeting with a stern look at Mr. Morrows. "From my discussion with T.J. and interviews that I had with his other teachers, I feel that T.J. may have Attention-Deficit Hyperactivity Disorder, ADHD. If we agree at this meeting to label him with ADHD, we can do you a favor and postdate him into the Special Education department. If we do that, we can conclude the meeting about expulsion and turn it into what we call a *Manifestation Determination* meeting."

His mother was stunned. "You want to label my son with ADHD and put him in Special Ed? Won't that mar his school record? What about next year in high school? Will he still be Special Ed? Won't that ultimately ruin his chance to go to college?"

Ms. Maher responded, "Yes, he will have to be in the Special Education program in high school, but that does not mean he will apply to anything other than regular classes. Being in Special Education does not mar his school record. All it will mean is that he will have a case manager who will monitor his progress and address any of his needs with the teachers."

His father leaned forward and asked, "So our options are either to let T.J. be expelled or to allow him to be placed into the Special Education program, which will ultimately have no further consequences?"

For the first time in the meeting, the Special Education teacher spoke. "There will be a consequence. If you allow your son to enter the Special Education program with an ADHD label, then this meeting turns into a *Manifestation Determination* meeting. That meeting will determine whether the behavior leading to the discipline action was a manifestation of ADHD, which would be a foregone conclusion. At that point, we would inform you that due to the severity of the action caused by his ADHD, state law requires that T.J. be prescribed mandatory medication to treat the disorder before being allowed back in school."

*****

Warren had insisted that the nuclear reactors would prove difficult to remove. After Ethan had been given the reactor design, he had surprised Warren by having the tail section of the first submarine lopped off. The tail section was not on the essential components list. It was lifted by crane to the scrap pile in the corner of the lair humorously designated *Phoenix's-crap*.

He and Warren now entered the sub through the large gaping hole that had been the tail. "I would not have gone about it like that," began Warren, "but it does make the reactor disassembly much easier. Could you have the other teams do similar demolition to the other submarine tail sections?"

There were four teams of six men that worked directly under Ethan. He set three teams to the job of removing the remaining sub tail sections. When he returned to Warren and the first team, he found them donning radiation suits and entering the rear compartment.

Air Force Major Jim Hunter, leader of the fourth team, helped Ethan into a suit. It was hard for Ethan to move around in the heavy and confining suit, but the other team members seemed to move quite efficiently. They entered the compartment.

Warren was instructing the team in the removal of the radioactive fuel rods. Once that was complete, Ethan took over the task of informing the team on how to cut the reactor sections away from the hull. He was thankful that the designers of this submarine kept everything compartmentalized. Each section had to be itemized and placed into specific plastic crates. He took thorough notes on the disassembly steps.

After instructing Major Hunter to have certain items removed, Ethan headed back out with Warren to check on the other teams. Ethan scrambled out of the radiation suit and was relieved to be out of its confinement.

Major Jim Hunter asked, "Are you feeling well?

"Nothing that a long shower won't cure," replied Ethan. "It does get hot being suited up, inside an enclosed steel compartment, during the Florida summer. Throw in some radioactive rods, and a man can really work up a sweat."

Ethan was pleasantly surprised to see that the tail section that had been previously placed into the scrap area was already gone. While he had been in the bowels of that submarine for many hours working with the first team removing the core, the lair's other inhabitants had cleaned up the disposed portion of what had been a fast attack nuclear submarine. The other three teams had completed their removal of the additional tail sections. The last one was now being hoisted by crane toward the s-crap.

He exchanged a look with Warren. It was official. They were no longer submarines. Now they were just a collection of parts to be harvested.

*****

T.J sat with his parents at their kitchen table and ate in silence. He still had three days left of his suspension, and the stress of the situation was becoming unbearable. His parents had taken the tentative deal the school psychologist had offered to defer the expulsion, but they had assured him that it was mainly to stall and buy time to come to a family decision.

"For the last time, I will not allow my son to be drugged," argued his mother. "He is an intelligent boy who just made a mistake! They will not be pharmaceutically lobotomizing the curiosity from him."

"You know I don't want that either," countered his father.

T.J. could see the strain in their relationship. His parents had either been fighting or not speaking since the meeting.

"I don't know that we have many options," continued his father. "They said that it would apply to the final few weeks of this school year, but more importantly affect him next year when he goes to high school. We either trust the system when they put him into the Special Education program, or find a private school to put him into."

"But they will have him drugged!"

"Actually, it is only a mild stimulant to address hyperactivity. He would be on it for two weeks, and then we would have the whole summer break. Hopefully, we can get them to change their minds at the high school; however, Ms. Maher and the Dean were adamant."

"When did curiosity and asking questions in school become so difficult for teachers that they wish the student to be labeled ADHD? Even Mr. Morrows was furious. Ms. Maher should be ashamed at shoving her prognosis down our throats and pushing the drugging of children! It is a pretty sad way to control children in the classroom. I would rather home school him than let my son be conquered by such a system."

T.J. just listened. It had been the same discussion for the last two nights.

*****

"My fellow Americans," began President Stephen Ryan from behind his desk in the oval office. "I have called this special address to inform you of a bill that will be introduced in the Congress tomorrow."

"First, I would like to thank all of you for electing me to be your President. I am here to assure you that your support is well founded and that I have been busy the past four months in office. As you hired me to champion education and the environment, I am here to tell you my vision for the United States to lead the world on both counts.

"The environment is a great concern for me. Our world is in perilous jeopardy of teetering to the point of no return with Global Warming. That is why I teamed up with Al Gore to find a solution to the mess the world was willingly accepting. Shortly after being sworn in as President, I signed the bill that mandates a carbon capture program. This program has incentives for quick implementation, and I want to inform you that the U.S. government will be cutting the first checks for captured carbon dioxide in the coming month.

"Who says that progress must take a lot of time? With proper incentives and inspiration, scientists and engineers found a way to make this happen. I want to personally thank those men and women for their hard work, and point out to America my reverence for anyone willing to work hard in school and achieve the highest level of education that they can.

"As you know, I came to politics from the field of education. During my tenure as Speaker of the House, I helped increase the education budget, worked to build state-of-the-art schools, and mandated a series of programs that promoted science. I have been worried about America's infrastructure. That would include its schools. Not only has America led the world in defining what freedom means, it has led in innovation and invention. That is why I am putting forward the NASA School Leadership Bill.

"NASA will take ownership of all public high school science programs. This will be the agency's new mission. At this point, I am cutting off all further assistance to the International Space Station. This program costs too much without sufficient benefit to justify it. Don't get me wrong; I am still a scientist at heart and wish the universe and solar system to be studied to the fullest. I just won't allow taxpayer dollars to go to such an obsolete program.

"NASA will still have the responsibility to research and develop advanced aeronautics and space technologies, but their new primary objective will be to nurture and develop the love of science in our children. The first four years of the mandate will be in our high schools. In addition to NASA assigning science curricula, the best of our students will have the opportunity to participate in a new program.

"The new high school select program will be called the NOTC, which is short for NASA Officer Training Corps. A select few of our smartest students will be intellectually challenged to the fullest in this program. Upon completion of the NOTC program, these students will be eligible to enter into the next phase of NASA's mandate. They will have the opportunity to attend a free NASA University. We will be creating scientists. We will be inspiring all students with our quest for knowledge. Once again, we will be leading the world.

"NASA has a new mission. *NASA is an investment in America's future. As explorers, pioneers, and innovators, they will boldly expand the frontiers of science to inspire and serve America and benefit the quality of life on Earth.*

"With this bill, we will be securing America's future."

*****

It was the last day of his suspension, and T.J.'s parents were not surprised to once again be summoned to a school meeting. His father suspected that the school wanted assurances that they would be taking their poison pill, and his mother wanted to tell them what they could do with it. It had not been an easy few days for him, but he knew he would soon be back in school, even if it was under medication.

This meeting was only attended by Ms. Maher and the school principal, Mrs. Smith, in whose office they now sat. Apparently, Mrs. Smith could sense his parents' hostility toward Ms. Maher. "Please let's just get right to it. Your son will be coming back to school tomorrow."

His mother shot back, "Labeled ADHD, entered into the Special Ed program, and drugged!"

"Please, Mrs. Gillooley. Let me continue. Today, we received his test score from the National Standardized Testing which he took the day before the incident."

His parents sat back in their seats waiting for the other shoe to drop.

"Ms. Maher, would you please inform them about the test and their findings."

Ms. Maher opened a folder in front of her, but did not read from it. "This year's test was different from all past tests. Apparently, hidden throughout the test sections were some additional questions. These questions amounted to a personality trait assessment test. Your son scored outside the norm for this assessment."

T.J. did not like the sound of this. He specifically remembered those parts of the test. He had answered each of those questions honestly.

"Based on his answers," she continued, "T.J has been assessed to have an ADT personality. ADT is new terminology defined by the Department of Education which stands for Adventurous Display Tendencies. Based on this rating and the high test scores in the other sections, T.J. has been recommended for the new NOTC program."

"The President's new program?" his father asked.

Mrs. Smith stated, "Yes. He has been selected for the program. Even Ms. Maher agrees that ADT supersedes the ADHD diagnosis she was recommending. T.J. has served his time off for the incident, and I feel the school will be honored to have him represent us in the program."

"What is NOTC?" asked T.J.

His father replied, "It looks like you will be in the NASA Officer Training Corps in high school."

T.J. was pleasantly surprised by the news. He couldn't wait to tell Mr. Morrows tomorrow.

*****

Ethan was a little fed up with the blind instructions. While Warren had spent the last few weeks working on upgrades for the nuclear reactors, Ethan had his teams remove the turbine generators, the electrolytic oxygen generators, the atmosphere controls, the carbon dioxide scrubbers, and all of the ballast tanks and pumps. Today, they had removed the Dry Deck Shelters which had been used to deliver Navy Seal teams while submerged. Once they finally got them crated up, all of the essential components from his Christmas list were wrapped up and ready for delivery. It irritated him that he still had no idea what they would be used for.

After another long day, Ethan and Warren sat in a quiet Air Force canteen enjoying a beer. Ethan was determined to find out what Warren actually thought of the project.

Ethan finished his first beer and ordered another round. "I just about completed my punch list for the subs. How about you?"

"The last reactor has been retrofitted and can be refueled. I am as far as I can go on them until given further instructions. It is not like them to leave us without work to do."

"We must be working faster than they expected," replied Ethan. "But to be honest, they had us chop up these subs every which way, and I still don't know what they'll be used for."

As the beers were dropped off, Warren added, "My whole career has been vested in building something for which I never really understood its ultimate use."

"Come on, Warren. They had me scrap all of the weapons systems."

"The subs had no weapons on board anyway. They don't store live torpedoes and missiles in a dead ship. You just scrapped the tubes."

"How do you explain the fact that none of the sonar or navigation systems were on our list of essential components?" asked Ethan.

"They were antiquated designs. You would never build them into a new boat." Warren laughed into his beer. "Besides, I don't think you know what we are really doing."

"Hell! I am an aeronautical engineer. I don't do submarines!"

Warren set his beer down. "Ethan, you look to me for answers because I am Navy. You're the Air Force top dog engineer. To be honest, I think you must be an idiot savant. Think about it. This is not a naval base. We have been working in another top secret Air Force base under the auspice of NASA. We are on their turf. We cut up my subs and collected the reactors, generators, oxygen generators, and atmosphere controls. You are the aeronautical engineer. Why do you think we are here in NASA's backyard?"

Ethan only stared at Warren. It was too implausible.

"That's right," continued Warren. "They won't be used to build a new nuclear submarine. They aren't even for underwater. They are for outer space!"

NOTC

This was T.J.'s first time at Disney World and he was really digging Epcot's futuristic flare. Wearing the NOTC cadet uniform, he had been allowed into the park accompanied by his parents two hours prior to the official park opening. Their only mandate was that he had to visit the attractions *Spaceship Earth* and *Mission: Space*. He was slightly surprised at the number of other cadets that he was seeing. They too were following their NOTC orientation agendas. Now that it was 9am and with his first assignments complete he left his parents to check in at *The Land* attraction.

A NASA representative stepped to the microphone in front of the assembled cadets. He also wore the blue, astronaut flight suit like T.J. and the others.

"Good morning, Cadets. I would like to welcome you to the first session of your orientation program. I am here to explain to you why *The Land* is a pertinent site to begin your training.

"Most people assume NASA has our eyes only on outer space. It is more correct to state that NASA's goal is scientific exploration. Mainly, this has been done through studying the heavens. However, often we learn more by using our assets to look inward toward the Earth. Our satellites have witnessed climate changes, atmosphere and weather fluctuations, and ecosystem dynamics. Our tools allow us to witness science from a different perspective.

"Why would one of NASA's objectives be to study the Earth? How can we expect to understand our place in the Universe, without first knowing our home, the Earth? I think we can all agree that there is value to be gained from understanding the world we live on.

"*The Land* was created to show man's interaction and responsibility to the Earth. We can learn about how humans can affect the land. More interesting is the demonstration of future technologies. Here, we can witness how the scientific process affects how mankind better learns to live off the land. If you witness this attraction through the lens of NASA, you might also see how the technologies shown here might be implemented into future settlements in outer space.

"Learning about the Earth and developing technologies to best utilize its resources is essential in furthering the sciences that will someday take mankind from our home on Earth up to new frontiers in space."

After breaking into groups, instructors led them through the gardens while emphasizing the pertinent technologies. They observed greenhouses, hydroponics, plant grafting, and hybridization.

T.J. was enthralled with the place. Tackling the issues associated with growing plants in space had peaked his curiosity! He wanted to learn more.

*****

T.J.'s next session took place at *The Seas*. This time the cadets were asked to enjoy the attraction. They would later participate in a discussion. He immersed himself in the surreal oceanic experience. He saw some wonderfully exotic sights. Now he was excited to hear from a different NASA instructor who stood before his group.

"From the looks on your faces, I can see that everyone is enjoying themselves. I will now tell you why this attraction is so very important to this program.

"Yes, I know what you are thinking. You just came from *The Land* and believe it runs along a common line of reason. Sure, NASA does watch the Earth's oceans. Yes, our interaction with the world's oceans can affect mankind's very existence. It is more than that.

"It is about exploration. This was an experience of adventure. Each of you has been selected for that very reason. You are adventurers. The most important criteria for your placement into this program is your disposition to explore new things. You also scored very well on the tests, so you are smart.

"One of NASA's main objectives is to inspire the next generation of explorers. Just as we can learn about other worlds by studying our own, mankind can fuel the adventurous spirit to explore our Universe by starting from the bottom of our oceans."

*****

The last morning session T.J. attended was held at *The Energy Universe*. Here he learned about the past, present, and potential future of Energy. The NASA instructor gave his speech and concluded by stating, "Energy is the lifeblood of a technological society. Whether on or off the grid, powering transportation or delivering information, it is imperative to Earth's survival and the future of mankind to find new means for energy. This can only be accomplished through the inventiveness of scientists. You have been chosen to be those scientists."

Following the morning sessions, T.J. reconnected with his parents and enjoyed lunch on the World Showcase side of the park. They stopped first in the area representing Mexico and sampled the fare. As they walked through the region representing China, they realized almost everybody was just passing through to the next area. It appeared that people were still too sensitive to the casualties in Argentina to want to experience Chinese culture. They finally arrived at the American Garden Pavilion with plenty of time to get good seats for the final orientation presentation.

Another man wearing the blue, NASA flight suit stepped onto the stage and up to the podium. "My name is Paul Hogan, and I am NASA's Associate Administrator of Science. When one thinks of NASA, it is typically associated with space operations, space exploration, and aeronautics. One of NASA's most important objectives, since it is the directive that I am in charge of, is the advancement of scientific knowledge. The President reasserted this objective when he gave NASA the additional curriculum responsibility for high school science programs and to oversee the newly created NASA

Officer Training Corps program.

"I hope you are enjoying the venue NASA chose for your orientation into the NOTC program. I am sure you can appreciate the significance of this site. Not just because of the beautiful weather. Not only for the fact that it is only an hour from the Kennedy Space Center, which you shall be visiting tomorrow. Epcot's theme is to inspire technological innovation. The acronym EPCOT actually stands for Experimental Prototype Community of Tomorrow. It is the perfect place to discuss the inception of the NOTC program.

"NOTC, the NASA Officer Training Corps, was mandated three months ago by President Ryan. Its mission is to instill core principles of science into special select students. You have tested to be intelligent. You were found to have a spirit of adventure. Now you shall have the resources to foster those traits that champion science.

"What does participation in NOTC mean for you in high school? You will continue to have standard high school courses such as English, math, and history. Further, you will participate in science classes with the rest of the school population; however, the science curriculum will now be under the purview of NASA. Most importantly, you will participate in the Core Training Principles program, of which you got a glimpse today.

"At the attraction, *The Land*, you saw how humans can affect the Earth. You will learn the *value* of science by gaining an understanding of the land. In this core training program you will become Master Gardeners. You will learn about plants, of course. More importantly you will learn about agriculture, ecosystems, and biospheres. The most important biosphere you will discover is the world on which we live. I want to emphasize that this is a core program of NOTC. You will be discovering plants, while learning the value of science.

"You visited *The Seas*, which was an exciting view of the world beneath the oceans. It encouraged exploration of the world in which we live. To that end, you will be given the core training to become a Master Scuba Diver. You will become great swimmers. You will have some adventures. You will learn many skills. You will gain the spirit of adventure and exploration that NASA deems to be the essence of a scientist.

"You toured the Energy Universe and learned how energy is the lifeblood of technology. Innovations in science are essential for the continuation of mankind's trek into tomorrow. Our current path leads toward global changes, energy shortfalls, and economic stalling. Innovation gives us opportunity to create a new future. Toward that goal, you will be given the core training of Master Mechanic. The program includes mechanics, computers, and robotics. You will work with your hands. You will work with your mind. You will learn to create and innovate.

"You will take standard high school courses with a strong emphasis in science plus the core training program. For now, these core training principles may appear to you as mundane courses in gardening, physical education, and shop classes. Think of them as instilling and distilling into you the essence of the value of learning, exploration, and innovation.

"This is the NASA *Officer* Training Corps. Why do we use the term *officer* as part of the program name? NASA is a civilian government agency, but shares members with the military, specifically astronauts. Those astronauts have been its officers and have held the highest place of honor within NASA. They have been at the pinnacle of our organization. Now each of you will have the chance to be exemplary students. Initially you will be the symbol of scientific achievement in the education system. After graduating from the NOTC program, you will have the opportunity to lead our scientific search for what America will look like in our future's technological world. Whether you choose to become scientists or astronauts, you will have the opportunity to be a part of the NASA family.

"This program will be difficult. Your school day will be longer than most. This program will be rewarding. You will learn more than most. While all high school students will learn science, you will become scientists. You will be the exemplar students. The NASA flight suit will be the uniform you will wear each week on Friday. We will inspire you and you in turn will inspire the world."

The NASA administrator walked off the stage and T.J. and his parents started to file out of the theater with the rest of the group. Instructions were given over the loud speaker as to the time the buses would pick them up in the morning for their trip to the Kennedy Space Center to meet their new family. T.J. could hardly wait to discuss his thoughts with his parents. He was going to be an astronaut!

*****

Peter Owens, the Secretary of State, entered the oval office in a very serious mood. The President motioned him to the chair opposite his desk as he hung up the phone.

"Well Peter, I hope you have some good news for me."

"No, Mr. President. The Chinese have come right out and told me that they have no intention of leaving Ushuaia. They would not let us into the talks with Argentina. We had pushed to get invited to the table to promote a treaty. They took issue with the word *treaty*, denied our request to attend, and came away with a trade deal that they state legitimizes their presence in Ushuaia. It is unfortunate that, after all our efforts to keep Russia out of Cuba and Venezuela, the Chinese snuck their way into the neighborhood." Owens paused.

"We never thought they would leave anyway, after such a bold invasion," said Stephen, taking measure of his demeanor and determining that he was about to get the bad news.

"I just left a very disturbing meeting with the Chinese Ambassador." Again Owens paused. "The Chinese claim that our moves into Ecuador are escalating the situation and demand that we leave immediately. In the Ambassador's own words, he stated, *"We were there first.""*

"Now they lay claim to South America? They are making me second guess the decision not to send the carrier group down there to knock them off the continent!" Stephen stood up and walked over to the window. "What are the Russians doing?"

"Currently, they are just watching. They love the turmoil and may very well take advantage of the tensions."

Stephen sat back down. "Tell the Chinese that our trade agreement with Ecuador was in the works long before they invaded into South America. We will honor their agreement with Argentina, but will protect the sovereignty of our friends in neighboring Chile. Then, get the State Department to become friends with Chile. Get their president to Washington as soon as possible for a very public meeting to discuss our strong relations."

56

"Great tactic," agreed Owen.

"Have they made any actual moves to accompany their verbiage, *escalate* and *demand*?"

"No, Mr. President. They are still maintaining their current positions on land and have only their tactical submarines at sea."

"Well, let's try and keep this dialed down as long as possible. While the Phoenix project has been moving along quicker than I anticipated, we cannot afford another situation until I pull the trigger."

*****

It was late in the evening and time for his daily video conference with Dr. Kevin Scott. His friend appeared on a portion of the monitor. "Kevin, give me some good news for a change?"

"When have I ever given you bad news?" replied Kevin. "We have moved the vision from a concept into plan, and now it's a reality."

"Now if only all of the pieces come together to show the picture we envisioned. In the meantime, I have to avert war as we play our silly games."

"Mr. President, I think you will agree that nothing we have done can be called silly. It may be science fiction but never silly."

"Kevin, the Chinese have informed us that we need to get out of South America."

"But we can't. Ecuador is essential to our success!"

"I know. I had a long meeting with General McKnabb earlier this evening and informed him that he needs to complete the bases there as soon as possible. He told me that the carrier fleet has already set up in the Port of Guayaquil. The area is secure and construction of a base there would be a simple process."

"But it's the other base that is essential. What did he say about your timetable for that?"

Stephen pulled up some data on the screen for Kevin to see on his end.

"This is the timeline that I forced the General to agree to. To date, he had only sent scouts and the Army Corps of Engineers to evaluate the area. The engineers reported back in the kindest terms that orders to construct a base at that location are crazy. They don't recommend building on top of a glacier. They stated the air was too thin. They informed their command that the mountain is known as the highest point on Earth and that only one hundred of the six hundred annual experts that attempt the climb actually reach the summit. Their command passed that information up the ladder thinking someone had made a mistake."

Kevin interrupted, "But that is why we need it."

"In my meeting with General McKnabb, I informed him that the information was correct. While Mt. Everest is famous for being the tallest mountain in the world, Mt. Chimborazo in Ecuador is a dormant volcano that happens to be the *highest* point on Earth. I educated him on the fact that the Earth actually bulges at the equator, thus making the summit of Chimborazo two miles further from the center of the Earth."

"Doesn't he recall why we need it?"

"I reminded him," said Stephen. "The General assured me that he would have a team to the summit by the end of the week and claim it as our own. The Army Corps of Engineers has started rebuilding the rail line."

"An essential start if we wish to get all the materials from the port to the highest point on Earth."

"Kevin, General McKnabb agreed to my timeline. Can you assure me that you are meeting your schedule?"

"I am in Houston now. The mission appears to be a success and the assets landed intact. The Cats are ready to perform their tasks."

"That is some great news. I am just worried that the Chinese will prompt us to show our hand too soon. I need the Phoenix team to be prepared. If we show some transparency to the Chinese regarding our intentions in Ecuador, it will give us some valuable breathing room to get over the next set of hurdles."

"I will fly out in the morning and personally oversee the final project assembly."

*****

"Consider this the heart of the organization you now belong to," called the guide to the cadets and their families. "Welcome to NASA's Kennedy Space Center, where the adventure to explore outer space truly begins. We will start in an area called *Rocket Garden*. Be aware that all of these are actual rockets that have just never been launched into space."

T.J. walked in among the incredibly large rockets that stood at the ready. He came to the Apollo capsule which displayed three suited astronauts inside. He could see himself in one of their places. He looked up at an immense rocket labeled as the Gemini Titan. He imagined that it would have to be that big to contain enough power to get an astronaut in training like himself up to the Moon. He finally noticed the largest rocket in the garden. He had not realized the structure was an actual rocket because it was the only one laid on its side. It was labeled the Saturn-1B and it was enormous. He felt a thrill at seeing such a powerful rocket.

His group finished their walk through the Rocket Garden, and their guide led them off toward the IMAX Theater.

*****

Ethan Dire watched the new cadets attempting to maintain a professional composure. While he wore his Air Force uniform, he was amused that the guide and all of the children were sporting NASA flight suits. Only the parents of the cadets wore civilian clothing. He had been ordered to attend an afternoon meeting here at NASA's Kennedy Space Center, so he came early to tag along on one of the morning tours. He was impressed that the children seemed so attentive. Ethan imagined these NOTC youths would soon inspire the scientific community.

He decided to skip the IMAX movie about life in space. He had never been one to enjoy watching movies. In the Rocket Garden, he stopped where the actual Saturn-1B was displayed. It had been NASA's emergency vehicle in case the Sky Lab astronauts had required rescue. He wished that he had security clearance at NASA to get a closer look at the rockets.

While walking around, a large reflective structure in the distance caught his eye. Ethan came upon a giant black marble wall with a plaque entitled The Space Mirror Memorial. It was a tribute to those astronauts who had lost their lives in the service of the United States space program.

Reading the plaque, Ethan's chest tightened. As he read the illuminated names through the black granite, he stopped at the name of an Air Force test pilot. He could feel his eyes burn as he recalled the small wall of names kept at Area 51. He could remember each of the casualties that he attributed to his own work. It was this part of his job that he truly detested. He could handle the responsibility of making war machines to protect his country, but still felt incredible sorrow for the heroic men that lost their lives testing his theoretical principles of aeronautics. At least he could be grateful that he no longer had that responsibility.

Realizing the amount of time he had spent reflecting on the past, Ethan hurried back to catch his group coming out of their short movie.

*****

T.J. left the IMAX and walked over to board the tour bus. He could not get the images of the movie about life in space out of his mind. The special effects had given him the sensation of rocket propelled flight, taking him to the surface of the Moon. Only 12 men had ever walked on the Moon, but there he was experiencing the lunar landscape through the 3D effects of the IMAX. He had seen the futuristic lunar base where he might someday live. He had walked on the surface and visited sites that some might consider dangerous, but he considered magnificent. He truly had envisioned himself on the Moon.

He was barely conscious of his surroundings until the bus stopped and the guide called out, "We are at the Vehicle Assembly Building. This is the third largest building in the world. It is here that the shuttle orbiter is attached to the two solid rocket boosters and the external tank."

The other cadets were piling off the bus with their families. His Dad nudged him into the line. T.J. was impressed to see that the building had real activity going on inside. While he did not actually see the shuttle, the guide pointed out the mobile launch vehicle apparently loaded with two solid rocket boosters. The crawler-transport was positioned outside of the large bay doors. He was disappointed that the shuttle program had been cancelled; otherwise, he might have been watching the shuttle being attached at that very moment.

*****

Ethan flashed his credentials and told the guide that he would be leaving the group at this point. He headed over to the Launch Control Center for his meeting with Dr. Kevin Scott. He checked in with security and was escorted to a waiting room where he found Warren Poet already seated.

"I guess today is a good day to find out what we have been working on," stated Warren. Over the past few weeks, Warren had continued to avoid talking about his beliefs about the real purpose of the project. The door opened and Dr. Kevin Scott poked his head in.

"Gentlemen, please follow me."

Ethan walked down numerous hallways. They finally stopped before a door labeled Firing Room 4.

"I don't have to remind you of your top secret clearance," stated Dr. Kevin Scott before opening the door. "What you are about to become part of is currently our country's best kept secret."

Ethan entered and quickly surveyed his surroundings. He was in a high-tech auditorium loaded with computer monitors, wall sized displays, and a spectacular, full wall window view of the shuttle launch pad. This was the NASA nerve center. There were about twenty other people already seated behind monitors scattered about the room.

Dr. Kevin Scott ushered Ethan and Warren to their seats. "This was called *Mission Control*, back in the day when the shuttle program was still ongoing. You might be surprised to know that it is still called *Mission Control*. But now I will have to let you in on what the mission is that it controls. Dr. Kylie Williams, if you will please bring them up to speed on the details of Project Phoenix."

A younger woman stood and walked to the display wall which illuminated to a view of the world from space. "While you may believe the name Phoenix refers to one of the Los Angeles class submarines that you two have been disassembling, it actually serves a much higher purpose. I am talking about the mythological bird that symbolizes immortality and resurrection. NASA has been dying. People are no longer inspired by the science that NASA has been hypothesizing for the past thirty years. The cost benefit relationship has a large debt in the eyes of the public. Just like the phoenix, NASA feels its death approaching. It has thrown itself onto the pyre with the hope of rising up again with a resurrected life and new mission."

She turned to the display showing the world rotating on its axis. Extending from the Earth's surface into space was something that appeared to be the Seattle Space Needle. "Our mission objective starts with the concept sometimes referred to as the *Space Elevator*. The theory works just like it sounds. We propose to build a structure that would transport materials into space without the need of launching them from the ground on rockets."

Dr. Kevin Scott joined her at the front and added, "Space launches are expensive. They are also very dangerous. I don't think many would accept a position where the odds are one in every fifty flights would result in catastrophic death."

Ethan found himself nodding agreement as Dr. Kevin Scott sat back down in the front row.

"The theory has been around for a while, but the technology did not exist," continued Dr. Kylie Williams. "Now we have what we believe is a multipronged solution to the problem. The design strategy previously failed because there was no known material capable of sustaining the stress of such a large structure. We thought we had found a material that could handle a much greater tensile stress, but it had still been insufficient to support the structure. Our final break came when we found a special benefactor. He has given us a means to push from the realm of a theoretical solution into reality."

The display changed from the mock-up to a schematic of the space elevator. "The elevator does not work in the typical fashion of an elevator. The transport compartment does not get pulled up and down by the cable. It is actually a climber that crawls up the cable. The enormous length of the cable requires it to be extremely strong to handle all of its weight below. The cable needs to be much thicker at the top than at the bottom, making it impossible to use a movable cable. Only the powered climber will move. Due to the length of time to transit from the ground into space, most often it will move in one direction. Up."

"What will be the purpose of the space elevator?" asked Warren.

"The climbers can actually speed up enormously the farther they get from the Earth. They can reach the escape velocity required to leave Earth's orbit. The initial use will be toward saving the world from the threat of global warming. We will be launching captured carbon dioxide into space. Once built, this type of launch will be extremely reliable and affordable."

Ethan found it comforting to shift his thoughts from building weapons to a paradigm of working to save the environment. He was still anxious about what he was doing there.

"While the cable is the most important and expensive part of the structure, we plan to have two running up into space. This way there is the extra support for the climber in case of a catastrophic incident such as a meteorite, space debris, or even a satellite that could sever a cable. This also allows us the opportunity to power the climbers through the two independent cables."

Warren asked, "What keeps the cables from falling back to the ground?"

Dr. Kevin Scott stepped forward and replied, "Good question, but I should inform you that you both have been working on that portion of the project for the last six months. The plan is to place your *Submarines* into geostationary orbit. Their angular momentum will act as a counterweight to the cables."

Dr. Williams laughed. "That's just like Kevin to oversimplify the challenge. It would actually be wonderful to place some of those Los Angeles class submarines up there as the counterweight. Unfortunately, that would be impossible due to their incredible weight. How heavy is one of those subs, Mr. Poet?"

Warren responded, "Six thousand tons."

"Currently, our Delta IV heavy lift rocket is capable of bringing 10 ton of payload to geosynchronous orbit. Even dismantling it into pieces as you have done would take six hundred launches at an incredible cost."

"It is too bad you couldn't use the cables to hoist up the components," Ethan chimed in. "If you could manage to get sufficient initial ballast for the counterweight, then you could slowly pull up the components and add to the counterweight."

Dr. Kylie Williams turned toward Dr. Kevin Scott. "I like them already. They'll be a superb addition to the team." She winked at Ethan. "That is the plan. We plan to have the three space shuttles carry the cables up to geostationary orbit."

"Wasn't the shuttle program grounded?" inquired Warren.

"They were grounded and shipped off to various museums around the country," agreed Dr. Kevin Scott. "Unfortunately, NASA forgot to remove some critical, high security components which happen to be surrounded by asbestos. We thought it best to bring them back here to remedy the problem. Once they are back, we might find something that needs to be shuttled."

"Actually, the shuttle program is still cancelled," replied Dr. Kylie Williams. "They will no longer be in use for ferrying supplies and components to the International Space Station. This will be their last launch, and once they are up there they are never coming back down. We intend to link them together as the ballast for the initial counterweight. They will lower the cables to the ground base. At that point, we will have a very low weight capacity space elevator until additional ballast can be raised via the elevator to the space base."

"Space base? How high up is this geosynchronous orbit?" asked Warren.

"The International Space Station is in what we call *Low Earth Orbit* at two hundred miles up," responded Dr. Williams. "A *Geostationary Orbit* is exactly over the equator and is at a distance where the velocity of the orbit exactly matches the rotation of the Earth. An object in *Geostationary Orbit* always maintains its exact position directly over the same location on Earth. This orbit is about twenty-two thousand miles up, approximately one tenth of the distance to the Moon."

"Twenty-two thousand miles!" exclaimed Ethan. "I thought that the shuttle could not get more than five hundred miles from Earth."

Dr. Kevin Scott stepped over to join Kylie. "The shuttles could potentially go anywhere," he stated. "They just do not have enough fuel to do so, usually.

This time we plan on them bringing their external tanks into *Low Earth Orbit*. From there, we plan to refuel them by launching heavy lift rockets carrying liquid fuel. Once their external tanks are reloaded, it will be much easier for them to jump to the geostationary orbit from the low earth orbit than from the ground. It still expends an extraordinary amount of energy to get the shuttles and the cables up there, but the goal of the project makes it worthwhile. Besides, these will be the last launches ever planned by NASA." Dr. Kevin Scott was watching Ethan closely.

"How will the Astronauts get back down?" Ethan asked.

"They won't be coming back down, at least not for a while. The shuttles might not be able to safely reenter the Earth's atmosphere from such a high altitude. Once up there, the shuttles are staying up there. The three teams of astronauts will then have plenty of motivation to accomplish their mission and assemble the space base."

"I know astronauts are chosen for their talents," began Ethan, "but do you expect any old team to be able to put those submarine components back into functional service?"

"No, I would expect that a sufficiently competent team had already been assembled and that an extraordinary team leader had already been chosen."

Ethan felt a chill wash up his spine. He exchanged a look with Warren and returned his focus back to Dr. Kevin Scott.

"Warren will make a perfect ground base leader. You, Ethan, have been chosen to lead the space base team."

"But I am not even an astronaut."

"Your application is approved. Do you accept the task?"

"I don't even know the team of astronauts. What if they cannot accomplish what I ask of them?"

Dr. Kevin Scott smiled in response. "Yes, you do. You have been their team leader for the last six months. The four teams of six men that have followed your instructions to deconstruct the submarines will comprise the three shuttle teams."

Ethan felt shocked at the news but kept his composure. They were all good, competent men. He knew that they could do it. Could he do it? He had never put himself in the *test pilot* role previously. Other men had always risked their lives for his work. Did he have the courage to do what they did? Did he have what it took to be an astronaut? "I'll do it," he heard himself say.

*****

T.J. stood before another enormous rocket. It dwarfed everything that he had seen so far today.

"This is the Saturn V replica," began their guide. "This was the rocket that carried the manned Apollo capsule to the Moon. All of its incredible size was required to contain the millions of pounds of fuel needed to have enough power, just to get two men to the Moon."

The group walked among the museum displays dedicated to the Moon rocket. It concerned T.J. that it took millions of pounds of fuel for just two men to enter space. He thought about how many people it took to keep NASA running. He knew it must be very expensive to keep the program going. They had gotten so few men into space and fewer still to the Moon. Would the program still be around when he was old enough to participate?

T.J. climbed the stairway around the rocket. He felt grateful that he had been given a chance to participate in the NOTC program. Placing a hand on the rocket hull, he pledged to himself to be the best student in the program. He would one day be an astronaut.

*****

Ethan walked with Warren across the empty lair. They had overseen the loading of all of the crated, essential components onto a barge. The barge had just been pulled by a tugboat out of the hangar and toward the port, where the cargo would be loaded onto a ship headed toward South America. Now they stood alone in the place where they had so quickly finished the project, but had only just begun the mission.

"I can't believe that the rest of the submarine hulls have already been disassembled and removed," said Warren.

"It was apparently not too difficult," replied Ethan. "Considering the reactors were removed and nothing else was to be salvaged, they probably found it fairly easy to scrap the rest. They could have brought in a larger crew to do that."

Ethan and Warren had spent the last few weeks with the engineers from NASA going over the design for the Space Elevator. Ethan knew that it had not been the teams of astronauts that had completed the deconstruction. They were now in full astronaut training mode, and Ethan had been required to spend a few hours each day training with them. While he found it to be exhilarating to train with the astronauts, he had been instructed that it was even more critical for him to get up to speed on his mission assignment. That was fine with him, if it meant being able to spend many hours each day in the company of Kylie.

"I was so busy working with the ground base engineers that it did not occur to me until yesterday that the nuclear reactor won't work in space," stated Warren. "Reactors require a lot of water for cooling purposes. In the ocean, submarines obviously have plenty of access to it. In space, there won't be enough heat exchange to keep the reactors safe."

"They have it worked out." Ethan explained, "They plan on slowly bringing up tons of water via the elevator to act as ballast. While the shell that we will be assembling is extremely lightweight, it will actually be creating a double hull in many places. A large amount of water will be circulated inside the hull void. This will help maintain temperature for the living quarters, give extra protection from solar radiation, and allow for a larger surface area for heat exchange into space."

"That is a novel idea," agreed Warren. "They just need to make sure that there is enough. The reactors can put off an extraordinary amount of heat and there are four of them."

"The design calls for only one to be placed on the station. The space station will be built in three levels. The top level will be the three shuttles docked together with their noses facing toward a center. The next level down will be the doughnut shaped corridor that will allow access to the shuttles and lower sections. We are going to use the SEAL Dry Deck Shelters from the subs as the connection points to the shuttles and various watertight hatches to also allow each section to be segregated from the rest in case of emergency. The lower section of the base will be five tubes facing outward like spokes on a bike. Only two adjacent sections will be designed for human use with one as sleeping quarters and the other for general use. The section across from these will contain the reactor which will generate electricity. Its primary use will be for powering the electrolysis units to create hydrogen and oxygen, which will be stored in the last two sections on each side of the reactor."

"The reactor will have plenty of output to supply electrolysis units," agreed Warren. "That should create a surplus of oxygen to maintain an atmosphere up there."

"They even intend to have enough hydrogen and oxygen to refuel the shuttles," stated Ethan.

"I thought they would be too high up to reenter the atmosphere safely."

"I suppose it's better to have an emergency exit than to have none at all," said Ethan.

"It appears that NASA found an economical way to keep some sort of space program alive, even in today's economy. From everything I have seen, they will be combating global warming using a space elevator paid for using funds from my recycled subs and the retired shuttles. I head off to Ecuador next week to await the space components. When do they plan on sending you up?"

"I have been told that everything is ready for our mission to commence. It is all contingent on how fast you can get the ground base operational."

Warren shrugged. "The army guys sound pretty optimistic on the construction. The hard part apparently is the addition of a power plant. I suggested setting up a reactor, but was told that they were not going to add anything nuclear to the ground operation and jeopardize Ecuadorian relations."

Ethan grimaced. "As long as you guys can maintain a secure power supply for us up there, it won't matter what's over them as it will be twenty-two thousand miles away. By the way, I was given some additional design requirements last night. Guess what goodies were added to your supplies heading south on the frigate?"

"I assume it's nothing for entertainment up there."

"You are right about that. It's not. They will have you sending up modified ground to air missiles. These are solid fuel rockets capable of long distance flight but not far enough to travel back down to the ground. There are also a couple of high powered lasers. I am supposed to have everything mounted in the reactor section. That thing will be bristling with weapons, but for what reason I can't tell. Maybe they will be for entertainment after all, like destroying meteorites playing a live version of the arcade game, *Asteroid*."

"Well, I'll try not to be in the ground base on the day they are lifting them up to you, just in case you drop one," Warren joked.

*****

President Stephen Ryan once again sat in the War Room with the National Security Council. He listened to General McKnabb report on the incident.

"Last night, the Chinese were actually brazen enough to send a sub up Ecuador's Guayas River, attempting to get past our carrier group stationed there. Knowing that they were there, we cornered them up against a sub net which we had recently put in place to protect our naval base construction. Rather than directly confronting them, our guys drove them into the net. We are currently answering their distress signal to get them untangled. A second Chinese sub is currently being monitored by our subs outside of the bay area."

"Has the Chinese Ambassador contacted the State Department yet?" asked Stephen.

"Not yet. Since we are conducting a *rescue* mission right now, I do not see any point in calling them," responded Secretary of State Peter Owens. "Let's get them all in custody and the sub under wraps if we can."

Stephen turned to the National Security Advisor and suggested, "Why don't you tell them about the other little encounter?"

"Three days ago, we picked up a team of mountain climbers on Mt.

Chimborazo in Ecuador. They were Chinese mountain climbers attempting to get to the summit, which our Army had closed off to all tourists. The Phoenix ground base is well under construction, and it appears to have drawn some attention. The Army Scouts handed the group straight over to the CIA, which had been anticipating the move."

The Secretary of Defense banged a fist on the table and interjected, "They are testing our defenses!"

Stephen leaned forward and stated, "Maybe. They definitely want to know what we are up to. It's a perfect time to tell them. It is sure to relax tensions as their leaders laugh at our efforts."

*****

"My fellow Americans," began the President, "I called for this special address to discuss a grave peril that we all face. Carbon Dioxide levels are reaching the point of no return. Global Warming will be hastened and environmental changes will soon be seen at an unprecedented pace. Our world is in cataclysmic danger."

He was seated at his desk reading from a teleprompter but facing the whole world through the cameras. Behind him, through the oval office windows, the sun was setting in a spectacular blaze of magenta. It created the perfect imagery of the world on fire.

"Our dependence on fossil fuels has brought us to the brink of disaster. Al Gore sounded the warning. I heard it. The carbon capture program has commenced and I am happy to announce that the United States is committed to keeping our excess carbon dioxide out of the atmosphere. Furthermore, we have found a means to remove this hazardous waste permanently. I am about to tell you of a new innovation that could potentially save our world.

Stephen leaned forward and addressed the camera. "The United States is about to create the first Space Elevator. It will be constructed at the equator with the permission of the Ecuadorian government. Ecuador has always proven a champion of the environment as shown by its stewardship of the Galapagos Islands. This Space Elevator base will be placed on top of their Mt. Chimborazo, which happens to be the point furthest from the center of the Earth. Cables will run all the way to a base similar to the recently abandoned International Space Station.

"While the International Space Station orbits the Earth at two hundred miles up, this base will orbit at twenty-two thousand miles above the Earth. Containers of captured, solid carbon dioxide will be brought up the elevator and expelled at escape velocity into space. While it had cost thousands of dollars to launch a single pound of cargo into space, this technology will allow a continuous low cost means to expel this waste."

"I am proud to announce that we have the means to save our world. I am putting the retired space shuttles back into service and commanding that they make one final voyage. Three shuttle crews will be undertaking a mission to construct a high altitude base, which will act as a counterweight to the elevator. NASA will be given the opportunity to rescue our world. Their mission will commence with the launch of the first shuttle one week from today. Let all the world wish them good luck and our prayers."

*****

Mondays had previously been a hard day to get through school for T.J. Now it was the Tuesday, Wednesday, and Thursday schedule that exhausted him the most. They contained an additional three hour long class in one of the core NOTC disciplines. Friday was still the best day of the week as he and the other nineteen NOTC students sported their NASA uniforms for the rest of the school.

It was Wednesday, and T.J. stood among his classmates in the middle of a large dirt and gravel lot under the hot summertime sun. He wondered why the Master Gardener class couldn't take place in the early morning.

Their teacher, Mrs. James, pulled a flatbed truck containing potted plants alongside the school bus. She motioned for the students to approach as she lowered the truck's tailgate revealing a pile of shovels. "This lot has been donated to us. We will attempt to reclaim it and turn it back into a vibrant prairie. In this truck there are seeds and plants that should sufficiently cover this area. Grab a shovel and spread out. You have two and a half hours before we need to return to the school. It will rain this evening, so we won't have to water them. Just get them into the ground. Let's see what we can accomplish."

T.J. grabbed a shovel, a packet of seeds, and a potted bush and headed away from the truck.

"Wait up," called Billy. He came hurrying up as fast he could, considering that he was holding a flat of plants and was dragging his shovel behind him.

T.J. had been extremely pleased that his friends, Billy, Lisa, and Todd, had all made it into the NOTC program. Apparently they were looking for a few good troublemakers.

Billy scraped his shovel against the ground. It was hard packed with gravel. "Did you notice how there are very few weeds actually attempting to scrounge out a life in this dirt?"

T.J. poked his shovel at the soil but barely made a mark in the ground. "The soil is too compacted for their roots to break through. If we work an area of soil enough, we might be able to make a little planting bed for the plants and seeds that we took. Let's just set them aside and try to break up this patch of ground."

The two started to work together turning the soil. They slowly but steadily were able to break up a six foot by six foot bed in just under two hours. Quickly during the last thirty minutes, they spread a couple of seed packets and planted the flat of plants. As they were working to get the bush planted, Mrs. James approached.

"We are almost done," Billy said. "Just a couple more minutes and our bed will be good to go."

"Don't rush," said Mrs. James. "I just came over to admire your work. It appears that you two accomplished quite a bit."

"We decided to tackle the horrible topsoil first. Once we had a small area broken up, it was much easier to actually do the planting."

"Good idea," agreed Mrs. James. "Finish up and we'll see you on the bus." She headed back toward the other students who were collecting around the bus.

T.J. dropped the bush into the hole and helped Billy push the dusty soil back around the root ball. As they headed back toward the bus, he noticed that there were very few plants scattered across the lot. He hoped the seeds would fill in the voids. Otherwise, it wouldn't end up looking much like a meadow.

*****

"Final check of flight controls," announced a voice over the speaker.

Ethan was suited up and strapped in. It was not a simulator practice session this time. He was on the shuttle *Discovery*.

Major Jim Hunter, the shuttle commander, called back to him, "Do you know what the Discovery was named after? It was for the ship in 1610 that attempted to find a northwest passage from the Atlantic to the Pacific Ocean. It instead discovered the Hudson Bay."

Ethan called back, "I wonder what we will be remembered for." He could see the pilot flipping switches.

"T minus one minute."

Ethan had nothing to do but wait.

"T minus 31 seconds." He saw the on-board computers power on.

"Discovery's computers are now controlling," announced the pilot.

"TEN, NINE, EIGHT, SEVEN, SIX…"

Time slowed for Ethan, and he wondered if this is what it was like just before you died. He felt the shuttle begin to rumble as the engines ignited. He realized that he had forgotten to say a prayer as the countdown continued.

"ENGINES START, FIVE, FOUR, THREE, TWO, ONE, ZERO, LIFTOFF!"

The shuttle was really rumbling now. He had expected to feel the moment of liftoff but had instead learned of it from the announcer. He was being pushed down hard into his seat as the shuttle accelerated away from the Earth.

"Our speed is now eleven thousand miles an hour and the engines are at full throttle," called the pilot. "Our altitude is fifteen miles and we are at twenty-one hundred miles an hour."

Ethan could not believe the gut retching acceleration. Suddenly, a jolt was felt and then the violent rumbling subsided. He broke into a cold sweat as he feared the shuttle engines had failed.

"Solid Rocket Boosters are away," announced the pilot.

Ethan thought he was getting used to their speed but was then pushed back into his seat as the shuttle once again accelerated. Finally, as he began to feel that he could no longer handle the pressure, the engines were throttled back. The shuttle had found its temporary low Earth orbit.

A cheer went up among the astronauts. They were beginning to unbuckle themselves from their seats and float around the room. Ethan realized the feeling of weightlessness after experiencing such violent G-force. His hands reached for the clamp controlling his seat belt. He attempted to remove the grimace from his face before anyone noticed, but it ended up not mattering as he vomited in his helmet.

He was floating in space.

*****

The feeling of weightlessness was disconcerting. He began to float upward and waved both of his arms around wildly while trying to maintain his balance. He floated back downward. He was almost overcome with excitement at this new sensation. Luckily, he had nothing to do but watch the instructor show them how to maintain neutral buoyancy. He exhaled deeply and watched the bubbles rise to the surface of the pool.

T.J. was enjoying this portion much more than the first part of the Physical Education class. It had started with the whole class having to stay in the deep end of the pool and float or tread water for ten minutes. That had been a lot of work for him. While most of the other kids were casually floating on their backs, T.J. alternated between treading water and swimming in small circles.

"Are you having some trouble T.J.?" asked the instructor, Mr. Graca.

"Not really," answered T.J. "I just don't float."

"Are you nervous? Sometimes that can keep a person from floating."

"Nope," replied T.J. "I feel perfectly comfortable in water. I just don't float. I didn't even float a few weeks back when I was in the ocean down in Florida. This is tiring though. Would it be OK if I hold my breath and sit underwater for a while?"

"Sure. I suppose that would be enough to prove that you are comfortable in water."

T.J. sat in a yoga position suspended under the surface, occasionally surfacing for air. He was not going to allow himself to be disqualified from the Scuba diving program just because he could not float. He had also decided not to be embarrassed about it either. None of the other students showed such composure in water by holding their breath and staying underwater for as long as he did.

The next portion of the class required each student to swim eight laps of the pool. T.J. quickly outpaced his group with sprinting freestyle speed. He completed four laps far ahead of the others, but was completely out of breath and had to stop and hold onto the side.

"Don't worry," called Mr. Graca. "There is no time limit on this exercise. Just catch your breath and then complete the remaining four laps at a more leisurely pace."

Before the first student could finally catch up to him, T.J. started off on the second half of the swim. He completed two more laps freestyle, but had to complete the last two laps performing the backstroke. He was still pleased with himself that he had finished first. He was so tired that he could barely pull himself out of the pool. Luckily, T.J. had been in the first group, so he was allowed plenty of time resting on the side of the pool while his other classmates completed their swims.

When the last student finished, Mr. Graca motioned them over to the bleachers.

"That may have felt like the hard part. Trust me. You will become extremely good swimmers. Each day that we meet, you will swim for me. On Thursdays, we meet for three hours and get to do additional activities, but you will always swim. Swimming is probably the best exercise that you can perform. It strengthens the entire body.

"Being in the NOTC program, you should know that astronauts are constantly floating around in zero gravity. They can lose a lot of their muscle mass and as much as one to two percent of their bone density each month that they are in space. NASA requires their astronauts to be very fit. In space they must exercise hard using treadmills and resistance systems to maintain their strength for when they return to Earth's gravity. Hard work also counters the bone loss.

"Here on terrestrial Earth, swimming will be your challenge. You will become fish in the water. You will also join the swim team. You will enjoy it. You will become stronger. Otherwise, you will not survive the NOTC program. Think of me as your drill sergeant.

"Now we come to the fun part. This will be the beginning of your NOTC adventure training. We will start scuba diving." He proceeded to show them a complete set of scuba equipment, including a diving computer. "You will each get your own dive computer compliments of NASA and a logbook to document all of our underwater activities."

T.J. raised his hand and asked, "Where is the diving knife?"

"Why do you need a knife?"

"In case I encounter a shark," responded T.J.

Mr. Graca laughed. "The only way that it would save you from a shark is if you stab your dive partner in the arm and swim away. No. You will not be getting dive knives. To be truthful, knives are never used for underwater defense. They are tools that can be helpful in the unlikely event that you get tangled up in something and need to be cut free. Most often they are used to communicate underwater. Tapping a metal knife on the bottom of your metal air tank is a great way to get someone's attention underwater." He continued to explain how to use the computer, regulator, and vest.

After helping them into their gear, Mr. Graca got everyone into the water and instructed them to hold onto the sides at the deep end. "Remember that the surface is in your mouth. Stay calm. We will go down and I will show you how to get neutral buoyancy like we discussed. Watch me, and when I signal to go up, return to the surface."

The class sunk to the bottom of the pool. The feeling of weightlessness was somewhat unsettling to T.J. Their instructor demonstrated how once the air volume had been properly adjusted in his buoyancy control vest, breathing in deeply would allow him to rise and exhaling would allow him to sink back down. T.J. watched Mr. Graca, floating vertical over the bottom, slowly rising up and back down. He saw the signal to return to the surface. T.J. responded by adding too much air to his vest. He rose too quickly and popped out of the surface along with the rest of his classmates.

"Just add a little bit of air to carry you up," instructed Mr. Graca. "This time when we go down, I want each of you to go to the bottom and attain neutral buoyancy. I will point to each of you, one at a time, and you will perform this buoyancy control along with the breathing exercise. Remember that the surface is in your mouth. Stay calm."

They sunk back down to the bottom. T.J. adjusted the amount of air in his vest to just allow him to rise up when he breathed in deeply and drop back down when he exhaled. He watched as the instructor moved among the students and had them demonstrate their buoyancy. The instructor pointed to his friend, Todd.

Todd instantly floated up to the surface. Mr. Graca swam up and pulled him back down to the bottom. He helped him adjust his vest, demonstrated the activity, and again pointed to Todd. Todd floated back to the surface. Apparently, Todd was getting so excited that his breathing was buoying him upward. Mr. Graca followed after him and was unsuccessful at pulling him from the surface.

T.J. was laughing uncontrollably. Bubbles were coughing through his regulator. As he lay on the bottom of the pool laughing and watching his bubbles rise to the surface, he recalled that the surface was in his mouth. He also realized how comfortable he was in this strange underwater world.

*****

"Are you ready?" asked Major Jim Hunter.

"The hatch is open, so I am technically outside already," Ethan called back, trying to sound confident. He stood looking out of the shuttle's open airlock. His gloved hands held tightly to the rails. This would be his first spacewalk. Two other astronauts were waiting on him to cross the eight foot chasm of empty space from inside the partially constructed corridor. He let go of the rail but still did not step out. He continued to stare and let his mind wander to what had already been accomplished.

The other astronauts had all been out on numerous spacewalks. For the initial walk, a pair of astronauts from each of the shuttles had gone outside for what had been the longest spacewalk in history, eight hours. They had managed to permanently tether the shuttles together using long poles connected in a tinker toy fashion. The shuttles now stood facing one another in an equilateral triangle approximately one hundred feet apart.

"Ground Base Phoenix, this is Space Base Phoenix. Do you copy?" called Ethan over the radio.

"Ground Base is here. It is good to hear your voice, Ethan."

"It is good to hear yours too, Warren. I am reporting that the scaffolding stage of the space base construction is complete. The shuttle level grid is secure. We are ready to commence stage two, the dropping down of the cables."

"We are glad to hear that. We'll be ready to secure and power them up when they finally make it down. Kylie Williams told me to tell you that she sends her regards."

"Is she there?" Ethan asked.

"She visited us upon the completion of the ground base but had to get back up to Houston. She told me that she would be back for the open house when you guys complete construction of the space base. She asked me to give you a message."

"What was it?" asked Ethan curiously.

"Hurry up."

The next stage began with Discovery opening its cargo bay doors. Ethan and two crew members monitored the display showing numerous camera angles of the action unfolding. The rest of the crew was at the airlock. Two astronauts, who had just completed their first spacewalk, were assisting the next two into their suits. Time was critical, and stage three would begin soon.

The bay doors were fully open, and Ethan could see what appeared to be a miniature spaceship dropping into view. Momentarily, its small booster engines ignited. It moved away from the shuttle and off into the blackness of space. He continued to watch the cargo bay doors and realized that he was seeing the essential elevator cable unfurling after it into space. He watched for an uneventful half hour. The counter on the bottom of the screen had grown to twenty. There were still twenty-two thousand two hundred and sixteen miles of cable to unwind.

Another display showed the bay doors to Atlantis swinging open. It too dropped a small rocket which propelled out in the opposite direction from the first. Its counter began to grow showing the status of the second cable unfurling into space. It would be nine more days of unwinding the cables before the rockets would propel them toward the ground where they could be attached to the ground base.

Ethan watched as Major Jim Hunter gave the order to begin execution of the third stage of construction. On the main display, Endeavor's cargo bay doors began to open. The next set of spacewalkers from each shuttle headed out of their respective airlocks and converged on the Endeavor bay. They withdrew the construction supplies and began constructing the base's corridor section. They appeared to be in a synchronized dance, slowly flying through space. In reality, they were each attached by lanyards to multiple points on the scaffolding of the shuttle grid. A spider web of cables had also been laid across the interior for them to traverse by battery powered wenches.

Work seemed to proceed very slowly. Two members from each shuttle crew were outside, two were monitoring them, and two were sleeping. Each spacewalk lasted just under six hours. It took over a week of rotating shifts for the fragile shell of the corridor to be laid out. Ethan had felt like a bystander with nothing better to do at this point than sleep, help the others into and out of their spacesuits, or assist in monitoring the progress of the spacewalkers so that the two crew members next in rotation could get some additional downtime.

"Space Base, this is Ground Base. Do you copy me?" called an unexpected voice over the speaker.

Ethan was surprised to realize how bored he had become over the past week, even though he was floating in the safety of a space shuttle. "This is Ethan Dire. We copy you."

"How is everything proceeding up there today?"

"I am told we are almost on schedule. Most of the corridor pieces are in position."

"I know you realize the urgency of the situation, being stranded up there with limited resources until the elevator is operational." The voice paused. "We thought that you would like to know that the cables have been acquired and attached to us here at Ground Base. We are powering them up so that you can recharge your batteries. The very first cable walker will immediately start carrying small volumes of water for ballasting your base. Expect the first shipment in approximately five days. Be ready to receive it. We now have the capability to get you additional supplies, but you still must continue to build and ballast the station as quickly as possible."

They had a lot yet to complete before it got here, Ethan thought.

Suddenly, Ethan was pushed from behind, and his mind snapped back to the present. He slowly jogged across the empty space to the waiting astronauts.

"Sorry about that," called Jim Hunter, following after. "The first step out is always the hardest. You OK?"

Ethan caught his breath and nonchalantly played off the incident. It had been a lot like tripping and then pretending that you intended to start running. "Sure. I was just appreciating my personal historic moment."

He wasn't upset with Jim for he knew that he had been frozen in place and needed the push. Now that he had crossed the open space, he found himself inside the confines of the constructed corridor. He realized that he could not easily get to free floating outer space from his present position.

Ethan began instructing the first team in the connecting of the SEAL Dry Dock Shelter to the corridor and mounting it to the shuttle. When they were busily performing the task, Jim led Ethan further down the corridor to the second shuttle team waiting at the next shelter connection. Again Ethan laid out the required task before being pulled to the third team. When he finished with them, he was not surprised to find Jim leading him once again to the first team.

Ethan and Jim met the team and assisted them in completing the assembly. After Ethan had thoroughly inspected their work, he was led to the second team and finally the third team for review. He entered his own shuttle through the newly installed hatches of the Dry Dock Shelter and was greeted by the cheers of his entire shuttle crew.

"Congratulations on your first spacewalk. At ten hours, you just broke the previous record."

Ethan was assisted out of his suit and wanted nothing more than to take a long hot shower. Unfortunately, there was not enough water on board to allow for more than a wipe off with a damp cloth.

Before Jim left he said to Ethan, "I know that you need to bunk down after that, but Ground Base wants you to call in with a status report."

Ethan headed to the front of the shuttle and called in. "Ground Base, this is Ethan Dire of the Space Base."

"Ground Base acknowledges you. We are patching you through to Houston Control."

"Congratulations, Ethan," responded a familiar voice.

"Kylie?"

"Yes. It's me. I have received reports that you and the team are about on schedule. The beanstalk is connected and the ballasting stage is underway. I just wanted you to know how proud we are of all of you. You are in my prayers."

"Thanks. You don't know how much it means to hear that."

"Well, I hate to cut this short, but I know how tired you must be. I also know that you will be out there again in twelve hours. Get some rest."

"I will. We will have this place habitable in no time," said Ethan. "You will have to come up for a visit."

"I would love to. Now, sweet dreams."

The next day was just as exhausting for Ethan. The teams were installing five watertight hatches in the corridor down to where the future compartments would be located. One final SEAL Dry Dock Shelter was also being installed to allow access from the space base into outer space. Even though Ethan now had the experience of being out of the shuttle, he could not quite get the chilling thought out of his mind that free space was on the other side of each hatch they were installing. He watched as a team worked a gasket between the corridor shell and hatch. He reached outside through the hatch and positioned a bolt through an opening. Using a torque wrench he began to work the nut into place.

*****

T.J. pulled hard and finally exerted enough torque on the wrench to break the nut free from the last bolt. He peeked out from beneath the Ford Focus and gave a "thumbs up" to his awaiting classmates. They hoisted the crumpled fender off the frame and placed it along the wall with the other scrapped parts. T.J. crawled out and joined the other students who were gathered around their teacher.

"Now that we have broken the shell of this egg, let's take an inventory of what is left inside for us," suggested Mr. Roedel. "While the body of this car looks fairly rumpled, that was not the reason that it was donated to us. It has worn tires, bad brakes, a slipping transmission, and a cracked head on the engine. To be honest, I would not recommend this car to any of you, even as a fixer-upper. It would be a horrible mistake. It is, on the other hand, the perfect candidate for your initiation into the Master Mechanic program.

"What we'll be doing this school year is dismantling this pile of parts and rebuilding a car from the ground up. Think "Pimp My Ride.""

A cheer arose from the students.

"We are going to make the most reliable, efficient, and modern vehicle that can be imagined, and I have a pretty good imagination. We will be putting the best parts that can be found into making it. Cost is not a factor." He smiled and added, "Mostly because we will be getting all of our parts from a junkyard."

T.J. found himself laughing alongside the others.

"There's one important thing to note about this car. It won't be running on petroleum fuels. Remember that this is the NOTC Master Mechanics program. You are here to learn and get hands on experience with machines with emphasis on the principles of innovation. This vehicle will be powered by a hydrogen cell. It will release zero emissions and be on the leading edge of technology in an effort to combat global warming. It will be less like the typical car's combustion engine and more akin to something that NASA would be building."

*****

"We cannot place our military into your countries at this time," stated President Stephen Ryan. He was seated in the Oval Office with the Presidents of Ecuador, Chile, and Columbia.

The Chilean President folded his arms and made his request again. "It could be just a token force to show the Chinese that we have your support. Chile has to be seen as an American ally. The Chinese are right on our southernmost border. We do not have the means to keep them out if they choose to also take our half of the peninsula."

"I can appreciate your request for assistance; however, if we move troops south right now, it might appear to the Chinese as a threat to their current tenuous position. They might feel the need to strike first to protect their newly acquired petroleum resources."

"But you have already made a major military movement into South America," pleaded the Chilean President.

"Our treaty and commitments in Ecuador had already been underway," refuted Stephen. "As the Ecuadorian President can attest, our treaty had already been signed before your country acquired its new neighbor."

The Ecuadorian President nodded. "We had negotiated the terms long before the Chinese joined us on the block. Now I am wondering if it was as good a deal as previously thought. My country now hosts a large American military presence with a potential enemy force in close proximity."

"With my country in between them," reminded the Chilean President.

"The United States does not want to initiate military actions against the Chinese," assured Stephen. "We have been working on toning down the situation through diplomacy. Unfortunately, the Chinese appear to be there to stay."

"Should not the President of Argentina be here with us?" asked the Colombian President.

"Unfortunately, my State Department has convinced me that Argentina needs to be put in a diplomatic time out for their participation with bringing in the Chinese. The South American nations need to make a strong joint statement to the Chinese, showing their solidarity against further encroachment and hostilities."

"Please, Mr. President, you must resume talks with the President of Argentina," stated the Chilean President. "It is true that the leaders in Ushuaia had been working with me toward seceding from Argentina to become part of Chile. That could have potentially brought conflict between our two nations. Even though we had anticipated the additional tensions, it made the most sense that the oil should have been pushed north through our oil pipeline on the northern half of the peninsula. We had been willing to give economic concessions to stave off any hostilities. Now that is a foregone conclusion. The Chinese ruthlessly took control of the situation. There is a steady stream of refugees entering Chile. Now, my country is in a very dangerous situation with an army on its border. We need your assistance."

Stephen nodded sympathetically. "I have been informed that the Chinese have fortified their positions in Ushuaia with an additional thirty thousand troops."

The Chilean President stood and walked over to the windows. "If you still believe that this is about oil, what is to stop them from moving their forces north and taking over the Chilean half of the peninsula? They would acquire our oil fields and give themselves geographic security by controlling the whole peninsula."

"We are aware of that possibility. That is why we urgently called this meeting. My intelligence analysts believe that the most likely scenario, based on recent Chinese actions, will be the complete evacuation of the Argentinean population from the peninsula. You may soon find a huge influx of refugees."

"My country cannot support such an influx of refugees who have had their livelihoods stolen from them. We will need the United Nations to step in and stop this," pleaded the Chilean President.

"That will be impossible, since China is on the UN Security Council," responded Stephen. "What we need is a treaty creating an organization similar to NATO, but for the Americas. Unfortunately, many of the South American countries are not true democracies and lean toward socialist allies such as China and Russia."

The Columbian President asserted, "It is time that we team up and work around them toward a common security. My country is tired of standing alone against neighbors that support guerrilla rebels and drug lords. They use socialism to protect the elite groups in power. We need a union of true democratic countries to stand together. Now we have an even bigger threat. That should help us toward this common goal."

"Yes. That could potentially stave off the Chinese moving northwest. At this time, the United States cannot act militarily to stop that action. It could escalate too quickly into a full-fledged world war. It needs to start with the South American democracies. Your countries along with Brazil need to show a combined military presence. The next step would be to have the Central American nations join your league. Finally, the United States and Canada could join and bolster the show of force. But everything needs to move quickly before more territory is taken by the Chinese. Unfortunately, I am not sure that we actually have enough time."

*****

The bus stopped and the NOTC students began to file off. T.J. was eager to see the progress on the prairie that they had planted last week. As he stepped off, his eyes looked for signs of their work. It looked just like the dirt and gravel lot that it had started as. He and the other students roamed over to the areas where they had personally worked.

No new sprout could be seen from the seeds. Of the live plants that he and Billy had planted, only the bush still had a small number of green leaves. After all of their hard work, it was still a barren landscape.

"Congratulations," greeted Mrs. James loudly, as she walked up to T.J. and Billy. The other students converged, curious about what had gone wrong and who was being congratulated. "This bush is the only sign of life left on the lot. Let's presume that we had been planting this area in a biosphere on another world to support us with a food supply. This would have been a dismal failure and we would likely all die. I find that it is often best to learn from our mistakes. Let's attempt to figure out what went wrong here."

"Don't you think it is as simple as not enough water and an extremely hot sun?" asked Billy.

"It's possible, but these were all sun loving plants. Also, it rained every other day, including the evening after they were planted. Come on. Play detective. What did you notice while you were planting?"

"The ground was extremely hard," offered T.J.

"Interesting point, and yet the ground seems fairly loose around this bush that is the last living relic from the very hardy plants that I gave you," rejoined Mrs. James.

"Billy and I really worked the soil before attempting to plant it."

"Maybe that has something to do with it still showing some signs of life. If the ground is too hard, even rain will just wash over and not penetrate the ground. Also, new roots cannot take hold if the ground is too hard. What else?"

"Well, there were an awful lot of rocks," stated Lisa. "When you finally went to fill in the hole, the soil was like a powder."

"Good observation. You call it soil. Why?"

"I guess that dirt would be more correct," responded Lisa. "It did not really seem like soil."

"Now we are getting somewhere," agreed Mrs. James. "Let us investigate that point. I have a bunch of soil test kits to determine what type of soil we have here." She ordered the students into groups of four and began to hand out boxes of test kits.

"First remove the kit labeled *Soil Type*," she requested. "Open the box and find a quart mason jar and measuring cup. Using a shovel, dig a six inch hole and fill the measuring cup with soil. Place the soil into the jar along with two cups of water. One of you should then shake the jar vigorously for several minutes and then allow it to sit still until the end of class. The soil composition will be determined later by how it settles."

The class was given a few minutes to perform the first test. T.J. again found it difficult to get the shovel through the top layer of soil, which was so compacted.

Mrs. James called out the next instruction to the groups who were spread out across the lot. "Fill the hole you dug with water and time how long it takes to empty. Document the time on the worksheet your group has been given."

Billy poured water into the hole and Lisa started the stopwatch which she had found on the bottom of the box. The water quickly disappeared from the hole.

"Please continue to document the observations that we are making on the worksheets," directed Mrs. James. "As you can see, there is very quick drainage. It appears that we have compacted ground that would make water penetration difficult. Once the water penetrates, it drains very quickly from the root level.

"Now, take out the *Composition* test kit. Remove the individual test tubes labeled pH, N, K, and P. Very carefully, without disturbing the sediment that is settling in the jar, use the eye dropper to fill each vial to the mark. Empty an indicator capsule matching the color of the cap into each vial. Shake for one minute and then determine results based on the included comparison charts."

T.J took one of the vials from the box and passed the others to each of his group. He filled it with solution from their mason jar and dumped in the indicator capsule. While he was shaking his, Todd danced past shaking his own vial. Mrs. James wandered over to witness their results.

"What did your group determine the pH to be?" she asked for all the groups to hear.

T.J. looked down and realized his vial was labeled pH. He compared it to the chart on the box and replied, "It looks like it has a 9 reading."

Mrs. James informed the class, "Most plants require a neutral soil pH. Neutral soil has a pH of 7. A result of 9 indicates very alkaline soil, which would make it difficult for plant roots to absorb nutrients. Higher pH can probably be attributed to the limestone rocks mixed into the soil. Let's look at the available nutrients. What's the nitrogen level indicated on the vial?"

She called out each of T.J.'s group's nutrient levels and informed them that the soil was deficient in each. She told them how nitrogen was essential for new plant growth and that low nitrogen could halt plant growth. Phosphorus was important for root and seed development. Potassium was important for sturdy stems. Deficiencies in any one of these macronutrients could severely stunt plant growth. "This soil is deficient in all three macronutrients. They are completely washed out, and due to the high pH level it would be difficult for the plants to take them up anyway. If we are short on the macronutrients, it would be a good guess that the micronutrients are also in short supply in this soil."

"Now, looking back at the mason jars, we can see about two inches of the bottom layer and a quarter inch each of the top two layers. The bottom layer is sand, a course material that allows for fast water drainage. The middle layer is silt, which is a mid-size particle good for water retention, plant root growth, and cohesive enough to retain nutrients. The top layer is composed of the smallest particles of clay. Healthy soil is typically composed of equal amounts of each to make a good loamy soil. This soil is unfortunately composed mostly of sandy particles.

"So why did our prairie fail? What we have is compacted, sandy soil that drains moisture too fast. The pH is too high for most plant types. The soil is virtually devoid of essential nutrients. I would say that we would be hard pressed to get anything to grow in this barren ground. You have just experienced the first challenge to growing food on another world.

"How do we overcome the challenge? We either pick plants that can survive in such harsh soil conditions or we fix the conditions. There happens to be a very easy means of correcting this soil's problems and that is to amend the soil with compost. Part of your schoolwork will be to run a community compost project and create enough compost to amend this lot and make a living prairie."

*****

Ethan watched with the others as the first cable walker lost velocity as it approached their space base. The powerful electromagnets, which were positioned around the shuttle grid, switched on and captured the walker as it released itself from the cable. The walker appeared to magically fly toward waiting spacewalkers, but in truth the coordinated efforts of the electromagnets carefully moved it into position. The walker was hooked onto the shuttle grid as a dress would be hung on a rack. It contained a paltry thirty gallon canister of water.

Ethan thought back to his harrowing experience installing the electromagnet array. It had been his first outer spacewalk. He and a team of astronauts had placed an electromagnet every ten meters around the one hundred meter circumference of the shuttle grid. Even being connected by lanyard directly to the grid, Ethan had not been able to shake the fear that he would float off into outer space. Then things had gotten drastically worse for him.

He had finished wiring the last electromagnet and had given the thumbs up signal to his partner. Suddenly, he found himself falling backwards away from the grid. Arms flailing, he had tried to catch hold but could not. It felt as if he had been pulled backwards away from the scaffolding. Luckily, he appeared to be heading directly toward his shuttle Endeavor. It had not been until he was caught by a laughing Major Jim Hunter, waiting at the shuttles airlock, that he realized that he had been played. They had used him to test the ability of the electromagnetic array to accurately move objects.

Time was of the essence to the spacewalkers. During the cable walker's transit up, power from the cable had heated the water in the canister. Having been released from the cable and floated in empty space, they had to pump off the hot water from the canister into the corridor hull before it froze. A pair of astronauts attached an umbilical hose to a section of hull sleeve that had been warmed by heat trace. The insulated and heated umbilical wound its way up toward another astronaut attached to the shuttle grid. This astronaut connected the umbilical to the canister, which repowered its internal heater. The pump switched on and the hull sleeve section began to inflate as it filled with water.

From the security of the shuttle's control room, Ethan watched the team of astronauts work quickly. He marveled at the coordination with which they worked. They only had one hour before the next cable walker would reach their base and require the same attention. With the canister now empty, the team began to move the heat trace from the filled hull sleeve to a different sleeve section. They completed the task just as a new crawler released from the cable and floated toward the awaiting astronaut attached to the shuttle grid. They made the required umbilical connections and the second hull sleeve was filled with water.

Ethan could not believe the exhausting pace that they had set for themselves. One small canister of water was to be received and emptied into the hull structure every hour for the next four days. They even found time to replenish their water supply and pump a few canisters of waste water into the hull.

The corridor was taking on its final shape as the expanded sleeve sections froze into a rigid structure. The hundredth cable walker hung empty from the shuttle grid. The space base received an additional dozen canisters directly to the shuttles. It was their replenishment supply of food and oxygen. The first receipts to the base were complete. The corridor now had a solid ice frame and they had ballasted the base by an extra twelve tons. Now they needed to send all of the walkers on a two day trip back down to the ground base where they would be refilled. It would be a full week before they expected shipments to their base again.

While the astronauts got some well-deserved rest, Ethan was busily studying the designs for the other structures that would be added to the space base. He would hold small training sessions to give them the scope of how they would assemble the two living quarter sections. He explained how they would implement the atmospheric controls. Ethan worried over the upcoming responsibility of installing the nuclear reactor and weapons systems.

*****

"A Master Gardener always knows the condition of his soil," called Mrs. James from the pinnacle of a large dirt mount to her students amassed below. "It is essential in getting the optimal growth for your plants. Optimal conditions do not mean I recommend the use of synthetic fertilizers. As a matter of personal preference, I rarely use synthetic fertilizers or pesticides. I find them unnecessary when you add one magical ingredient to your soil. This magic ingredient improves just about every variable responsible for a plant's optimal growth. Does anyone care to guess what it is?"

They stood in an industrial yard just outside of their city's landfill. T.J watched as a parade of garbage trucks wound down a path in the distance. He called out, "All plants need sunlight."

"Yes they do, but what ingredient improves soil for plants?"

Lisa answered, "Water does."

"Yes, both water and sunlight are essential ingredients for plants. However, I am talking about something that universally amends soil. I am standing on a pile of the magic ingredient, compost."

Someone called out, "Cow manure! Icky!" The whole class took a hesitant step back from the base of the compost pile.

Mrs. James reached down and grabbed a handful of the compost. "Yes, you can get composted manure. It happens to be a great source of potassium for plants." She sifted the compost through her fingers. "Gardeners often refer to this as *Black Gold*, because of its value in improving garden soil. Please get over your fear that it is poop and pick some up."

T.J. reached down and scooped up a handful. It was dark and crumbly. It did not resemble manure. He decided to smell it and discovered an earthy aroma.

"Compost is any kind of decayed organic matter. In the case of the pile you stand around, it was made from disposed yard waste. Let's consider all of the issues we had with the soil in our prairie.

"That was sandy soil where the water drained too fast. Never consider adding clay to sandy soil to amend it or vice versa. That would just create cement. Compost helps sandy soil by binding soil particles together and clay soil by making it looser. Compost creates ideal soil structure, allowing for roots, air, and water to penetrate easily. It helps retain water and nutrients long enough for the plants to access them.

"Our prairie soil was devoid of nutrients. Adding synthetic fertilizer would boost Nitrogen, Phosphorus and Potassium by a large amount for a short time. Compost adds a full spectrum of nutrients and releases them slowly over a long period of time. It adds the required macronutrients plus micronutrients such as trace elements that are essential to a plant's health.

"Soil pH is buffered by compost. As organic matter decays, it also adds a small amount of acid to the soil. Soil pH is critical to allowing roots to absorb nutrients. We will additionally use oak leaves and pine needles to lower the high pH of our prairie soil.

"Lastly, our compost will add a large amount of organic matter to our soil composition. A five percent addition of organic matter quadruples the soil's ability to hold water. The organic matter also attracts beneficial insects, worms, and organisms which break down organics into available plant nutrients. They also eat harmful pests. Composts actually helps plants defend against diseases. This is organic gardening, nature's intended way. Compost allows us to fix the soil without using synthetic fertilizers and pesticides.

"Now if we wish to improve the soil on the Martian or Lunar surface for NASA, compost would be the miraculous cure-all required. We will use the same fix for our prairie. We will come to this community compost location frequently during the semester to work a pile of organic matter. We will take grass clippings, tree leaves, sawdust, and manure into our pile. I will teach you how to properly maintain it. We will be monitoring its moisture level and temperature to properly cook it. We will help decompose organic material into our own black gold. This experiment will conclude next spring when we add it to the soil for another attempt at reviving our prairie."

T.J. squeezed the compost into a ball in his palm. He broke it up and let it fall through his fingers. They would be reviving lifeless soil just like could be done on the Moon.

*****

Steven watched as Kevin casually reclined in a chair at the Presidential residence in the White House. He could tell by Kevin's relaxed nature that he was very pleased with the progress report he would be giving. He was glad that he had asked his friend to meet here rather than in the more formal setting of the Oval Office. He recalled the days when they had sat over a chess board and discussed the impact of the symbiotic relationship between science and education. Now they were plotting world domination over the future.

"Well, Steven, it is going much better than we had anticipated. Looking back at how efficiently they disassembled the submarines, we should have known the team was capable of it. The space base hull is inflating like a jiffy pop."

"It didn't hurt that once they left low Earth orbit they were required to build it fast in order to survive," chided Steven.

"They are now tethered to the ground base, powered by the cables, and resupplied. They have more resources than the International Space Station ever had and at a fraction of the cost."

Stephen nodded his agreement. "Speaking of the International Space Station, which we unceremoniously placed out of service, I have had numerous offers of assistance on our Space Elevator."

Kevin sat forward excitedly. "Excellent. Who offered what? Have you accepted?"

"Of course I have not accepted. Remember what our ultimate goals are. We really can't let anybody in on the ground floor."

"Won't they be angry at being snubbed?"

"Considering how amused they were when I initiated the program, I decided to let them participate in the carbon capture program."

Kevin laughed and reclined back. "Good one. They mock you on the international stage for your carbon capture program. You counter punch by defunding the International Space Station. We begin construction on a grandiose space base that puts their space station to shame in functionality. They offer to help, and you allow those that had been ridiculing to participate by donating the carbon dioxide for the elevator which will be shooting it out into space."

"It is an absolutely ironic situation. Russia, who lost the most prestige with scrapping the International Space Station, pledged their carbon donations first. Most other industrialized nations followed suit. They will be making token donations to show their support of our program to save the world."

"You said Russia made pledges. Did China?"

"China is surprisingly quiet. It may be due to perceived tensions evolving from South America. We installed the naval base in Ecuador. Now they are fortifying the position with their own naval base and additional troops. They have expelled all of the Argentinean citizens from their half of the peninsula and Chile is readying for the potential incursion north."

"Seems like a dangerous situation," replied Kevin.

"We are trying to keep *friendly* communications open. We really need to change the whole conversation with them. How soon before the elevator is operational?"

Kevin opened his laptop and brought up pictures of Phoenix Space Base. "The shuttle grid and corridor level are in place. The cable is attached from the Phoenix Ground Base. The elevator is operational but at a very limited weight capacity. The first deliveries were only two hundred fifty pound cargoes, which gave the corridor hull an ice exoskeleton and added twelve tons of counterweight. We just completed the next set of deliveries to the station with cargoes of three hundred and thirty pounds each. It gave them enough water to create a nine inch ice wall around part of the corridor. Only seven more sets of deliveries over fourteen weeks before the corridor section is complete and the station is ballasted with over two hundred tons of ice."

"Then we can start on the lower compartments?" asked Stephen.

"Actually, they are already underway. The Station can receive one hundred twenty crawlers before reaching capacity and needing to send them back down. Since the cable can take crawlers only in one direction, turnaround time for them to come all the way back down and start to be received up there again is one week. Rather than giving them a well-deserved week off, I decided that would be the opportune time for them to perform construction. The first hundred crawlers carry water for filling the hull and ballasting. As the total weight goes up, the station can counterweight and bring up larger cargoes. At the end of a round of shipments, we deliver five cargoes of dry ice and ten of essential life support and construction supplies."

"Dry ice is being brought up already?" questioned Steven.

"It is as good a time as any to try out our CO_2 jets. We are mounting them around the shuttle grid to be potentially used for repositioning the Space Base. As we add weight, we will need to make orbital adjustments. The shuttles can do it, but they won't be there forever. The last five cargoes contained construction parts for the nuclear compartment. No time off for the weary."

*****

This was Ethan's first spacewalk in over two weeks. While the other astronauts had been busily rotating in and out of the shuttles to capture crawlers, he had been preparing in the background for this moment. At least he didn't have to don the extra radiation protection over the already cumbersome spacesuit. Not yet.

Ethan allowed the electromagnet tractor beams to carry him across empty space from his shuttle to the gaping opening of the base's first module. Upon reaching it, he connected a lanyard from the compartment and disconnected his shuttle lanyard. Six astronauts, two from each shuttle, were awaiting his instructions in this partially constructed nuke compartment.

Ethan was glad that they would be working at the farthest point from the opening. Moving toward the back, he looked up at the closed corridor hatch that he had helped install. He need not have used the tractor beam to get to this compartment. He could have left his shuttle and traveled here through the corridor. He would have had to be careful in the tinfoil thin areas not yet protected by twelve inches of ice, but could have traveled in the safety of an enclosed space. He had chosen not to. The other astronauts handled each spacewalk with confidence and bravado. As their team leader, he would work as they worked. Still, it scared him to be outside.

This module of the space base was at least fifty meters long and ten meters in diameter. He was pretty sure that the dimensions were similar to the submarine compartment that had originally housed the components. One difference that stood out to him was that instead of the cold steel of the submarine, he was in a tube comprised of a cold, twelve inch layer of ice to protect him from micrometeorites and solar radiation. The inner end of the compartment had been left open to space. That was the access point to get the equipment inside from the elevator via tractor beam. The compartment was currently strewn with crates.

He started by combining two of the teams and ordering them to unpack and inventory the first of two electrolysis units. He chose the men who had initially disassembled the units, months earlier. Once they were busy at their task, he headed back to the last team.

Major Jim Hunter patted him on the back and asked, "So I guess we got assigned the dangerous job since we have to work directly with you?"

Ethan smiled, as he fully knew that Major Hunter had never shown the slightest amount of fear. "You got that right. If we do this wrong, we're dead."

Major Hunter's eyes widened slightly. "You mean we are working on the nuke already? Shouldn't we be suited up appropriately?"

"No, the reactor does not make it up until the next shipment. We are going to be working on a special addition that they had me design into the space base. We will be installing a battery of solid fuel rocket ground to air missiles and some high powered lasers." Ethan had the pleasure of witnessing Major Hunter's eyes grow even wider. It was nice to see that even the bravest knew fear.

Major Hunter shook his head and expressed what Ethan had been expecting, "I thought we knew the mission objective. We're not up here to start a war, are we?"

Ethan assured him, "These missiles would never make it back down to the ground. Unfortunately, it indicates that they believe we are in danger from meteors and space debris. This is some high tech weaponry that they have given us."

"I used to shoot missiles back when I flew the B-2, but I never installed them before," confided Major Hunter. "I hope you know what you're doing."

Ethan smiled back more confidently. "I built the B-2. I know what I am doing here."

*****

"This is serious," T.J. stated to Billy, Todd, and Lisa. "We have only ninety minutes to complete construction and it needs to be exceptional."

Their hair was still wet from the thirty minute endurance swim during the first half hour of their Physical Education class. Normally, this would be instructional time on health, exercise, or more often than not scuba diving. Today they had been brought to the library to discuss the project that they were required to perform during Thursday's three hour class.

"I don't see what the big deal is," replied Todd. "We have been scuba diving in the pool all year. We are all pretty good at it. They need to take us into a lake to see if we can really do it, but that won't be until the last weeks of the school year."

"Yeah," said Billy. "This is just a little contest to see which team can build the best giant Lego structure underwater. We've played with them plenty of times in class already."

"This might be our only chance to show how good we are!" implored T.J.

Lisa rolled her eyes. "I think that we're all getting A's anyway. The structures will probably not even be graded."

"That is my whole point. We are probably all getting A's anyway. I'm working harder than I ever have to maintain a straight A record. From what I can tell, the whole NOTC group is working equally hard. Everybody does their homework and studies. We all do our very best on everything they ask us to do. We even excel at the daily swimming requirement. In fact, the swim team is comprised almost exclusively of NOTC members because they told us that it would be considered later for our college NOTC applications."

"And this is bad?" asked Billy.

"If we are all getting A's, then how will they be able to tell who among us is best? Not everyone can go all the way in NASA and become an astronaut. It is contests like these that will differentiate us from the rest. We need to win."

T.J. saw Billy give him a slight nod of agreement. A baseball hat sat on the table between them, alongside the discarded pieces of paper containing each of their ideas. Billy picked one up and said, "I still don't know why you don't like my castle idea. I used to build with Lego blocks all the time and can build a pretty elaborate structure."

T.J. leaned closer toward the group and quietly said, "I have been thinking of the criteria for the scoring. I have an idea that will definitely distinguish us from the rest." He looked over at Billy and added, "Maybe we can still use your castle concept within the design."

By Thursday, they had met twice more to go over pictures, sketches, and ideas for the underwater, giant Lego competition. They had even met that morning to set up and organize the blocks that they would be using. Two other teams were also there doing practice builds by the side of the pool.

Class began with their teacher going over the ground rules. There were five competing teams consisting of four members positioned around the pool. Each team would have a dive master judge in the water with them to ensure that all of the rules were being followed and to deduct points for infractions. The main rule was that you could not stand or sit on the bottom of the pool. Each diver had to maintain neutral buoyancy and control so as to only make incidental contact with the bottom. Teams had to get into their gear together, dump whatever giant Lego blocks they would need to the bottom, and begin building. They only had ninety minutes, but that required them to monitor their air supply so that they did not run out. They were each allowed to exit the pool only once for an air tank change and to potentially obtain more blocks.

The competition would be scored on four criteria: originality, complexity, dimension, and teamwork. Only giant Legos were to be used, so deductions would be made if other objects were used for construction. At the start, the blocks could be organized but none could be connected together. All construction would need to be performed in the water.

The teams gathered in their designated areas. Lego sets were reviewed by the dive master prior to entering the water. Finally, the buzzer sounded and the students helped each other into their diving gear.

"Remember to stay calm and in control down there," T.J. told his team as he helped Billy get his vest on. "Our design already takes into account originality, complexity, and dimension. We have gone over all of that. Maintain buoyancy and don't touch the bottom. We have to work in a coordinated fashion to get all of the teamwork points."

"We went over our roles," assured Todd. "We will put on a good show for the scorekeepers."

His team began to dump piles of blocks into the pool at various sections along the wall. They each rolled into the water and sunk to the bottom. They quickly reorganized the blocks into piles according to specific type. As the block suppliers, Lisa and Todd hovered over the piles. Billy took center stage. He would be constructing the central structure, an elaborate castle.

T.J. presided over the group giving block requests to Lisa and Todd by holding up fingers to differentiate which pile and again for the number of blocks needed. He had the design memorized, but occasionally messages were transferred between the team by using underwater writing tablets. The designed construction occurred quickly.

After forty-five minutes, Lisa and Todd exited the water to change their tanks out. T.J. quickly moved down to pull the last piles of blocks over to Billy. They made the final placements on the structure and turned to see another load of their blocks raining down to the pool floor. Lisa and Todd returned to the bottom to sort the new supplies while T.J. and Billy left to replenish their own air.

Back on the side of the pool, T.J. patted his friend on the back and said, "You really have done a lot of Lego building. It looks incredible so far."

Billy shook water from his hair and put his mask back on. "Well, now we will see if your elaborate addition to my castle wins the prize." They changed air tanks and dumped the last pile of blocks into the pool. When they got back down they saw the castle's dual spire that almost reached to the surface. Lisa and Todd were busy constructing short segments, floating toward the surface, and adding to the spires.

T.J. and Billy got to work on the last part of their design. Floating inches above the pool bottom, they worked to create a large doughnut. On top of this they added five sections positioned like blades on a fan. They flipped the structure over and started working on its other side. Billy built a small plane structure and handed it off to T.J. before returning to work on their last small pile of blocks.

T.J. placed the plane on top of the doughnut. He surreptitiously reached into his swimsuit pocket and pulled out a large Lego block. As Billy placed two more planes onto the doughnut, T.J. positioned his special block on top. Painted onto the block was the word "PHOENIX". Together they lifted the structure and swam it to the surface. Lisa and Todd were waiting, each holding a spire. T.J. and Billy hoisted their own space base out of the water and positioned it on top of the spires.

"We have created our own Space Elevator from the pool bottom, up through a watery atmosphere, and into air space," announced T.J. to the dive master judge.

Billy whispered to the team, "Hopefully, the structure lasts long enough to get judged. Swim away slowly and don't make any waves."

T.J. perused with the other students around the pool to check out the competition. At each team site, students laid on the pool edge with their masked faces in the water. T.J. knelt down at one structure and put his head underwater. He saw an elaborate carousel. At the other sites, he observed a Stonehenge replica, the Statue of Liberty, and the Coliseum. He grew more excited as he got around the pool. Most of the other students were gathered around his structure which reached up out of the water.

Pictures were taken of the competition entries. The judges made the circuit around to each structure. The scores were totaled. The win went to the Phoenix Space Elevator.

*****

The Phoenix Space Base had grown by seven hundred and fifty tons in just thirty weeks from liftoff. The elevator now had the capacity to lift one ton cargoes. The highest level which comprised the shuttle grid had already been vacated by the astronauts. The middle corridor was a giant hamster trail that allowed access to all areas of the base. Five compartments hung below and were attached to the submarine, air-tight hatches. Each of these compartments had the additional protection of a twelve inch layer of ice to shield from micrometeorites and radiation.

The electrolysis units were running at full capacity with power from the cables. Generated oxygen was pumped to the corridor and compartments. Excess oxygen and hydrogen were pumped into the storage compartments that stood adjacent to the Nuke Compartment. The carbon dioxide scrubbers were functioning.

Two of the compartments now housed all of the astronauts. They were commonly referred to as *LQ* and *RQ*. At first, Ethan had thought that these referred to their left and right position on the base. Major Jim Hunter enlightened him that *LQ* stood for Living Quarters and the *RQ* stood for Recreational Quarters.

Ethan could not believe the spaciousness of their Living Quarters. It could bunk up to eighty people as compared to only the six that used to live on the International Space Station. It also had a large mess hall. The Recreational Quarters really blew his mind by how luxuriously it had been furnished. A full third of it was a high tech gym with stationary bikes, elliptical riders, and a multitude of resistance weight lifting machines. The next third comprised a state of the art multimedia room. It housed a dozen computer consoles, several flat screen televisions, and a larger theater area. The last section was the control center for the base, and it too had amphitheater seating for up to twenty. The astronauts had plenty of room to spread out and relax after being cooped up for so long.

The last deliveries had brought up nearly a hundred tons of water to fill the inner liner of the corridor and the two habitat compartments. This water circulated throughout the base and radiated heat for the living. Currently, energy drawn up from the ground base powered super-heaters to warm the water, but soon this requirement would be replaced by using the radiant water as the cooling water for the nuclear reactor.

"Are we there yet?" asked Warren over Ethan's communication headset.

"I just made it into the compartment. Can't you see where we are?" replied Ethan. He hoped that Warren could see more than he was letting on, if he was to assist with the reactor assembly.

"I can see well enough to tell that your hands are shaking," Warren chided.

"Nothing could scare me more than working on radioactive equipment stationed in open outer space!"

The Nuke Compartment had just received its last shipment, the reactor and uranium fuel rods, but was still missing the final wall to enclose the compartment from outer space and allow for life support. He had still been required to float in space from the shuttle to the compartment.

Major Jim Hunter floated in behind and slapped him reassuringly on the back. He too was fully decked out in extra radiation gear. He appeared confident to Ethan, and should have since he had actually volunteered to assist him with this dangerous mission.

"Well, let's get to it," said Warren. "I sit in the comfort of the ground base on terra firma, but from my display I see your suits as being cumbersome. This might take longer than I anticipated. Did I tell you that I had dinner with Kylie last night?"

Ethan shook his head knowing that Warren could see the movement. Warren had dinner with Kylie. Here he was stuck in outer space and his friend was taunting him about life in the real world. "Is she there now?"

"No. She got in yesterday and left today."

"I thought that maybe she would stick around until the upcoming Phoenix open house," said Ethan, disappointedly.

"She will be around for that," replied Warren, positively.

They had just about completed construction on the base. It would be fully operational with the installation of the reactor. He had hopes of being allowed back down the elevator to participate in the upcoming open house and of actually seeing Kylie in person. She had become his full time pen pal, even if the content of the messages mainly pertained to the progress of the base.

"Okay, let's crack these packages open and see if we have everything," instructed Warren, referring to the crates they had so carefully packed almost a year ago.

Ethan knew it was all there. He had gone over the inventory lists for each crate. He had also studied the schematics for the reactor so many times in the past month that he was sure he could assemble it from memory. It was still good to know that Warren would be observing and could lend his expertise.

They worked slowly for what seemed like hours assembling the components. "Now for the fun part," Warren intoned. "Open the case with the big yellow hazard stickers all over it."

Ethan opened the crate containing the enclosed uranium rods. He noted that even Jim Hunter stepped back before reaching in with him to lift them out. They carefully slid them into the reactor core. Now they began the work of buttoning up the reactor. As they made the connection of water cooling lines to the reactor, a red flashing light came on at the back of the compartment. Ethan imagined hearing a corresponding blaring siren if only air was present to carry sound. His heart was pounding in his chest.

"Hold on guys," said Warren's voice over their headsets. "I have been told to tell you to just sit tight and don't move. I am not sure what's going on yet, either."

Even floating in zero gravity, Ethan felt the hull suddenly shake violently. After approximately a minute, the red light went out.

"All clear," said Warren.

"What happened?" asked Major Jim Hunter anxiously. "Did we have a radiation leak?"

"Actually, it had nothing to do with the reactor," answered Warren. "I have been told that it was the Phoenix weapons system. Your laser system just took out a Russian satellite, and you fired a missile which destroyed a Chinese satellite. Hopefully this isn't the start of World War III!"

*****

Even though they had been announced by his secretary, Stephen was startled by the way the National Security Advisor and General McNabb barged into the oval office. He could tell that they had bad news. He calmly got up out of his chair and walked around to sit on the front corner of his desk. They waited anxiously for him.

"Gentlemen, let's have it."

The National Security Advisor blurted out, "They may just have started World War III!"

"The Chinese?" asked Stephen.

"No, it was us. Or more specifically, the Phoenix group did."

Stephen stood and asked defensively, "How the hell could my project have already escalated things up to World War III?"

"They just destroyed two satellites."

"Whose satellites were they?" Stephen asked, concerned.

"That's the worst part. One was Russian and the other was Chinese."

Stephen turned to General McNabb and asked, "How could this have happened without our approval?"

The General stepped forward and stated, "Phoenix Ground Base is under military protection. As you are aware, we have had numerous military actions to protect its security perimeter. Unfortunately, this took place in outer space under what NASA felt was their jurisdiction."

"A military assault on a foreign country's assets should not have been left up to NASA," replied Stephen incredulously.

"It is too late to undo the damage. We armed them and somehow left them the discretion."

"Did the decision go through Dr. Kevin Scott or Dr. Kylie Williams?" probed Stephen.

The National Security Advisor responded, "Both had been completely out of contact when this occurred. The decision came from the NASA Deputy Director. From what I can tell, we might have come to the same conclusions as he did. They were both spy satellites, probably sent to get a closer look at what we have built."

Stephen ran his hand over his face. "State has warned everybody to stay out of that region of our geosynchronous orbit. The International Telecommunications Union awarded us the orbital slot upon our treaty with Ecuador. We also own the orbital slots on either side of the elevator. How and why would they invade our space?"

"Like I said, we think that they were spy satellites. The Russian satellite entered our space but actually kept a safe distance from the Space Base. It was the Chinese satellite that was sent way too close for comfort. The NASA Deputy Director was informed of its distance and trajectory and correctly made the decision to remove the threat to both the base and astronauts stationed there. One SM-3 missile took it out. Since he was taking action to clear the area, he had the high powered laser disable the Russian satellite at the same time."

"Have we heard anything from either country?"

"Not yet."

Stephen walked back around his desk and plopped back down into his chair. He held his head in his hands as he considered his options. It was way too soon for Phoenix to be causing world tensions. "I will have State go on the verbal offensive. I'll have them tell both countries how dangerously close those illegal satellites came to hitting our world-saving carbon dioxide elevator. We will scream about the safety of our courageous astronauts. It will, hopefully, wash itself out in public opinion.

"General McNabb, my immediate concern is to insure there is no retaliation on the Phoenix Ground Base in Ecuador. If there is a successful attack on it, it would also destroy the Space Base and our mission. Bring your forces in South America to full alert."

*****

The hydrogen fuel cell had been delivered.

"I promised you a fuel cell," began Mr. Roedel, "and I have delivered one, care of NASA. Let's see if any of you have done some homework on your own. Does anybody know what a hydrogen fuel cell does?"

A few students raised their hands. T.J., who had hurried to get to class early and now stood at the front of the congregated students, was called upon. "It converts hydrogen and oxygen into water and creates electricity. It will power our electric engine."

"Correct," responded Mr. Roedel. "Hydrogen is the fuel which is introduced on the anode side. Oxygen, which for our purposes is taken from the air, is introduced on the cathode side. The concept is a lot like a battery, except batteries discharge stored electricity and fuel cells create electricity while consuming fuel that must be replenished. What is the benefit of hydrogen fuel cells?"

Todd blurted out, "There are no greenhouse gas emissions."

"Correct, although that is somewhat misleading" added Mr. Roedel. "The hydrogen fuel cell itself has no greenhouse gas emissions. Unfortunately, today's technology mass produces hydrogen using natural gas reacted with steam and electricity while burning fossil fuel. So, in truth, there are still about the same amount of greenhouse gas emissions."

"Then why bother?" questioned someone from the back.

"One of my directives is to teach innovation. This may turn out to be a dead-end technology. It doesn't make much sense to pursue it if fossil fuels and emissions are still part of the equation, but that does not mean that it is not a promising concept for scientists to think about. Since you are all scientists in training, we will be looking at alternative ways to make this a zero emissions project. Anybody have ideas?"

Billy raised his hand. "Can't we create hydrogen ourselves using electrolysis?"

"Interesting idea, but how would we power the electrolysis unit?"

"We could just plug it into the wall," responded Billy.

"But the electricity comes from the power plants which may be burning coal. I want a zero emissions project."

T.J. interjected, "There would not be emissions if the power plant was nuclear, hydroelectric, wind, or solar."

"True. Those sources would allow our project to be zero emissions. I guess that the only way to be sure is to create it ourselves. We don't have access to a river. Nuclear power is the most reliable, but a nuclear reactor at the school might draw attention. That leaves us average Americans to choose between two clean renewable energy sources, wind and solar. As an employee of NASA, I have to lean toward the more abundant source of sunlight, since there is not a lot of wind in space. It is an especially convenient choice, since I have had a large solar panel donated by NASA and installed onto the roof of the school. It is of sufficient size to produce enough hydrogen for our fuel cell electric car to make a typical daily commute."

"You had this whole conversation already worked out," accused Lisa.

"Scientists work their way through problems," agreed Mr. Roedel.

T.J. felt like the project was coming together into something a NOTC student could be proud of. Thinking about it, he decided that every American home could probably maintain a solar panel mounted on their roof, creating enough of a personal hydrogen supply to provide power for their daily commute. Where needed, there could be nuclear power plants creating enough electricity to power electrolysis units at hydrogen service stations. The concept could even work outside the confines of the planet in outer space!

*****

Ethan and the other eighteen astronauts had been off the Earth for two hundred ten days. He had become accustomed to weightlessness. He no longer woke up in a cold sweat with a feeling of falling and was now used to sleeping strapped to a bunk. The novelty of the glamorous recreation quarters had not worn off, and they spent most of their downtime watching movies and communicating with people on Earth. Ethan realized that he was spending more than the required time working out on the exercise equipment. He was beginning to get anxious.

The construction of the Phoenix Space Base had been completed. He spent the past four days verifying the status of the life-support systems. The nuclear reactor was online and fully powering the base. The reactor core cooling system integrated with the base's radiant heat system performed perfectly together. Monitoring the air quality had Ethan traversing the base but completely from the inside. Surprisingly, everything had gone according to plan.

Now he was done. While he had the respect of the other astronauts, he no longer had to lead them. He wondered if they too felt like they had passed the point of usefulness. They did not appear concerned. It probably had to do with the fact that astronauts go up, do a job that nobody else can, and then go back down. They appeared to know that they had completed their mission and were anticipating going home. The next scheduled crawlers were bringing up their replacements.

Ethan had been told that ten astronauts and ten scientists would be arriving to take over residency of the space base. The current astronauts would then be going back down. Unsure as to whether they now considered him to be one of those astronauts, Ethan asked Major Jim Hunter whether he would also be going down.

Jim shrugged and told him, "You are kind of the commander of this base. It wouldn't be up to me to know. You will have to ask your bosses what their intentions are for you."

Ethan called down to the ground base and talked to Warren about it. Warren was even less helpful. All he could say was that he would have to wait and talk to Kylie, but that she was currently inbound for the open house.

This infuriated Ethan. The irony was that he was trying to be allowed back down to see Kylie at the open house but now had to wait for her arrival to even attain permission. By then it might be too late. He believed that all of the astronauts going back down would probably attend and be hailed as heroes, while he would be stuck up here as the maintenance man.

He was told that the first crawler would be arriving within the hour with five passengers. Even though crawler cargoes had reached a one ton capacity, the passenger elevators had to also allow for life support. He imagined five days stuck in an elevator. Regardless, Ethan wished this torture for himself but would have to await his fate. He headed off to clean up for the base's newest guests.

The first crawler arrived and was locked into place on the corridor's external SEAL Dry Dock Shelters. Its passengers were met by a welcoming committee and led through the corridor toward RQ. Ethan watched as Major Jim Hunter entered through the hatch leading the group. Shock registered on his face when he laid eyes on the woman of the group. She smiled at his recognition. This newcomer was Kylie!

Kylie stepped from the confines of the corridor into the larger area of RQ and floundered for control in zero gravity. Ethan reached out and took hold of her hand, and she grabbed onto him for dear life. He was very pleased with this serendipitous opportunity to help her.

"What are you doing up here?" he asked.

"I told you that I would be at the Phoenix open house. Did you think we would miss such an opportunity and have it on terra firma?"

Suddenly, Dr. Kevin Scott tumbled into view and stopped upside down before them. "I am here to tell you that maneuvering in zero-G is very difficult. Do you mind helping me turn right side up so I can congratulate you to your face rather than to your boots?"

Ethan helped him to rotate around and positioned him by one of the theater chairs. He continued to personally help Kylie. "It doesn't take long to manage getting around with some degree of competency. At least your stomachs appear to be handling it. I am told that space nausea can be common and can take a day or two to get over."

Kylie blushed and admitted, "We were weightless in the elevator for the past four days. I had an air sickness bag on hand for two of them."

"I ruined a perfectly good spacesuit helmet," admitted Ethan trying to make her feel more at ease.

"I think we are past our time of space sickness. Now it would be nice to freshen up after five days confined in the elevator. Over the next four hours the base should have received the full influx of visitors and replacements. Then the festivities can begin."

Ethan offered to lead them over to LQ. He showed them the galley and dorm, and Dr. Kevin Scott explained that the newly arrived scientists would be setting up a biosphere experiment in a section of the dorm. They would be testing species of plants to see which survived the best in a zero-G environment.

Leaving them at the dorm, Ethan headed back to RQ and killed time by watching the movie that was playing. Kylie soon returned and requested that he give her a personal tour of the base. He had a slight sensation that his space nausea was returning.

Ethan showed Kylie all of the perks built into the Recreational Quarters before leading her out into the corridor. He pointed out the hatch that led to the hydrogen storage compartment.

"While we can access the compartment, there is only a limited area where there is life support and radiant heat. Here the hydrogen gas created by our water electrolysis units is collected, chilled, and pressurized into liquid storage. A compartment on the other side of the nuclear compartment does the same for the oxygen used for life support."

They arrived at the nuclear compartment and Ethan opened the hatch for her. Inside, he proudly showed her each of the essential systems that he had built into the space base.

"It is pretty impressive that you managed to become an expert on each of these systems," said Kylie. "Plus you put this together while in the confinement of a spacesuit. That is no easy feat."

"I had Warren right here with me to assist," Ethan humbly replied. "It was mostly put together and compartmentalized for me anyway."

"You are too modest. Kevin made the perfect choice in you to lead this team. You completed the task quicker than we thought possible, carrying the stress of being an astronaut. You're an extraordinary man, Ethan Dire."

"Now that the base is constructed, what intentions do you have for me?" Ethan probed. "Do you intend for me to come back down with you and the others?"

"Well, there are not a lot of people qualified to be an astronaut and also capable of putting this type of equipment together," Kylie stated while gesturing to the reactor and electrolysis systems. "Do you think that you could do this type of mission again?"

Disappointed but not wanting to lose her respect, Ethan responded, "I can do whatever you need. I was looking for a challenge and you gave me an opportunity that surpassed my wildest dreams. What have you got in mind?"

Kylie then proceeded to tell Ethan what the real goal was that they were working toward. Ethan kept a poker face, but inside he was completely shocked by what he was hearing. What was she asking him to do?

Later at the celebration, Kylie and Ethan were inseparable. Whenever possible, they secluded themselves in private discussions. They talked late into the night, long after the others had strapped themselves to their bunks. A few days later he would actually find himself seated next to her on the elevator for the trip down to Earth. Ethan could not get enough of Kylie.

*****

It looked like their experiment had worked. Everywhere they looked, plants were growing. It had required them to figure out the lacking essential ingredients and to engineer circumstances to promote optimal growth. What had been lifeless soil was now on its way to become a prairie.

T.J. was satisfied with the progress his class had made toward becoming master gardeners. With their initial attempt at gardening, hard work had availed them nothing. The soil lacked root system sustainability. Through that failure, they had learned the essence of discovery. They had discovered the basics required to grow plants.

Throughout the fall semester, the class had managed the community compost project. During weekly trips, they had monitored and maintained the decomposition of yard waste into their personal mound of black gold compost.

Just before spring had arrived, the compost was relocated to, spread over, and tilled into their lifeless lot. Mrs. James had the class once again test the soil. Drainage was great, the pH problem was fixed, and nutrients were available. They had created the rich loam that their text book had stated was perfect for plants. They had been given another chance at planting their experimental prairie.

T.J. had gone to Mrs. James to make a special request. He described the special place in his previous school's garden library where he would relax under a majestic Bald Cypress. He asked if it would be possible to incorporate this type of tree into their prairie. She told him that the Bald Cypress was a very hardy tree that could grow under most conditions and she would consider his request.

When the spring day had come for planting, T.J. was rewarded with a twelve inch Bald Cypress sapling to plant. He picked what he felt was the optimal location on the lot and worked the soil the best he could. He planted, watered, and admired his diminutive tree.

That spring had been a rainy one. They had not been able to attend the prairie lot for three weeks straight due to coincidentally rainy Wednesdays. On the fourth week they arrived to find, not an empty lot, but a true prairie.

This had been T.J.'s first terraforming project!

*****

Ethan followed Kylie as she gave him a tour of the Phoenix Ground Base. From inside its walls, he imagined it would look like a medieval fortress set atop the pinnacle of the highest mountain on Earth. He had been told that the U.S. military was spread thickly outside its walls.

"This is where the crawler containers are filled with water," stated Kylie. "The water is pumped up from a steam further down the mountain."

"I hope the residents downstream didn't mind us acquiring nearly seven hundred fifty tons of their water," responded Ethan.

"It was really a drop in the bucket for the amount of water that comes off this mountain. We take a little at a time and will continue to take it for the next few years."

"Are you still loading canisters now?" asked Ethan.

"No. If you look over here, you will see the long line of railcars holding the inventory of capture carbon dioxide that the elevator has already begun sending up. The dry ice has been captured at power plants throughout the United States, shipped down to Ecuador on freighters, railed inland and up our mountain, and finally sent into outer space on our space elevator."

"That seems like a lot of energy expended to get the carbon dioxide removed from our atmosphere," said Ethan. "Has anyone done the math on how much carbon dioxide is generated just to do this?"

"It is a token effort by our government to lead the way in saving the environment. Crunching the numbers for carbon dioxide captured from cities along the west coast actually works out fairly well. It is when we add cargoes like these that our numbers really fall apart." She gestured toward a group of railcars on which Ethan could see the flags and country names of France, Germany, and Russia.

"Are they participating in the project?" asked Ethan incredulously.

"They want to. They don't know what we are really doing but see the potential of this elevator. They were allowed to make carbon donations to show their support."

Later that afternoon, Ethan stood with Kylie in the Phoenix Ground Base control room. The room was crowded with a small group of people standing expectantly before displays. Suddenly, Ethan was lifted off the ground by large arms from behind. After he was set back down, he turned to find the barrel chested Warren exuberantly shaking hands with Kylie.

"For a minute there, I thought that I was back in zero-G," stated Ethan, smiling broadly at his friend.

"Glad you could make it down for the commissioning ceremony. We actually had the first part three days ago, right after you arrived back down. They even broke a bottle of Champaign on the crawler before it went up the cable. In the next few minutes, its cargo will be jettisoned into space."

Warren led Ethan and Kylie over to his workstation. "The crawler is already well past escape velocity. Before it reaches the space base, it will release its cargo, undergo a braking sequence, and will be captured by the base to be sent down at a later time. The cargo itself will hopefully pass through the base with enough velocity to escape the Earth's gravitational pull. We will have sent the first ton of carbon dioxide packing."

A quiet fell over the room. "The cargo has been released," announced the person to Warren's right. The room stayed fairly quiet as a counter displayed the time for it to pass the base toward space. As it reached zero, a cheer rose from the group.

"Now we just have to be careful where we point this gun. We wouldn't want the cargo to hit the Moon," said Warren loud enough to be heard over the clamor.

Suddenly, uncontrollable laughter erupted in the room. Ethan and Kylie shared a knowing smile. Confused about the mood of the moment, Warren signaled for quiet to get a better listen at the open speaker from Houston Control. As the room quieted, Ethan realized that the tinny static sound coming from the speaker was a room full of laughter on the other side. This again caused their group to break out in hysterics.

'What's so funny?" asked Warren.

Ethan sympathetically patted his friend on the back as Kylie said to Warren, "It is time you too knew the rest of our plans."

*****

T.J. struggled to get the heavy equipment down to the miniature beach. He set his bag on a corner of a picnic table and went back to the bus to gather his air tank. In spite of how heavy it was, he eagerly swung it over his shoulder and started the trek back down to the water. He had been anticipating this test for months.

The school year had flown by for him. Was this how all freshmen viewed their first year of high school? He remembered how exhausted he had felt after the first weeks and now the rest were past. At least he had some memorable accomplishments during the year. Just yesterday, he had ridden his bike past the garden lot to see the very top of his Bald Cypress poking above a lush prairie accented with flowers. It was too bad that he had another year before being old enough to drive; otherwise, he might have gone by in the high tech car that he had helped build.

He felt the deltoid muscle in his shoulder flex under the weight of the tank. The year of swimming had been very good for his physique. He had even competed in the state swimming meet with a couple of his NOTC classmates. Their daily workouts had paid off, but now all he could think about was scuba diving in the open water of this quarry.

T.J. hurriedly placed his tank by his other gear and moved into the semicircle around his teacher at the water's edge. The students were given the ground rules for making the four dives required to obtaining their open water certification in scuba diving. The class broke up into smaller groups, each with a pair of dive masters.

T.J. helped Billy on with his equipment. They stood beside a large boulder jutting out of the shallow water. Lisa and Todd were also in his group.

Their dive master climbed up onto the rock. Like an actor on a small stage, he stated, "The first rule to remember is that you work in a buddy system. Each of you will be paired up and responsible for the safety of another diver. I will be paired with another dive master."

T.J. and Billy moved closer trying to assure that they would be paired together.

"From the surface, I will instruct the group on the diving skill that you will need to perform. We will go down at a controlled rate and equalize. I will point to each of you one at a time. You will become my buddy while I witness you perform the skill. My buddy will become your partner's buddy until you have completed. You have practiced these skills in the confines of a pool. Now we will see your competency in open water."

With this he rolled backwards off the rock and disappeared underwater. The other dive master ushered the group into the water. T.J. filled his buoyancy control bladder with air and swam with his fins to meet the two dive masters away from shore. With Billy as his partner, they slowly descended to perform their competency dives.

An hour later, T.J. and Billy surfaced and fully inflated their buoyancy bladders. They casually snorkeled back toward shore where the class was beginning to gather around Mr. Graca. T.J. took off his gear, placed it on a rock in the water, and sat down beside it.

"Gather around," called Mr. Graca. "During those four dives, each of you managed to perform the skills required to receive your Open Water certification. Congratulations. You now have the competency to dive on your own down to a sixty foot depth. Today, along with the basic skills of maintaining buoyancy and control under water, there was a common theme that the tasks required. Anyone venture a guess at what that was?"

T.J. called out, "It was safety and staying calm."

Mr. Graca agreed, "Yes. Most of your training for the Open Water certification was about what you should do when you encounter certain circumstances while you are underwater. For example, your mask fills with water. What should you do?"

The whole group simulated the act of clearing water from their masks by putting pressure on the top of their mask with their hand. Then tilting their heads back while blowing air into the mask, the imagined water was displaced.

"Correct. You wouldn't want to waste the limited time of an underwater dive going to the surface to empty your masks. With regards to safety, imagine that you run out of air. What do you do to survive? Or what if you get tangled in some seaweed? We taught you to be prepared and drilled you for these possibilities. You dive in a buddy system and work for the safety of your partner. Most importantly, we taught you that scuba diving is about exploration and adventure in what many would consider a dangerous environment, underwater. Remember that the surface is the air regulator in your mouth. Stay calm and enjoy the adventure."

Mr. Graca finished the class by informing them that next Thursday would be their last class of the year. They would again have an opportunity to dive at this quarry, but this time they would be in possession of their Open Water Certifications and have the opportunity to dive on their own. He handed out maps of the quarry's topography showing a sunken boat, a lost underwater crane, and the forbidden eighty-five foot deep hole.

Even though it was not Friday, T.J. and his classmates were allowed to proudly sport their NOTC uniforms on this last day of the school year. Even better than being the last school day was the fact that it was the last extended class for physical education. Today was the day that they would be allowed to scuba dive and explore on their own!

They arrived at the quarry and the class hurried off the bus with their equipment. Mr. Graca carried a cooler over to the picnic area. While Mr. Roedel started a grill and prepared to barbeque for them, Mrs. James put out some appetizers. This was a celebration for the NOTC.

T.J. and Billy hurried into the water wearing their dive equipment and wetsuits. They had memorized the underwater map and had made their plans. Just as T.J. had predicted, the other divers started out exploring along the shoreline. T.J. and Billy headed out alone across the center of the water. Snorkels in mouth, they stayed on the surface with their destination being a floating volleyball in the distance.

Reaching it, T.J. felt around beneath and found a rope leading down to the depths. He showed Billy and got a mischievous smile in return. Each of them opened an additional equipment bag which was tied to their wastes. They put on diving hoods and gloves and pulled out underwater flashlights.

"Are you ready?" asked T.J.

Billy took a quick look around. "Nobody is watching us as far as I can tell. Let's get under."

They dropped down to fifteen feet while keeping the rope in sight. After a quick pressure equalization and equipment check, they continued down. At thirty feet they hit the thermal cline. T.J. was amazed that he could actually see the depth where the water changed temperate to cold, enough to require the wetsuit. It looked like a cloud layer in the water. He stopped short and placed his arm down into the colder zone. They took another equalization stop before proceeding through it.

At the next stop, T.J. pointed to his depth gauge which indicated forty-five feet. They were now deeper than they had previously gone with the dive masters. Billy gave him a high-five.

At sixty feet, they experienced an uncomfortable feeling as the sunlight faded away. They switched on their flashlights and continued down. By seventy-five feet, they were in complete darkness, other than the small light beams streaming from their hands. They both grabbed onto the rope for the final decent into the unknown.

T.J. pointed his light straight down and was rewarded with the first sighting of a wooden platform. They touched down and saw that they were at eighty-two feet deep. It was pitch black and extremely spooky down there. Billy signaled that he was cold. T.J. felt like his exposed face might be freezing.

He signaled for Billy to stay put and watch him. With some trepidation but a greater thrill, T.J. swam away from the rope and off of the platform. He settled down on the silt bottom. Holding his gauge to the lowest point he could reach, he saw that he had attained the maximum depth of the quarry, eighty-five feet!

T.J. followed Billy's flashlight beam back to the rope. Billy took the opportunity to leave and made a small circuit around the platform. While T.J. was alone, he let his mind wonder. What if their lights went out due to the pressure? Would they be able to find their way up? With their visibility limited to only a thin beam, anything could sneak up on them. Next time he would bring a diving knife. Even if they said that it was mostly useful for communication, he felt that in this instance it would give him a feeling of security.

Billy returned and T.J. pointed to his dive computer. They had only been underwater fifteen minutes but had already exceeded the time allotted for a safe deep dive. They couldn't spend any more time underwater without risking a dangerous dose of nitrogen in their blood. They performed a last high-five and slowly headed for the surface making decompression stops at thirty and fifteen feet before reaching the surface. They snorkeled their way across the surface back to the beach.

Approaching the picnic area, T.J. belatedly realized that they were the first students back from diving. Mr. Graca gave them a surprised, concerned look as they approach. T.J. quickly pealed the diving hood off of his head. He could see that Billy's face was red from where it had been exposed to the extremely cold water.

"Man, are we hungry," declared T.J. sitting down at a table.

"Did you run out of air already?" asked Mr. Roedel. "You were only gone a half hour."

"No. We visited the shipwreck and then decided to come back for some lunch," replied Billy evasively.

T.J. exchanged what he believed to be a knowing look with Mr. Graca while Mrs. James placed some burgers on the grill.

FLY ME TO THE MOON

Kylie held the door open and Ethan followed Warren into the Flight Control Room. There was an immediate smattering of recognition and pointing directed his way. It had been like this ever since he had arrived at the Johnson Space Center campus in Houston. People acknowledged him wherever he went. It was a little disconcerting, but he still walked a little taller when it occurred in the presence of Kylie.

She had brought them to the Flight Control Room for a mission update briefing. Ethan was struck by the similarity of this room to its twin at the Kennedy Space Center in Florida. Even Dr. Kevin Scott could be seen giving a nod in his direction from the front of the room.

"I am kind of having a déjà vu moment here," joked Warren. "It makes me wonder if it was all a dream or did we actually complete construction of a spaceport."

As Kylie led them toward the front, Ethan could hear Dr. Kevin Scott saying that they were just waiting on their guest of honor.

Kylie leaned into him and whispered, "It is not you that he is talking about this time."

With this, the doors opened and a couple of extremely serious looking men in black suits entered and took positions on each side of the door. One spoke into a transmitter and soon President Stephen Ryan entered the room. Applause erupted from the gathered group. Ethan found himself clapping heartily along with Kylie and Warren.

Over the applause Kylie remarked, "Meet our benefactor. He's the reason that NASA has been given this extraordinary opportunity."

The President walked up to the front, shaking hands along the way. He was given a seat of honor at the front and center of the control room, only three seats down from Ethan.

Dr. Kevin Scott began, "Mr. President, NASA would like to take this opportunity to thank you for your generosity and vision. Just as we were reaching the point where our existence was being threatened by society's judgment based on our cost verses value, you designed a whole new paradigm for the purpose of NASA. Not only does this paradigm define a new mission, it defines a whole new reality for the United States."

The display behind Dr. Kevin Scott changed to external camera views from the Phoenix Space Base. Ethan was reminded of how familiar he was with the views.

"I have a couple of demonstrations to go along with the mission progress report," he continued. Another display showed a large representation of the Phoenix elevator with the numbers 320, 321, 322, and 323 blinking near the spaceport section. Higher numbers were shown further down toward the ground base. Each number also had a column designated with miles and times which were rapidly counting down.

"As you can see on that Cargo Locator Display, our three hundred twentieth cargo should be releasing from the Phoenix Spaceport within moments." He pointed back toward the display with the live camera angle and an object could be seen hurling up the cable. Within seconds it passed. The camera view changed, showing the braking crawler with its cargo fading into the distance.

"Cargo 320 is at escape velocity and will take only two more days before it impacts into our acquisition zone on the Moon," finished Kevin proudly.

Warren shyly raised his hand and asked, "If you are shooting it straight up from the equator, wouldn't it actually miss the Moon?"

A slight murmur began in the room as engineers clamored to answer. Dr. Kevin Scott raised a hand to regain silence. "It is true that the Moon does not orbit around the Earth's equator. The elevator achieves the escape velocity and projects the cargo out the distance to the Moon. Additional means of propulsion are needed to acquire the angle of trajectory."

"So there is a rocket incorporated into the cargo package?" asked Ethan, joining his friend in questioning.

"In a manner of speaking, there is a propulsion system. The cargo is the core of the delivery package. It is enclosed in a carbon dioxide, dry ice filled casement. This spherical casement has exhaust valves all around it. An onboard micro-navigational system powers lasers to sublimate the carbon dioxide into a high pressure gas. The cargo's trajectory can be altered by the CO_2 push. We even give a final burst to reduce impact speed into the Moon. It is the same technology we tested on the space base to alter orbit. It took us a couple of weeks of practice shots to work out the kinks. The first week we shot the carbon donation from foreign countries into deep space, and the next week we rained down our own onto the Moon trying to hone in on the AZ."

"So, if the cargo is encompassed by a dry ice casement, what is the actual cargo being sent to the Moon?" asked Warren.

"Right now we are mostly sending up water," answered Kevin. "That will be our most valuable basic resource. Some cargoes will be liquid nitrogen and others will even be just dry ice packages."

From the middle of the room, someone called out, "It is time." The main display changed to show a moving barren landscape.

"This is a view from Cat 1, which is about to pick up a cargo which left the elevator a couple of days ago," informed Kevin. The Cat's view locked onto an object protruding from the Moon's regolith. "The name Cat stands for Cargo Transport Vehicle. We have two of them on the Moon. Given the small window of time we have to shoot objects toward the Moon, it is incredible that we have been able to achieve sending four one ton cargoes daily. The Cats are continually retrieving cargoes and transporting them to stockpile sites. They have already retrieved over three hundred tons of lunar shipments to date."

The display showed craned arms hook onto the package and lift it from the soil. Once again the barren landscape began to move on the display. The President started to clap, followed by applause from the rest of the room. The President stood and spoke quietly with Dr. Kevin Scott who indicated for Kylie to follow.

"Excuse me," said Kylie to Ethan, as she quickly stood and followed the two men through a side door.

*****

"Great speech you gave out there," said Stephen while taking a seat at the large conference table. Kevin and Kylie sat down across from him. "Did you ever consider going into politics?"

"I am close enough to it just participating in your grand scheme," answered Kevin. "What was so urgent that you had to escape Washington just to attend a pep talk?

"I need to know the minimum amount of preparation time you still require to achieve our goal."

Kylie leaned forward and impulsively blurted out, "Mr. President, we are way ahead of the original timetable, but we had allotted three years before handing you your legacy."

"I know the original timetable," replied Stephen calmly. "I created it and still hope to hold off until just prior to reelection time. Unfortunately in the world of politics, just like in chess, I have come to learn that sometimes your opponent forces you to make plays which you had not anticipated."

"Did something happen that we should know about?" asked Kevin.

"Let's just say that I need to know my options here. When is the earliest that I could make the move and announce that we are going back to the Moon?"

Now it was Kevin's turn to look nonplussed. "But that will ruin everything. Once they know what we are doing, it will cause a space race long before we are ready to go. We will have to stop the supply banking before achieving critical mass. We can't be raining down cargo in an area settled by astronauts!"

"Kevin, I agree. It is not my intent to scuttle the mission, but daily reports I receive about the world we actually live on have been downright scary. Superpower tensions have been very high. If it had not been for falling oil prices and the current surplus on the market, we might already be at war. I had to do some major arm twisting to get that surplus into play and it can't last much longer."

"But we need more time," insisted Kylie.

Kevin solemnly contradicted her. "No, Kylie. This was one of the aspects of the paradigm we designed. It was intended to kick off a space race in order to alleviate political tensions and focus superpower attentions on the goal of conquering the Moon. Last time we challenged the Russians and beat them there. This time it won't be for just a stroll on the Moon. We will be there to claim it and stay there for good."

"I thought everything was contingent on getting the supplies up there before they knew," said Kylie.

Stephen agreed, "That is what we would like to achieve. The best scenario is for us to stealthily get everything in place, make the announcement to the world that we intend to go back to the Moon, and participate in a global space race. Russia and China are sure to take up the challenge. We might even find some other countries wishing to contend. There will probably be many offers from our allies to assist and participate in a joint venture. That is what I had intended to happen."

"But you need to know your options," finished Kevin. "The original plan was for us to still have two more years before you made the announcement and touchdown before election day. If we alter the supply ratio now, potentially in one year we could have sufficient assets in place to make a go at a much more modest habitat. If you had to make the announcement today, we would beat everyone back to the Moon, but only for a stroll."

"I understand," said Stephen. "I anticipate that you should still potentially have at least a year. Plan accordingly. If I can get the full two, then you know that I will."

*****

Ethan saw the President reemerging from the room with Dr. Kevin Scott and Kylie. He had been milling about making small talk with various engineers in the hope that they would be back. He saw the President look his way and then walk directly toward him.

"Ethan Dire, I know who you are," stated the President extending his hand and shaking Ethan's firmly.

"I know who you are too, sir," replied Ethan. Realizing that he had just responded to the President so simple mindedly, Ethan blushed. Of course he knew who the President was!

Kylie stepped forward and said to Ethan, "I bet you did not know that while we gave the President credit for creating this opportunity to go back to the Moon, he was actually the scientist that came up with the means for doing so. He is the idea man."

The President gave a nod of thanks to Kylie. "I might have put the pieces of an intellectual puzzle together, but it takes courageous and smarter men than I to actually bring the concept into reality." He patted Ethan on the shoulder. "Thanks for what you have accomplished. We expect great things from you."

*****

T.J. was excited. This school year promised to be even better than his freshman year. Already in master mechanics class, they had started learning about heavy machinery. He was told that later in the year they would even participate in a construction project. The first physical education class turned out to be an exhausting period of swimming laps, but they had also been promised that they would be performing an open water dive at the quarry later in the week. Today was the three hour master gardener class, and Mrs. James had promised them something special.

Mrs. James led the class out the back door of the school and across the track field. It appeared that their destination was a set of glass structures that T.J. had never noticed before. She marched the class into the first spacious greenhouse.

"These are a new addition to the school," she began. "There are five greenhouses, and they will be yours. They will be differentiated as biosphere one through five and each designated to a team assigned by me. Your teams will compete by planning, planting, and maintaining your biosphere."

"If it is a competition, then what are the rules?" asked Lisa.

"You will be growing food. You will be allowed all of the water, soil amendments, and nutrients that you want. The school will reimburse for any supplies that you deem necessary. The total existence of your garden must remain within the confines of the biosphere. The most important rule is that you most grow everything from seed, not transplants or cuttings."

"How will the competition be judged?" asked Billy with a reassuring nod to T.J.

"The Biosphere Challenge will be judged on four criteria of incremental importance, in accordance with the competition rules. The first will be originality and it will be up to you to figure out what constitutes originality. Next, you will be scored on flavor, so if you grow all lettuce then include tomatoes and carrots for the various salad accoutrements. You will be scored even higher based on the total biomass of the food that you are able to produce. The last criterion, weighted the most points, is on the total nutritional value of the food."

T.J. watched as Mrs. James walked the perimeter of the greenhouse. Some of the other students followed her, inspecting the biosphere confines. His mind was already racing through various strategies. He could not wait to get to a computer to investigate potential plants.

Mrs. James gave one last bit of advice. "This competition is about producing food. In addition, you will be participating in a service learning experience. You will be providing a service to the community by donating the food you produce to various local food banks. Remember that scoring is based on originality, quality, quantity, and nutritional value. I have posted copies of the assigned teams and scoring criteria back in the classroom. Choose your plant seeds wisely. Let's see which of you will be the master of the master gardeners!"

T.J. walked with the class back to the classroom. He collected a copy of the Biosphere Challenge rules and scoring criteria.

"You're going down, T.J.," called Billy.

T.J. moved over to some students gathered around the posted Biosphere team rosters. He was in Biosphere 4 along with Todd. His friends Billy and Lisa were on separate teams.

*****

Ethan was just leaving the fabrication facility at the Johnson Space Center when he heard his name called out. Looking around, he saw Major Jim Hunter hurrying across the lawn toward him.

"Ethan, I am glad I caught you. They told me that I might find you here."

Ethan was glad to see his trusted friend and warmly shook his hand. "Yeah. I have been spending my mornings in meetings at the Mission Control Center and the afternoons working with engineers in the fab shop."

"I heard that they have been keeping you busy," said Jim. "I was hoping that you might be free to join the boys on a little excursion."

"What do you have in mind?" asked Ethan hopefully.

"Would you be up for an all-expenses paid dive trip down to Belize?" inquired Jim. "All astronauts are required to log SCUBA diving hours. Occasionally, the boss signs off on an official R&R to get some quality dive time under our belts. It's your team of astronauts going. Are you in?"

"But, I'm not certified to SCUBA dive."

With this, Jim laughed. "Sorry. It just strikes me as funny that you spend seven months in space with a guy and spend hundreds of hours outside during extra vehicular activity and it turns out that you don't really know a guy after all!"

"I guess that I can use that as an excuse for my fright factor in the opening days up there."

"Trust me. We all had varying levels of fear up there," said Jim more seriously. "All of the other astronauts are dive masters. NASA actually requires it of us. That is why I was surprised that you aren't. I happen to be a certified master instructor. I have the capacity to judge your experience as sufficient to rate a certificate in open water diving. That is good enough for you to be able to join us. So what do you say?"

"I guess so. Do I need any special approval?"

"It has already been taken care of. Let's just head over to the Neutral Buoyancy Lab where you can do some practice dives and I can give you some official training."

*****

He followed his instructor down the rope line. This was very familiar to him. As he passed through the thermo cline he wondered how many of the other students in his group had gone this deep. T.J. and Billy exchanged a knowing look. He was energized by Mr. Graca choosing deep water diving as the first dive training in the Advanced Open Water diving certification.

As the class passed through the depth where the sunlight started to fade, Mr. Graca had them stop for another pressure equalization and turn on their flashlights. T.J. noticed some of their small group crowded closer to their teacher while holding tight to the rope. Flashlight beams sliced sporadically through the unknown darkness.

T.J. also moved in closer to Mr. Graca while actually abandoned the safety of the rope line. His intent was to show their teacher his competency to control his descent and confidence to venture into the unknown. Fortunately, it was not really the unknown for him. His flashlight beam shown straight down to the platform below.

After they completed the deep water dive, they sat on the beach waiting for the next group of students to return. Mr. Graca had them calculate their nitrogen absorption from the dive and informed them that they were done diving for the afternoon. He told them to relax and enjoy the warm August day.

When all of the other students finally congregated on the beach, Mr. Graca stated, "I decided that the deep water dive would be a good way to start this year's curriculum. You can appreciate the warm day after experiencing the chill of the depths. Anybody here find that dive to be exciting?"

The whole class quickly raised their hands.

"Deep Water Diving is the first specialty training of the year. It is most important to adhere to all of the safety requirements when doing this type of dive. Awareness of the amount of air in your tank is no longer the only factor. The Nitrogen level in your blood is of critical concern. Anybody here think it was awesome when the sunlight faded to pitch blackness?"

Again, the whole class quickly raised their hands.

Mr. Graca nodded. "Yeah, that additional unknown added to the environment really raises the thrill level. Lucky for you, that will be one of our next required specialties, night diver. Next week's dive will cover underwater navigator. The following week will require your parent's permission to attend a late evening, night dive here at the quarry. We need to get in as many open water dives as possible before winter quarantines us to the pool again."

*****

Late Friday afternoon, T.J. found Mrs. James in her classroom. He had spent all of his free time obsessing over the project details. He intended putting in a considerable amount of time with his team this weekend to get a jump on the others.

"Mrs. James?" called T.J. from the doorway. "Do you have a moment to talk about the *originality* portion of the challenge?"

"I'm sorry, T.J. I thought I made it clear that it was up to individual teams to decide what was meant by originality."

"I am not asking for help or hints about being original. I want to know if there is any way to protect the ideas that my team comes up with from other's scrutiny."

"Are you asking to patent your idea with me?" questioned Mrs. James.

"I was thinking more in the realm of putting a moat around our greenhouse," responded T.J. "Is there any way that we can keep the other teams from seeing what we are doing inside of our biosphere?"

"I don't think that is really necessary. The greenhouses are made of glass,

128

so you could see inside no matter."

T.J. countered, "But they will be able to see our setup."

Mrs. James was unconvinced. "Your most critical decision will be the type of plants you choose, and the other students will not be able to distinguish the type of seed from outside the window."

T.J. was not pleased with her position. "Could I still patent my idea with you?" he asked.

"No." She turned back to her work at her desk and dismissively added, "Good luck to you and your team."

On Saturday morning, T.J. met with his team at Todd's house. Stacey and Tom had previously been on the team that had created the carousel in the underwater giant Lego competition.

"Where were you yesterday?" Todd asked T.J. "We met last night to go over some preliminary ideas, so that we could each investigate different concepts without duplicating each other's work."

"Sorry. I was working on something for the project. Can I see what you guys accomplished?"

Accepting his answer, the others pulled out binders containing data they had acquired on the internet.

Todd stated, "I pulled up a list of the most nutrient rich foods. Then I pulled up their individual growth characteristics and optimal environmental requirements."

Stacey opened her binder and added, "I have a lot of experience gardening at home. I explored alternative planting strategies, such as companion planting of crops. I figure that will give us more bang for the area and help with our originality score."

Tom supplemented her information with his findings on the square foot gardening strategy. "This strategy shows how closely you can plant things to get the maximum yield per square foot. I have created a chart detailing minimum requirements."

Todd put their flash drive data onto his computer and merged it into one chart. "First, I will filter out the plants with the largest space requirements via the square foot garden strategy, removing the ones that don't perform in small spaces. Next I will group plants that can work under companion planting strategies. Lastly, I will sort the list with the most nutritional on top." Turning to T.J. he added, "I guess we can leave it to T.J. to work out some health food recipes to increase our quality score."

"That's what you think? I should contribute food recipes and promotional strategies!" T.J. laughed derisively. "Granted, I like everything that you have done so far and think it should all be incorporated. I even like the idea of promoting our produce with healthy recipes. I think it is time you hear what I have planned."

*****

Ethan lay in a lounge chair waiting patiently for the Corona that he had ordered. Jim had told him that he could only have one beer during his time out of water. He and Jim had logged a lot of dive time this morning, making a boat dive along the barrier reef. Now he was required to stay out of the water and let his blood nitrogen level fall to a sufficient level so he could make a night dive. It was a perfect day to relax on the tranquil beach.

As Jim was leaving, he mentioned that he had arranged for another master instructor to take Ethan out on a beach dive after sunset. He wanted his protégé to experience the novelty of a night dive. Luckily, his afternoon Corona was just being dropped off.

A familiar voice approached, "Is this where the astronauts hang out?"

Ethan turned his head to see Kylie in a bathing suit and sun hat scooping up his beer and taking a long drink. His first thought was *"Hey, she's drinking my beer!"*

The thought was quickly replaced by the realization that he was alone with her on a semi-secluded beach. His thoughts raced, *"What was it that could happen to me if I absorb too much nitrogen? It was called nitrogen narcosis. Jim had explained that warning signs could include a false feeling of well-being, inappropriate laughter, and apparent stupidity. I have two out of three. That must be it. I'm dreaming."*

"Wipe that silly grin off your face and offer your instructor a chair."

Finally realizing that he was alone on a semi-secluded beach with her, Ethan jumped up and pulled over another lounge chair. He quickly ordered a replacement beer.

"What are you doing here?" he asked. "Jim only mentioned that astronauts were coming here to log dives."

"I think he also told you that the trip was at the boss's approval. I'm the boss." She settled down in the chair next to him. "I also happen to be your dive instructor for the night dive you have to make this evening. So, do you want to make something of the fact that you're some big honcho astronaut?"

"Not at all. If I have to lay out on a beach with a beautiful woman until this evening when she takes me out diving, then I will."

Suddenly, they both blushed.

"Sorry boss," Ethan said shyly.

"No offense taken," she replied with a warm smile.

*****

T.J. sat with his biosphere team in the school cafeteria eating lunch and once again discussing their project. During the past week they had spent an enormous amount of time together working on their biosphere. Construction of the planting strategies had taken them longer than any other team. This drew humorous comments from Lisa and Billy, who now sat at different tables with their respective teams.

Mrs. James walked into the lunchroom and over to a bulletin board labeled Biosphere Challenge displaying the contest rules. She pinned a paper to the board and retreated back out the door. NOTC students from around the lunchroom raced to the board to see what was going on.

After reading from the sheet, Billy turned towards T.J. and called, "What sort of cheating is this, Gillooley?"

T.J. worked his way through the crowd to see for himself that the first scores had been posted.

"There is no way that you could have tallied produce onto your score already," continued Billy. "It has only been a week since we started the contest. Our seeds have just germinated and you already have a harvest?"

All T.J. could say was "When you're good, you're good," before rushing from the cafeteria toward Mrs. James' office.

He barged into her office with "Mrs. James, why did you publish early results?"

"Why wouldn't I? This contest goes for the duration of the school year. Don't you think it's fair that a *challenge* should have progress reports for spectators and contestants alike?"

"But they are going to figure out what we are up to!"

"Mr. Gillooley, I can barely figure out what you are up to most of the time. I approved your outrageous list of supplies. I even acquired the gases that you requested. You still cannot patent your ideas with me, but trust me. If anybody else tries to pull off the stunt that you are attempting, I will be sure to give you more originality points, even if it doesn't work."

The following morning, T.J. and Todd unlocked the door to their greenhouse. This week they had the early shift before school. T.J. quickly surveyed the area to make sure that nobody was around before opening the door, which bore the sign "Warning. Authorized Personnel Only."

T.J. poked his head into the room and read the monitor on the wall. It showed the oxygen level at twenty-one percent and carbon dioxide level at one thousand parts per million. The alarm was silent. Mrs. James had required the extra precaution of the monitor when he had requested the use of carbon dioxide tanks in the greenhouse.

"I see our competition looking in the windows all of the time trying to get a look at how our production is so high already," stated Todd. "The sign on the door and the paper completely covering the bottom half of the greenhouse is driving them crazy."

"Yeah, all they can see are typical greenhouse plants on the top half," agreed T.J. "Billy even tried to follow me in a couple days ago. It is too bad we could not have patented the idea so that we could also benefit from sunlight rather than depend on the twenty-four hours of grow lights."

"At least we can tell that all of the other teams are using the grow lights, too. You can see their biospheres glowing at night."

"Yet nobody has put up a single point on the scoreboard except us," gloated T.J.

They got to work on the *top secret* lower section of their biosphere. Along one side ran one hundred and forty-four mason jars hung upside down on a rack.

"Until they figure out how we used the rules to our advantage, the contest is ours to win," continued T.J. He started filling jars with water and then shaking the water back out through the screened lids and onto the traditional square foot garden above. "Mrs. James said we had to use seeds. The seed actually holds an abundance of energy for germination. We are just germinating the seed, bringing sprouts to salad in less than a week."

"These sprouts are little vitamin factories and they also contain thirty-five percent protein," said Todd. "When Stacey brought the first batch to the soup kitchen, she was almost turned away. They didn't want any bland old sprouts. She actually put on a pretty good presentation and left information packets with them about their health benefits. They had no idea that our broccoli sprout had such high protein and fifty times more antioxidants than mature broccoli. She told them that, to get the same nourishment as in one ounce of sprouts, they would have to eat three pounds of full grown broccoli! That sold the soup kitchen coordinator who spread the word. Now they can't get enough of them."

"We have twenty-four jars of sprouts to deliver every evening. We just need to keep rotating the crop," stated T.J. "Luckily, we weren't limited by the number of seeds we can use. One pound of seeds yields five pounds of broccoli sprouts in six days. It's the easiest gardening you can do. Heck, they don't require light until the fifth day."

"We will actually get seven pounds when we switch to alfalfa," added Todd, "but it has a slightly lower nutritional rating. Best to mix it up though, so our customers don't get bored. That is why I suggested the button mushrooms being grown directly under the mason jars to collect drained water. They're high in fiber and potassium and taste good on a sprout pita."

Finishing the work on the sprouts, they turned to the three large fish tanks running along the floor on the other side of the greenhouse. They were up on blocks, so that grow lights could be positioned on all sides including the bottoms of the slimy green broth. Todd used a strainer to place large amounts of slime into glass cooking trays.

T.J. optimized the tanks' growing conditions. First, he added a little water to each and verified the heaters were set to a hundred degrees Fahrenheit. He placed a probe into each tank and decided to add a couple of alkalinity tablets to raise the pH to the optimal ten. He added some organic fertilizer, as their entire biosphere was growing organically. Lastly, he verified the carbon dioxide gas tanks were delivering the essential carbon to the bubblers at the tank bottoms.

As they locked up the biosphere, T.J. commented, "The excess CO_2 from our algae farm really seems to help the rest of our square foot gardening. Even our traditional plants seem bigger than everyone else's."

They headed to the kitchen to dry the collected blue-green algae.

*****

Warren poked his head in the doorway and asked, "How was your vacation?"

Ethan looked up from the small mock-up of a space shuttle sitting before him on the table. "What vacation? That was all work. We astronauts need to be working on our mental state at all times. The scuba diving was all part of my mental preparation."

"Did it work?" asked Warren as he entered the room and walked over to get a better look at the model.

"I suppose it did. The experience brought me to a place I thought that I would never be." His mind wandered to Kylie.

"Sounds like you are ready to go back up into space."

Ethan contemplated that statement. "I suppose I am. I'm really not afraid anymore. I know what I need to do."

Warren allowed Ethan time to reflect before asking, "What are you doing? It looks like you are back to making toy models."

"Actually," responded Ethan, "I prefer to build a model before fabricating the final product. I'd have a whole collection of them if it weren't for their top secret classification. They keep taking them away when I'm done."

Warren walked around the model and inspected it. It looked just like the space shuttle but with an exoskeleton structure over the wings with a circular array at each end. "I might not be an aeronautical engineer, but I can't see how that can fly."

"NASA is no longer using me as an aeronautical engineer. Since the shuttles will never be in air again, the principles change. Space has no atmosphere to hinder or, in the case of aviation, to help. Conversely, there is usually relatively little gravity to work against. Our shuttle no longer needs wings and the engines at the back only propel it forward to a destination with little in the way of steering."

Ethan pointed to the end of the wings. "Adding a circular potential propulsion array at the wing tips allows us the maneuverability to push up, down, left, or right. The best part is that we can stop or even go backwards. Think more along the lines of a Harrier jet."

"On a sub, we could always turn the screw backwards to go in reverse. Wouldn't it be easier to put an engine on the nose of the shuttle to push backwards?"

Ethan laughed. "You would have had to stop moving backwards already. Think about the consequences of firing up the forward engine while you are propelling forward, right through the flames and heat. You would burn up. These jets are placed at the wing tips and always pointed away from the shuttle."

Warren nodded his understanding. "I always tell everybody how brilliant you are."

"They already had the concept. I just need to implement it."

"So you are going back up?" questioned Warren.

"I go next week," answered Ethan, "just as soon as they complete the next round of cargo deliveries."

"They are stealing more water from the Chimborazo streams?"

"Actually, they are sending up the captured dry ice," answered Ethan.

"Why? I thought that was just the cover story for the elevator."

"Apparently, it will be needed for something on the Moon," responded Ethan.

*****

T.J. handed Billy a wrench and watched as he worked on the crane's transmission. The master mechanics class was at a yard for heavy machinery. They had been broken up into groups, each assigned to a piece of equipment that required some type of repair. Mr. Roedel walked among the groups and advised the best way to accomplish each task.

T.J. thought about how little he and Billy hung out lately. They had drifted apart as friends ever since being placed on different teams for the biosphere competition. The competition had taken much of the NOTC students' time this year. Surprisingly, T.J. had come to realize that it seemed to take up significantly less time for his team, even though they were in the lead for points.

"Are you excited about the field trip that Mr. Graca is planning for us?" asked T.J.

Billy's face lit up at the mention of scuba diving. "Heck yeah! I can't believe we get to perform a cavern dive."

"It's called spelunking," corrected T.J. Immediately, he could see the smile leave Billy's face. He apologetically asked, "So, do you think you would want to be my dive partner for it? I don't know anybody that likes to explore as much as you do."

The compliment seemed to soften Billy's demeanor. "Sure. We make a pretty good team at that." As T.J. took a turn removing some bolts, Billy continued, "It's too bad that I can't get my biosphere team to have as much fun as we do."

"What do you mean?"

Billy acknowledged, "Ever since your team pulled so far into the lead, it's taken all of the fun out of the master gardening class. It was supposed to be

136

a competition to inspire us in the quest for knowledge about optimal plant growth. Instead, I think it has ended up hurting the learning ego of the rest of the NOTC class."

T.J. was surprised by the comment. He had noticed that the class did seem less motivated. "Well, it's not my fault just because my team is winning the competition."

Billy considered this a moment before saying, "Remember your theory about how everybody in NOTC is in fierce competition to be number one in the group. You were right about our grades. I think that everybody got straight A's last year. The only things differentiating us are these little competitions. This time, the competition is having a much bigger effect. Instead of just winning, your team is crushing the morale of the class. I would be surprised if there is not a drop in grades this term."

Later that evening, T.J. and Todd were on their daily trip to the shelter. They were making a delivery of sprouts and Spirulina powder. Along the way they discussed the issue of the morale of their NOTC classmates.

"Now that you mention it, I have even noticed that it is getting harder to motivate myself. Everyone's attitude is bringing me down," agreed Todd.

"I have been considering a solution," said T.J. "Our team has more than twice the points of any other team and there is only one month left of school. What if we just share with them what we are doing? They could never catch up, so we're in no danger of losing."

Todd was in complete agreement. "I'll talk with Stacey and Tom."

The following Wednesday, T.J. stood with his team outside the door to their biosphere. The rest of the class was gathered expectantly around them. All eyes scanned the now revealed lower half of the greenhouse. The paper cover had been removed to reveal the fish tanks filled with what appeared to be bubbling pea soup. Even Mrs. James was anxiously waiting for the explanation.

Stacey began. "The top half of our biosphere is very similar to all of yours. It is a high density planting of vegetables. Mostly, we followed square foot gardening guidelines with some additional companion planting strategy. To reduce the plants' stress from being grown so close, we needed to closely monitor and supplement their light, water, and nutrient requirements."

"Our biosphere breaks away from the norm in the lower half," added Tom. "Over there you can see a rack of mason jars. That is our sprout garden. Every twelve hours, we soak the seeds and rotate our crop. There is a constant rotation of starting new seeds and harvesting. It takes six days to grow a seed to a nutritional sprout."

Todd took over. "Sprouts contain thirty-five percent proteins. Compare that to just twenty-two percent protein in beef. They also contain more vitamins, minerals, and enzymes than any other food per calorie. The broccoli sprout we grew also contains an enormous amount of antioxidants, fifty times more than mature broccoli does. All of that nutrition is contained in the little seed that only requires water at first and then light after the fourth day."

T.J. stepped forward. "The last section of our biosphere was the most experimental. It also turned out to be the most productive. In the fish tanks, we are growing blue - green algae called Spirulina. It is a single celled plant that grows prolifically in warm, alkaline fresh water. It is probably going to be known as the super food of the future."

T.J. led the class into the greenhouse. "As you can see, each tank is absolutely choked with algae." Stacey, Tom, and Todd each used a strainer to begin collecting a harvest. T.J. continued, "Each morning it grows to the point where it requires harvesting. The typical land plant has a photosynthetic conversion rate of three percent, whereas our alga has a rate of almost ten percent. So it grows at three times the typical rate, but even more important is the fact that it is one hundred percent edible and packed with nutrients."

They slopped the algae into baking dishes. Tom stated, "We dry it in the school's cafeteria oven and make it into powder form in a food processor."

Stacey added, "We deliver it with the sprouts to a shelter, where they add it upon request to orange juice they serve for breakfast. They are really pushing the healthy aspect of our donations to their clientele."

"While beef is twenty-two percent protein and sprouts contain thirty-five percent proteins, Spirulina contains an incredible sixty-five to seventy percent complete proteins. It is loaded with vitamins, contains protective phytochemicals, and is one of the few plant sources of B12 which is typically found only in meat. It is also low in fat."

"How easy is it to grow?" asked Billy.

T.J. was glad for his friend's question. "It requires warm water, so we have a heater. It requires light, so we surround our tank with grow lights. It requires an alkaline pH. It also has a voracious appetite due to its reproductive rate. We constantly monitor the nutrient levels in the water and add organic green sand as fertilizer to maintain levels. The last tricky part is that its growth rate is dependent on the amount of carbon dioxide in the water. It grows so fast that it would consume all normal levels present in the water and stop growing. We actually bubble a constant trickle into the water from gas tanks. The extra amount released from the water elevates levels in the greenhouse, spurring growth in our other plants. It actually turned out to be a good companion strategy."

"Excellent job, Biosphere 4 team," complimented Mrs. James.

"One more thing, if I may," said T.J. "While I know it was originally set up as a competition between us, we kind of have a good thing going. We make daily food donations to a homeless shelter that is very thankful to get them. We were hoping to keep it up throughout the summer, but need some help with that. Also, if it is OK with Mrs. James, we could help your teams implement some of what we do here. If we ever got to the point where the shelter had enough, they are affiliated with a food bank. For the greater good of humanity, I think NOTC should work together on this."

*****

Stephen left the oval office and headed toward the residential wing of the White House. He was glad that his presidential duties were done for the day, if it could be said that the President was ever really off while serving in office. In fact, he was expecting to meet with Kevin to discuss progress of the project.

"Stephen," called Kevin, who came rushing down the hall towards him.

"Excellent timing," replied Stephen. "You can join me for dinner."

The two entered the presidential suite as a server was pushing a cart toward the dining table.

"The best part about being President is that the service is great. They seem to know exactly what I want, when I want it." He poured a couple of drinks.

"I have good news about our progress," said Kevin while accepting a drink. "We managed to use the Elevator to place six more rovers onto the Moon, two Cats, two Dogs, and two Bulls."

"You lost me," interrupted Stephen. "I know Cats are the Cargo Transport vehicles. The two additions make a total of four on the Moon. What are the Dogs and Bulls?"

"The engineers wanted to keep the animal naming motif. *"Dogs"* simply stands for a small unmanned rover, which is for exploration purposes only. "Bulls" are the bulldozers that are leveling the sites on the Moon. They incorporate microwave cones that sinter and melt the lunar soil, making an extremely hard glass surface. They're preparing the landing site and base."

"So activity on the Moon is progressing more quickly, and we are still working under everyone's radar. That is great news," stated Stephen. "The world is still a dangerous place, but I haven't had to light the wick for the space race."

"That's good," said Kevin. "The longer you hold off, the more we'll accomplish toward our final goal. That Warren Poet is turning out to be the best asset we have in Houston."

Stephen was surprised by the statement. "I thought Ethan Dire was our most important asset."

Kevin corrected himself. "Of course, Ethan is still our Golden Boy. He just got back down from the Phoenix Spaceport after making the modifications to the shuttles. Now they are truly spaceships made for moving outside an atmosphere. Once the bulls complete the landing zone, we can go at any time."

Kevin allowed that good news to sink in before continuing. "When I said that Warren has become invaluable, I was talking about his contributions to the Power teams. We had three different engineering teams waiting for access to Warren. Each wanted to incorporate one of his nuclear reactors into a process they had designed. Once Warren heard of their intended uses, he surprised everyone by incorporating all into one process. Apparently they can all work in conjunction with each other. He almost tripled our potential capacities."

"Incredible news," agreed Stephen.

As they served themselves dinner, they discussed the technologies that would allow their project to become larger than they had ever anticipated.

*****

The summer off had actually been hard on T.J. He missed the challenges that school offered. He still worked the greenhouse and made the donation runs to the shelter, but that had only been once a week. Many other students had volunteered to be part of a rotation manning the biosphere. He saw all of his NOTC classmates at various times when he went to the school's pool to swim laps. Best of all was that his friendship with Billy had strengthened. They had gotten to the quarry every weekend to get in dives and practice the navigational skills they had learned that year.

Now that T.J. was a junior, he was starting to think about his future. While other juniors in his school were visiting with counselors to discuss their potential futures, T.J. and the NOTC students had just received a one on one pep talk with a representative from NASA. Their college acceptances were assured. There futures were bright. T.J. had asked without much of a response about NASA's future for space exploration.

On the first day of school, he was given some disappointing news about the master gardening class. Their biosphere access was being taken away. The greenhouses were being handed over to the sophomore class. The silver lining to the news was that Biosphere 4 was still going to contain the Spirulina tanks and sprout garden. They would be maintained by the sophomores and donations to the shelter would continue. Apparently, Mrs. James knew that the knowledge of its success could not be kept from her new class and decided it would be best to continue that project with them.

Physical education class promised to be a challenge. They would start out with CPR training and move into lifesaving classes. They would be incorporating those skills into the scuba diving curriculum, working toward getting certified as Rescue Divers. While receiving medical training, they would be pushing their endurance levels in the pool by swimming laps.

Mr. Roedel began this year's master mechanics class with a shocker. "You learned automobile and heavy equipment mechanics pretty well, but what would a NASA master mechanic be without knowing a little about gadgets? We will start with a crash course on computer hardware, software, and programming. Then we will be building simple machines, complex machines, and finally move on to robotics."

"The theme this year is innovation. I will teach you concepts, and you will need to apply them. I will teach you robotics, and you will create a robot warrior. At the end of the school year, I will not be giving you grades. I will be giving your robots' grades. Their performances will be judged during our Robot Wars."

The class erupted with conversation. T.J. could not believe the challenge that had just been revealed. It looked to be another exciting school year of hard work.

Mr. Roedel allowed them to talk for a full minute before beginning again. The class went immediately silent. "Here are the ground rules, which will also be posted. You will work in assigned teams. Maximum robot weight limit is thirty pounds. I will supply all electronic radio controls. No radio jamming devices will be allowed. You have a maximum budget of one hundred dollars. The rest of your supplies will be obtained at the garbage dump."

"Prohibited weapons are guns and explosives. Other projectiles must be tethered. Combat will be conducted during a five minute match and will end with the thirty second immobilization of the opponent. If neither is immobilized, then it goes to the judge, that's me, to decide the winner of the match."

Mr. Roedel put on a mischievous grin and rubbed his hands together in eagerness. "Now, who is ready to build robots?"

The classroom jumped to their feet and cheered exuberantly.

*****

Ethan saw Warren busily working over a drafting table. He marveled at the fact that an exceptional engineer like Warren would be using old school means rather than software to design for NASA.

142

"Hey. Do you have time for lunch with an old friend?" he called.

Warren looked up from his work and his serious face brightened to a smile. "I didn't know that you were back up to the States already. Or should I say back *down* to the States?"

"I got back down from Phoenix over two weeks ago. I made a stopover at Kennedy to visit there with the fabrication guys. I wanted to go over the modification of the shuttles with them and discuss some additional ideas I had. It's their birds after all. While I was there, they mentioned that you were causing a whole lot of commotion here."

"I'm just trying to help out," defended Warren.

"Actually, I heard you made some phenomenal suggestions that are causing the stir. The other engineers are worried for their jobs," joked Ethan.

"I didn't do too much. They consider me the owner of the three remaining nuclear reactors destined for the Moon. I had to meet separately with three different teams of engineers, each with a design to support a technology run on nuclear energy. I was to assist them in incorporating the reactor into their systems. The funny thing was that once each team explained how their design was intended to work, I realized that all of the systems were interrelated. I figured out how to raise their efficiency."

Ethan was impressed. "So the old seadog taught these young studs some engineering. Well, you might as well teach me, too. How do you get more energy out of the power plants?" He started reading over the drawing on the table.

"They're actually production plants," corrected Warren.

"Sure," agreed Ethan. "I understand how they will be used to create electricity and also power the electrolysis units like they do on Phoenix. What else did you guys come up with?"

Warren proudly continued. "The first team needed to power a massive array of electrolysis units to turn water into oxygen and hydrogen. The oxygen is essential to the planned biosphere, and both hydrogen and oxygen are required to refuel the shuttles."

Warren fumbled through the pile of drawings and pulled out another. "The next group wanted to create water from the lunar soil or *regolith* as they like to call it. Did you know that the Moon is comprised of forty-two percent oxygen? It is bonded to silicates and metal oxides. There is also a small amount of hydrogen which has been implanted by the solar winds. This plant was to heat lunar soil to release trapped hydrogen, which in turn would react with the silicates and metal oxides to release oxygen in the soil. The end product is water."

Again, Warren fumbled for another drawing. "The last group intended to use a reactor's energy to produce building material for the base out of minerals mined on the Moon. They intended to purify these using heat and large electromagnets. Well, once I heard their concept, a light bulb went off in my head."

Ethan felt proud for his friend who was standing there knowingly. "OK. Why don't you connect the dots for me?"

Warren turned back to the page he had been working on. "It all starts with one reactor powering electrolysis to generate oxygen and hydrogen from water. The oxygen is a useful byproduct for the biosphere. I was wondering, what they could do with the created hydrogen without its companion oxygen to burn it? There would always be an excess of hydrogen.

"Then there was the second team's requirement of heating regolith to generate small quantities of hydrogen to create small quantities of water. If we were to use the excess hydrogen from the first process, you could capture a lot more oxygen from the soils and create more water. The water could then be recycled into the electrolysis system to continue the cycle of generating water and oxygen.

"The last team's requirements caused the whole design to gel." Warren excitedly pointed to his design. "They propose to manufacture the lunar outpost's building material almost completely out of the regolith. Along with the large quantity of oxygen, the regolith on the near side of the Moon is mostly composed of silica and iron."

"So they can make glass and steel?" asked Ethan.

"Exactly," replied Warren. "I brought all three teams together to discuss a single system. Pulverized lunar soil is dropped into the top of a long tubular, rotating kiln. Iron oxide is separated out by strong electromagnets into a second column off the main tube. The long rotating tube has catalytic fins inside. The whole unit is heated by the reactor which serves as a furnace. The excess hydrogen from the electrolysis array is forced up from the bottom as the fine regolith is dropped in from the top. As the hot molecules meet in the presence of catalytic fins, the hydrogen and oxygen combine to form water which steams back out the top to be collected. As the regolith falls further down the column, the oxides are consumed and you purify silicon and iron.

Warren smiled triumphantly. "See, it is all one system. From the lunar soil you strip out oxygen and create more water. The purified silica is converted into quartz. Carbon monoxide converted from CO_2 will be added to the iron to make carbon steel for support structures. They will even be extracting purified aluminum from the silicate column and precious titanium from iron-titanium oxides on the iron column."

Ethan agreed. "So the nuclear reactors will create electricity, but they will also power production facilities for mining the Moon. Your all-in-one system just tripled their capacities!"

*****

Stephen entered the chamber to an eruption of applause. As he walked down the aisle, he shook hands with Republicans and Democrats alike. His popularity with the American people was at an all-time high, and that had translated into better relations between the parties. His programs in education and his work with the environmental groups had kept opinions favorable even if world tensions were high. He was looking forward to finally sharing his historic goals with the American people during this State of the Union speech.

He began by discussing the favorable economic environment of the past year. He discussed how the treaties made with South American allies had benefited everyone. He transitioned into the topic of world tensions and how Chinese and Russian provocations had severely strained relations between superpower nations.

"Now, I am about to make a historic announcement. School achievement scores have shown a dramatic rise. It appears that NASA's involvement boosting scientific learning in our schools has translated to improvement in all curricula. I would like to thank the people at NASA for their efforts, as everyone can agree that our children's educations are a valuable investment in all of our futures.

"On a related note, I would like to thank NASA for their involvement in helping to stave off global warming. They have been able to remove over a thousand tons of carbon dioxide from our atmosphere and launch it into space. Their courageous effort at building the Space Elevator created the means. It is also a strong platform for the scientific study of space. It has the capacity to house up to a hundred scientists. Over the past year and a half, NASA research teams stationed on the Phoenix Space Base have made tremendous accomplishments. Their discoveries and insights have led us to the next phase of exploration.

"And with that, I am proud to state that NASA will be taking the United States back to the Moon within the next two years. They are at this very moment working on the means to create a lunar outpost for our astronauts. From there, we will be able to conduct research from afar. We have seen that by injecting our school curricula with a healthy dose of science, we can raise the learning potential of our children. By adding the essential ingredient of science into American society, we will attempt to raise the standard of possibility for mankind."

*****

T.J. sat at the table reviewing the tactical plans for their robot with his teammates. Now that NASA had reinstated its space program, he was once again determined to be ranked the best NOTC student and thus improve his chances of becoming an astronaut. This Robot War was another opportunity to show his creativity.

T.J. began, "Let's go over our strategies one last time. Peg, Jeff, and Brent will be stationed as scouts in left, right, and away positions around the field, calling in flanking observations via walkie-talkie. I will be the commanding general, stationed front and center. Billy will be with me, operating the remote control."

Their robot appeared to be quietly watching them from the corner of the room. It sat short and squat to the ground with a protective Plexiglas bubble shielding much of it. They had built it over the last few months. Tomorrow it would be tested, both in battle and for their final grade.

Billy stated, "I have practiced all of the moves. I have a dead on shot with the pneumatic harpoon and Taser. I can maneuver well and know how to handle the flipper mechanism. The dueling robotic circular saws are fearsome. I will take quick victories from our opponents."

T.J. irritably added, "You forgot to mention our Armageddon component!"

Billy responded, "I just think we might get in trouble using it."

"That is why it will be our last resort. These matches are like playing rock, paper, scissors. Everything that our opponent does needs to be countered by the appropriate move on our part. We don't want to show our next opponent too much either. I just wonder what surprises our classmates will throw at us."

The next day they arrived at the games. The arena was a fenced in platform in the center of the school football field. The bleachers were full as the whole school turned out for the spectacle. The first match was to pit T.J.'s robot which they had named *Overkill* versus the *Electrocutioner*.

The robots were placed into the arena. Their opponent was an unassuming robot with two circular saw arms.

"It's too bad our opponents were dumb enough to presumably give away their strategy with the robot's name. My bet is that we will be dealing with some high voltage," stated T.J. to Billy before they started.

"Unfortunately, they will need to get by my Plexiglas shield. Not only is it lightweight and strong, but it is resistant to electrical charges," replied Billy.

"Just keep the blades off of it or the shield is done for," said T.J.

The match began with Billy moving *Overkill* cautiously forward with circular saws engaged. *Electrocutioner* followed suit with its own circular saws. Billy fired a Taser to one of the opponent's saws and followed with a harpoon to the other. Both appeared to be disabled with the harpoon embedded in an arm. The *Electrocutioner* followed with a volley of Taser shots that bounced harmlessly off their shield.

"I see a rod extending out of the body," called Brent over the walkie-talkie.

"Beware their secret weapon," stated T.J. to Billy. "Try to bring it in close, but don't let it touch any components. It looks like a cattle prod."

Billy let the *Electrocutioner* in closer to *Overkill* while attempting to keep the prod at bay with the shield.

"Keep our saws back. Draw him in closer. Now flip him!" ordered T.J.

With a press of a red button, Billy executed the robots flipping mechanism. The low front edge of their robot had been positioned under their opponent's body. Suddenly, their robot jumped upward as if on a spring and *Electrocutioner* toppled over. Being immobilized, the match was over, with *Overkill* earning its position in the final.

They were now able to scout their next opponent during the second match between *Slasher* and *Tank*.

"*Slasher* is very impressive with three circular saws and a large chainsaw to boot," stated T.J. to his team. "I wish we would have thought of one of those. I see that monster doing some damage. Hopefully *Tank* can eliminate him for us."

The match began with *Tank* racing around its opponent. He danced a circle around *Slasher* while issuing a constant rain of spring shot harpoons. Being tethered, the harpoons tangled and entwined Slasher who quickly appeared to be in trouble. Just as quickly, the tables turned with the saws disengaging the lines and the chainsaw leading the way straight at *Tank*. It ended gruesomely with *Tank*'s robotic parts flying everywhere.

"Now we have to face that brute," said Billy. "It's too bad they could not at least have taken out some of those saws for us."

The final match began with *Overkill* again destroying a circular saw with a Taser shot. First a pneumatic harpoon and then a second one failed to do damage or even penetrate *Slasher's* hard armor.

"Don't attempt the flipper on this guy," warned T.J. "He appears to have a low center of gravity and those saws are too dangerous to bring in close. Keep him at a distance with the extender rod and see if we can get in position for a strike with our saws."

Billy slowly extended a pole out the center of *Overkill* that pushed into *Slasher* and held him at bay. *Slasher* responded by dismembering their extension rod. A second rod extended from *Overkill's* body, but it was also removed before it could make contact. Now it appeared to be a free-for-all with blades. The two sets of circular saws sparked off each other, but the chain saw was free to do damage at the center. *Overkill's* shield exploded away. The blade continued into the main body.

"Armageddon! Retreat and Armageddon!" yelled T.J.

Billy complied by quickly disengaging from the attack. *Overkill* got some distance from *Slasher*, who slowly pursued. Suddenly, a continuous stream of flame shot from *Overkill. Slasher* was doused in flames but continued its pursuit. It was too slow and the flame thrower continued its assault. In a blaze, *Slasher* shuddered to a halt and died. Excited roars of enthusiasm erupted from the stands. The combat was over and *Overkill* stood victorious within a ring of flames. Even parts of the football field grass below were burning.

*****

The President entered the situation room, quickly followed by other members of his War Cabinet. "Give us the full report, General."

General McKnabb started with "The Chinese have made a preemptive attack."

"They moved into Chile?" asked Peter Owens, the Secretary of State. "We have been pressuring them to stay in their half of the peninsula."

With a stern look, General McKnabb added, "They attacked us."

The room was silent. Finally the President asked, "You stated it was a preemptive act. How could it be preemptive? Did they believe we were an imminent threat?"

The National Security Advisor answered. "We believe they determined the space elevator to be a threat to their own exploration of the Moon. They must have figured out our intentions and decided to stop us. The fact that we already had the space shuttles gave us a great advantage in the race.

Previously, everybody thought it ludicrous to actually use a shuttle to go to the Moon. We have all three of them already stationed one tenth of the distance to the Moon. They are outside the Earth's gravity well and are in a position where they can easily be refueled. I guess it dawned on them that we had actually built a spaceport. If their attack had succeeded as planned, we would be back to square one."

General McKnabb took over. "We were informed that they would be putting a test rocket into space. Our intelligence knows that they are actively racing us to the Moon. We were closely monitoring the rocket as it left the atmosphere and became concerned when it started to track in orbit. It was not heading toward the U.S and was heading away from Earth, so it took us awhile to determine it was actually targeting the elevator."

"So they did not succeed? Did we take much damage?" asked Stephen.

"The Chinese missile was not even close. I guess they have some more work on their rocket technology. As we had armed the space base anyway, we destroyed theirs with one of our own missiles. They probably counted on the fact that, even if the missile was destroyed, charges would still devastatingly hit our base. It was probably quite intense for those stationed up there. Luckily, they were way off target."

The National Security Advisor added, "Our analysts believe that the missile had a heat seeking guidance system. Fortunately, the space base is insulated and shielded from space by an ice shell. Its heat signature would have been much too low to be detected by their guidance system and it just ended up in the general trajectory vicinity of the base."

"Well, any attempt made is too close for comfort," stated Stephen. "Peter, make it clear to them that our Phoenix Space Base is considered to be the property of the U.S. military and any further aggressions will have serious consequences. I am sure that they know we will not allow an attack on our Ecuadorian ground base, and they attempted to take out our soft, space assets once and for all. We have moved very quickly so far, but it is now time to ratchet up our timeline."

*****

"What's up, buddy?" said Ethan, poking his head into Warren's fabrication workshop.

"Hey, come on in, Ethan. They have me on packing detail once again. This time they need to send up the production plants that we built. I was asked to manage the three very competent teams of engineers building the three identical plants that symbiotically incorporated all of their needs."

"You got them completed already?" asked Ethan.

"Like I said, they were all very good engineers. They already knew what they needed. I just got them to work together. The hard part was keeping construction modular so that we could send them up in pieces via the elevator. Luckily, that is what submarine engineers do best. We make simple components that work together, but can easily be changed out and assembled."

"Well I hope they are really easy to assemble," remarked Ethan.

Warren nodded. "I know what you mean. I will be giving assembly instructions again, but this time from Houston. What do they have you working on?"

Ethan gave a wry smile. "I am actually packing up myself."

"What do they have you sending up?" asked Warren.

"Myself."

It took a moment for Warren to register the information. "Well, they picked the right man for the job. At least I will be assured that the nuclear reactors and the production plants will be assembled properly. How soon before you go?"

"I have been told that I go as soon as your fabrications are up. Some of the parts will be shot right to the Moon. The fragile components like the radioactive cores will go up on the shuttle with me. Right now there is a delay as they are attempting to get as much liquid nitrogen onto the Moon as possible. I was told it would be a few weeks yet."

"Liquid nitrogen? What could they need that for? I suppose it's cold and could be used for cooling, but the reactors are set up to use cooling water which is incorporated into the whole outpost survival. You'll need the heat so you don't freeze to death."

151

"I don't know what it's for yet, but they need a lot of it," responded Ethan.

"How is Kylie taking the news that they are sending you up?" asked Warren.

"She's the one that asked me to go," replied Ethan. He looked away from his friend and at the ground. "Apparently, she has always considered me to be an indispensable asset to the project."

Warren patted Ethan on the shoulder knowingly. "You are indispensable to all of us. Keep yourself safe up there."

*****

"My fellow Americans," began Stephen, "I called this news conference to give you some grave news. The Chinese have attempted an attack on our space elevator, the very same space elevator that is helping to alleviate the threat of global warming by removing greenhouse gases that threaten our planet. Fortunately, they had poor aim and missed this scientific research outpost.

"The Chinese have made it clear that they intend to take the United States up on its challenge to get back to the Moon. I want to make it clear that I welcome their working toward that goal. The advancement of science is just as good for their culture as it is for the United States. However, it becomes inexcusable when the Chinese decide to cheat to help their chances of getting there first.

"The space elevator serves mankind by helping to alleviate the growing concentration of greenhouse gases. It has become a center for astronomical research and a symbol of inspiration. The Chinese realized that it could be used for much more than that. For example, it could be used as a platform to go into space. They decided that they would take out this valuable asset to give them more time to reach the Moon first. They gave no consideration to the scientific researchers up there who would have been killed had their attack been successful.

"I am here tonight to inform you that the space elevator is indeed a spaceport. Being that it is run by NASA with many brave astronauts who also happen to be military officers, I have decided that the elevator will be defined as an installation of the United States military under the combined directive of NASA and the Air Force. It will be called U.S. Spaceport Phoenix. Any further aggressions toward the base will be deemed an act of war against the United States.

"Now I will try to lighten up this conference with some good news. When I announced our intentions to go back to the Moon within two years, I received some unexpected criticism. Why would I make such an ambitious goal that was supposed to occur during the next presidential term? It had to be so that I could get reelected, partisans said. Well, I stand before you today with some astounding news. I do not need to hold this over the American public during an election. I plan to name the date right now. I have been told that NASA wants to get to the Moon sooner rather than later. They will be ready in the next couple of months. I state here today that the United States will be back on the Moon on October 30th of this year.

"Some of my detractors might be brazen enough to say that now I am moving it up just to get reelected. It is true that October 30th is one week before the election, but NASA says they can be ready by then. I have chosen this historic day for America because it happens to be my birthday!"

*****

"So tell me, Mr. Gillooley. What are your intentions after high school?"

This was T.J.'s first interview with a NASA collegiate admissions representative. While other seniors were meeting with guidance counselors to discuss their futures and to decide at which colleges to apply, NOTC students were receiving more than just guidance. They were competing.

T.J. smiled confidently. "I intend to take NASA up on its offer to become part of their family. I want to become an astronaut."

"Completing the NOTC curriculum will guarantee you financial reimbursement for almost any university and admit you into their NOTC collegiate program. A select few of your group will be accepted into the newly formed NASA School of Higher Learning at the University of Florida. They will have direct affiliation with NASA. The best of you might even be accepted into the astronaut program."

"I intend to be the best. I want to be an astronaut," repeated T.J.

The NASA representative took some notes. "Let's look at your qualifications. Your grades and test scores are exemplary, but you are being compared to other NOTC students who also score highly. Let's talk about your personal achievements. You have done very well in the diving curriculum. Tell me about your freshman year win in the Underwater LEGO Challenge."

T.J. liked where this was going. "I wanted to design something that would capture the imagination of the NOTC group. Building the space elevator achieved that. It also helped that the structure grew from the bottom of the pool all the way to above the surface, reflecting the way the real space elevator climbs from Earth all the way to above the atmosphere."

More notes were taken. "Mr. Graca reports that you are very confident underwater. You have mastered all of the skills he has taught. He intends on giving you a lot of bottom time in the quarry throughout the year, especially during the winter. You will be given additional equipment training to include dry suit diving. Do you think you can handle diving through ice in the dead of winter?"

"I heard that you don't even get cold when you have on the dry suit over your clothing. It sounds awesome. I wish we could have done it the previous two years instead of losing time during the winter," answered T.J.

"Tell me about your success in the Biosphere Challenge."

T.J. was pleased to reply, "Seeds grow to more than five times their weight as sprouts in as many days. They are also concentrated nutrition. We used the fact that we could replenish as many seeds as we wanted. I figured that if nobody else did the sprouts, then we would have a big enough lead to try the algae tanks. That experiment paid off even better than the sprouts. I'm glad, because I think it is something that NASA could easily grow the Spirulina algae in space."

"Tell me about the Robot Wars."

"Well, we handled that like you would handle a match of Rock-Paper-Scissors. We just had to have more tricks up our sleeve than our adversaries," stated T.J. proudly.

"But you got in quite a bit of trouble afterwards. Didn't you?"

Reluctantly T.J. admitted, "Yes, sir. The last match started to turn bad on us. I devised a flame thrower out of a battery operated squirt gun filled with some flammable alcohol. While the plan was to douse our opponent into a flaming death, we did not anticipate how much damage a super soaker could discharge. We burned down the entire temporary stage and severely damaged the football field grass. We did not break any rules of the competition though, so we still won."

"You have gotten in trouble before. Tell me about what happened in eighth grade."

T.J. could not believe that incident had turned up in his record and was going to blow his chance to be an astronaut! "The school was one of the high tech magnet schools specifically designed without any distractions. I decided to solve the riddle of where they were storing the adult size chairs for the evening college classes. I deduced that there had to be a hidden passage. Once I found it, I determined that I had to explore it. I used a science project as a diversion to get into it, but the diversion ended up being much bigger than I had anticipated."

T.J.'s hopes sank as the NASA representative scribbled some more notes. "Do you recall the achievement test that you took that year?"

Remembering, T.J. perked up and responded, "Sure. It was the most interesting test I ever took. Throughout the test, there were these incredible questions that woke up the imagination."

"Do you recall the last question? *Should mankind expend enormous resources and face exceptional dangers to leave Earth and explore the Universe?*"

"I do recall it and I definitely think we should."

The NASA representative was staring hard into T.J.'s eyes. It was like he was trying to read his soul. "Those interesting questions that were sprinkled through that achievement test were personality profile questions. They helped NASA locate the people most likely to become inventors and scientists. That last question just as easily could have been stated as *Do you want to go to the Moon?*"

T.J. was excited by the prospect.

Then the NASA representative asked, "Well, do you?"

*****

The two day trip up began as sheer torment to Ethan. The constant rush of adrenaline reminded him that this small room was an actual elevator heading out into space. The initial feeling of acceleration was a reminder that he was being pulled away from something he had always sought. He had never felt truly needed by anyone before. Now he was championing the quest she had charged him. He had nothing but time to dwell on this inside the small compartment surrounded by his team members.

"Care to play some Texas hold'em?" asked Jim Hunter to his right. He had been sitting quietly for the past few hours, probably contemplating his future. Now the acceleration seemed to stop and they found themselves once again in zero gravity. He and the other astronauts seemed to snap out of their trances.

"You want to have a poker game in space?" asked a surprised Ethan.

"Sure. We could have played on our previous stint in space if I had thought of bringing the cards and chips. We each get a thousand dollars in chips. We keep our chips and the pot in clear Ziploc bags on the table. "

"Sorry, I don't have a thousand on me for the buy in," replied Ethan.

Jim laughed. "Money doesn't mean anything where we're going. You get that amount of chips, but we are playing for something else, time. The buy in is one hour of time off for the winner from each loser. "

"Now that is something of real value," agreed Ethan. "I just hope that none of you guys gets caught cheating and gets tossed from the game, or worse, tossed from the elevator."

"Just make sure you don't lose any of your chips my way in zero-G."

The next two days were a comfortable blur of poker and sleep for Ethan. As they locked onto the Spaceport Phoenix, he was pleased to find that he was still up four hours of time off. He wondered when he would get to redeem them as they went through the hatch, exchanged pleasantries with

156

the current spaceport inhabitants, and boarded directly onto the fully loaded and fueled shuttle Endeavor.

"Now let's see how your modifications to the shuttle perform," said Jim who now sat in the pilot seat. He had elected to pilot the shuttle away from the spaceport to get a live feel for the new Harrier type control system.

"I am igniting the wing jets." He flipped a switch and pressed a button. An indicator showed that a pilot flame was lit at each wing tip. A few more switches activated, and then he pulled the two sticks back toward him. The shuttle gently disengaged from its dock and backed away from the spaceport.

"Nice job pulling out," called Ethan from the seat behind Jim. "Now you just have to merge with traffic."

Jim turned the sticks and the shuttle rotated ninety degrees to the determined course. "It works just like the simulator anticipated." He ignited the rear jets and propelled them toward the Moon.

It was three days of solemn camaraderie, as the team got their game faces on for the mission ahead. These men were now Ethan's family. They would be relying upon each other's skills for survival. The Moon now appeared much larger through the window and Jim once again reclaimed control of the pilot seat. He maintained control for the trip around the back side of the Moon which used the Moon's gravity to help decelerate the shuttle.

"Now let's hope it's just as easy to land upside down on the shuttle's back," Jim called to Ethan. "Are you sure that you remembered to install the new set of wheels up top?"

"It is a little late to be asking that now," responded a smiling Ethan. "I modified it. You just figure out how to make it work."

The shuttle still had the external fuel tank mounted to its belly. Ethan had built new landing gear on top of the shuttle and into the extra wing supports for the Harrier jet system. Landing would prove an interesting first for the shuttle, as it could only be practiced in a simulator. Such a landing would only be possible under the minimal gravity conditions of the Moon.

Jim began to further decelerate and bring the shuttle closer to the surface of the Moon using the harrier jets. He had to maneuver to the outpost landing strip guided solely by the GPS display, as there were no landmarks, towers, or landing lights.

It was disconcerting to Ethan to see the Moon surreally approaching from above through the windows. As they made their final approach, his aeronautical sensibilities were telling him that the shuttles speed was way too slow. He had to remind himself that, since there was no atmosphere, aeronautics did not come into play. Jim had to deal with the low lunar gravity for landing.

Suddenly, they were down. Mankind had returned to the Moon. Ethan was on the Moon!

LUNAR U

Major Jim Hunter maneuvered the Shuttle Endeavor down the runway of solid glass. They approached the rim of an extremely large crater with steep walls. The runway led down the rim as a road would lead down into a deep quarry. This was to be the lunar outpost.

Ethan could see what appeared to be numerous pyramids positioned around the bottom of the crater. It took him a moment to realize that they were the supplies that had been neatly stacked by the Cats. Directly ahead was an enormous pile. Jim pulled the shuttle closer to it before coming to a halt.

Jim called back, "On behalf of NASA, I would like to welcome you to Eden, the new lunar outpost. Currently, the sun is shining on this side of the Moon and we register a balmy 35 degrees Fahrenheit at the base of the crater. Welcome to your new home."

The team of astronauts removed their harnesses and headed back toward the spacesuits. Ethan nervously fumbled with his harness latch. Jim passed with the comment, "Time to get to work, Ethan. Hurry up or you'll miss your chance."

Three others were already beginning the tedious process of donning their spacesuits. Ethan was helped into his by Jim. When completed, Jim tapped him on both shoulders and yelled into his helmet, "Be careful out there and have fun!"

The four suited astronauts were sealed behind a hatch before the outer portal opened. The lunar landscape was incredibly bright and the sky extremely black. Ethan stepped first onto the lunar surface.

He was slightly disappointed that the surface was not the fine dust in which Neil Armstrong had famously left his boot print. This surface was polished glass. The fine dust that had once covered the lunar surface had been transformed by NASA using rovers called the Bulls. The heavy earth movers made the runway and graded the floor of the crater. They actually looked similar to bulls walking in reverse. The Bulls' two hornlike probes shot out strong microwaves that turned the silica concentrated soil into the heavy duty polished surface that Ethan now stood on.

Ethan followed one of the astronauts along the rim toward the large pyramid. The other two astronauts followed a GPS signal toward an area where they would find the Horses, an acronym for Human Rover Systems. Ethan neared the stack and his GPS indicated that the supplies he required were to his left and in close proximity to the crater wall. He visually located them, realizing that they were in plain sight but just much smaller relative to the size of the main pyramid.

Written on the sides of the crates was, *"To the Moon or bust."* Yep, these were Warren's packages and that was Warren's writing. These crates had not been stacked but were strategically positioned by the Cats approximately where he would want to use them. Leave it to Warren to be so thorough. This trip out would be strictly to open them and remove the packaging. Surprisingly, the crates were composed of biodegradable foam surrounding actual wood. He had been told that it would later be somehow recycled.

After they had unpackaged the first few crates, the other astronauts pulled up on a couple of Horses. They dropped one of them off and both left on the other. They followed the runway back up to the rim of the crater, where they would find their own strategically placed packages. Ethan waved and wished them luck. Their construction project would be to zipper and glue large pieces of plastic together. These would be used to create a large biosphere lean-to along the rim of the crater. The rim wall also would require the microwave lazing to make a gas impermeable glass surface. If the equipment that Ethan was installing created oxygen and heat, they had to have some way to contain it so that it would not just bleed away into space.

After about three hours outside, they had six crates unpacked. They decided to clear the crate debris and load it onto the rear of the Horse. They drove it to the far side of the pyramid to the area the GPS display designated as the area for biodegradable waste. The other astronaut was at the wheel of the dune buggy type four-seat rover. Ethan finally had the time to just enjoy the view of the landscape as they traveled.

He was exhausted but still excited. This was real. He was an astronaut on the Moon. He was also the lead engineer constructing Eden. He had been given command of the lunar outpost.

*****

Stephen logged onto the video conference to find Kevin and Kylie there waiting for him. "Thanks for the birthday present."

Kevin smiled broadly on the display and stated, "The landing went perfectly. We now have all of the projected supplies in place along with seven very competent men working to fulfill our dream."

Stephen replied, "It was still a big risk doing this the week before the election. If the mission had failed, my reelection chances would have been over and the mission would have lost its focus."

Kylie jumped in, "The public loves you, sir. You own their hearts and minds with your pledge to science, education, and the environment."

Stephen was still on the road stumping for the upcoming election which the polls showed him winning by a landslide. There had even been recent pundits commenting that they were surprised that he was still expending so much time and money considering his lead. They did not know the fear Stephen had that something would go wrong with the mission to hurt his lead. "All the same, I owe those brave men another round of gratitude for saving our mission and me politically. It is unfortunate that we had to once again put them in the position where they need to succeed to survive."

Kylie responded, "I have every confidence that Ethan Dire and his crew can accomplish the mission."

"It's theoretical. If it can, this group will get it done." Kevin agreed.

*****

Ethan marveled at the large plastic tarp that formed a tent encompassing everything essential running from the shuttle, over his production facility area, and beyond the large pyramid. He estimated that it stretched about a quarter mile along the rim. While he found it to be incredibly large, it still enclosed less than ten percent of the crater and mostly just the pyramid.

"So you requested me on your nuke detail again?" asked Jim. "I thought we were friends."

"We are," replied Ethan. "That is why I am entrusting my life to you. Today we need to install the reactor, integrating it with the production plant. We cannot actually put it online until we have a large body of water."

"And when will they deliver the water?"

"It's already here. See the large pyramid?" asked Ethan pointing up at the summit. "This is a mountain of ice. They shot it to the Moon in large blocks. The Cats acquired them, removed their wrappers, and stacked the ice neatly for us."

"But it is frozen. How do we make use of it for the reactor?"

Ethan stopped working to answer. "That is the other reason I invited you today. I figured that you being the shuttle commander needed to know first. The plan calls for us to consume the rest of the external tank's fuel to melt enough water for initial startup of the reactor. Once it is operational, its heat will continue to melt the pyramid down into the Moon's first lake. There is sufficient water here to cool all three reactors, which will be powering the production plants. Eventually, we will have enough hydrogen and oxygen generated to refuel the shuttle."

Jim could only stare at Ethan as he continued to process the information that the shuttle would be with no means of returning home.

"Don't worry," stated Ethan. "Everybody believes that this should work. We will be fine, eventually."

Finally Jim said, "Let's get this done then. When this mountain of ice melts, where is all the water to go?"

"Actually, it is not sitting on level ground with us. It is situated in a crater within our crater. It is a large shallow crater that the Bulls had to work hard to remove the impart rim and level it with the rest of our base floor. Below the ice is another twenty feet of crater. It also slopes away toward the center of the main crater to where the melted ice will eventually flow."

"So this will be quite a large lake," said Jim.

"The area has already been dubbed Luck Lake by Houston planners. They figure that a crater impact within a crater basin is similar to lightening striking twice in the same place. They are hoping luck would have it as unlikely for another large impact in the same region."

"It is a perfect place to put the nukes then," responded Jim.

They began assembling the reactor. Ethan was sure that Jim was contemplating how he was going to tell the others that they would soon be stranded on the Moon.

The next morning, one team made a final inspection of the biosphere tarp which had been melded to the crater wall and floor. Jim and Ethan were again out by Luck Lake. The shuttle had been fired up for a last time and moved closer.

They ran fuel lines from the external tank down to the future lake. After attaching multiple heaters, they fired up the system and waited. Soon, steam was rising over the ice.

"Well, something is melting," Ethan told Jim. "Too bad some of it is escaping our lake, but at least the biosphere will keep it from escaping to outer space."

"We have about five more hours of fuel for the heaters. Let's hope that it is enough."

"Let's go inside and wait," said Ethan. "We'll need to get back out here before they run out and start up the reactor to keep the process going. Otherwise, we will need to be rescued."

Upon return, they found liquid water deep down in the crater. Ethan collected some and stated, "I am worried that it is still an ice slurry. I just hope the cooling pump of the reactor can handle it."

"I don't want to speculate," said Jim, "but what will happen if the pump clogs on a chunk of ice."

"I hate to say that we have no choice but to try. I have an idea though. The reactor specs have the intake line and the output line positioned at a minimum distance of a hundred meters. I think we should position them on top of one another and monitor the intake temperature. As it rises, we can move them further apart."

"Good plan," agreed Jim. "Let's get started."

Ethan went through the startup procedure for the reactor and then switched on the cooling pump. A meter registered the thirty-two degree water as it sluggishly began to flow. Ethan and Jim each held their breath as they watched the temperature reading holding at thirty-two. They stood like sentinels over the meter for three more hours before they saw the temperature rise up to thirty-four.

"It's working," stated Jim. "I feel like staying out here for a couple more hours just to be sure before letting the next team relieve us. Want to stay?"

"Sure thing," replied Ethan. It is not hard work, just stressful." The meter registered thirty-five degrees.

*****

Stephen had just been sworn in for his second term. His popularity with the American people was at an all-time high. The applause around him was thunderous, but all he could think about was the next step.

"You may applaud me, but I applaud you. It is because of you, America, that my job has been so easy. It is because of your hard work, America, that the economy is so strong. It is because of your commitment to the Earth, America, that our environmental consciousness is so alert. It is because of all the hard work being performed in our schools, America, that student achievement scores are on the rise and all of our futures are brighter. I thank you, America, for allowing me to be your president during such a great time in history.

"While the last four years have been remarkable, with the creation of Spaceport Phoenix and our brave astronauts returning to the Moon, the next

164

four year will be historic. NASA has done an amazing job resurrecting science and learning in the schools. They have also mentored a marvelous batch of high school students in their NOTC program. I would like to thank NASA for their ability to inspire.

"I have been asked "What is to become of this first crop of NOTC students?" Will they be granted the futures promised to them at the program's inception? I want to congratulate all of these fine students for their hard work. They have applications in to various universities and, like other high school seniors, are at this moment awaiting their fates. To reward NOTC for their achievements, they will all be given scholarships. Many of them will also be accepted into the NASA School of Higher Learning at the University of Florida. The very best and brightest of the group will be given a historic opportunity.

"They will be accepted into the NASA cadet program and will attend Lunar University. The university is currently under construction and the cadets will assist in its construction while receiving their educations. Why would I have students assist in the construction of their own university? Well these are not just regular students and this is not a regular university. As its name suggests, Lunar University will be on the Moon!"

*****

Ethan stood looking down at the glassy waters of Luck Lake. If it were not for the fact that he was wearing the bulky spacesuit, he would have put his feet into the water and found it to be extremely cold. It was still a brisk forty degrees with icebergs floating across its surface, but the majority of water had been melted and the first reactor was working at capacity.

The production facility was also partially functioning. It was powering a bank of electrolysis units which had already replenished their supply of oxygen and refueled the external tank of the shuttle. That had greatly reduced the stress level of the team. Now they no longer had the clock ticking while wondering how they were getting home. With the tanks filled, the excess oxygen was being vented into the biosphere tent.

Ethan turned back from the lake and started toward Facility 1 where they had already created an excess of hydrogen. It was time to start up the other production processes. Ethan flipped a switch and the tube started to rotate like a giant cement mixer. He flipped another switch and the temperature reading for the furnace slowly began to rise.

Two astronauts stood along the crater rim wall beneath a large tube that ran on a forty-five degree angle over the nuclear reactor. Ethan signaled one of the others who remotely started up a new rover which they had named the Mole. Large blades at its front started turning and it began to burrow into the crater wall. In time it would create a tunnel to an adjacent crater that had been designated for future outpost expansion. For now it was creating the pulverized regolith that would feed the plant. The third astronaut turned on a pump, which pumped water from the lake to the Mole and pulled regolith saturated water back into the processor.

At first the speed of the tube rotation was very slow. The furnace was not yet up to temperature. As the temperature rose, so did the speed of rotation. Regolith made its way down the tube. Electromagnets turned on and the iron oxide and titanium-iron oxide was pulled from the mix and diverted down a side column. Hydrogen began to be slowly pumped up from the bottom. Oxidizes were stripped of its oxygen and steam rose up the tube. Waters from the lake flowed through coils at the top of the tube and condensed the steam back down into Luck Lake. Electromagnets and smelting purified the silicon, iron, aluminum, and titanium as they fell further down the length of the tube.

Next the hot iron and titanium mix was reacted with a small amount of converted carbon monoxide from the dry ice inventory to form carbon steel and purify the titanium. The steel completed its journey through the plant as it fell into moldings. These would be the structural supports for the biosphere. The extracted titanium was invaluable as an aerospace metal for its light weight, high strength, and heat resistance.

The silicon and aluminum continued the fall through the rotating, smelting tube. Finally purified, the silica was reacted with superheated water to create quartz. Cerium oxide was injected into the mix to give the ability to absorb harmful UV rays. The molten quartz was formed into one inch thick plate glass triangles measuring six foot on each side. These would be used to create the geodesic structure of the biosphere.

Quartz plate glass was being produced. Steel supports were formed that would be used to connect and hold the plates. Aluminum and titanium were being extracted. The Cats were staging the newly constructed supplies. Hydrogen was being recycled to create more water for the cooling lake. The electrolysis units were making hydrogen and oxygen. The nuclear reactor was powering the whole facility. Ethan was pleased that Facility 1 was now fully functional. There were only two more facilities left to be put together.

*****

Stephen nodded at Kevin, who was sitting near the end of the table. He noticed that the rest of his cabinet members looked much more at ease than his friend. "First off, I would like to acknowledge all of the hard work done by the men and women at NASA. They brought my plans to fruition. Here representing them again is my good friend and confidant in the project from its inception, Dr. Kevin Scott."

Stephen stood and walked around the table to shake hands with Kevin. He continued, "I would like all of you to know that I am giving my Science Advisor a promotion to the newly-created cabinet position, Secretary of Science."

Numerous congratulations were thrown at Kevin who appeared completely taken by surprise. "Don't look so shocked, Kevin. The role of a Cabinet member is actually defined in the Constitution as advisor to the president for their respective department. NASA is now my Department of Science, and you have been placed in charge of NASA. It makes just as much sense as Sara advising me on Education and Greg on Commerce."

"Thank you, Mr. President," was all that Kevin could muster.

"All right," said Stephen. "Now that we have secured our newest member, let us get on with it."

The National Security Advisory stood and walked to the display. A picture of a rocket appeared. "We have intelligence of numerous activities of the Chinese space program. Analysts believe and the State Department can confirm that the Chinese government was very angry that we made it to the Moon first."

Peter Owens, the Secretary of State confirmed, "They actually accused *us* of cheating to get there first. They believed, when we announced our intent to go to the Moon, that it was a challenge for them to race us. Since we were already set to go at that time, they felt we were just using it as an opportunity to embarrass them. Yes, they were angry."

The National Security Advisory continued, "Even though we beat them, they still appear to be making a great effort to get to the Moon themselves. We know they intend to send probes and a rover to the Moon in the next few weeks."

"Good," stated Stephen. "The whole point of this paradigm is to inspire science. Let's see what they can do. I wish them success. With that said, Kevin, you need to keep the United States ahead of them in all aspects at all times. That is your first order as a Cabinet member. You're up. What do you have for us?"

Kevin stood and took over the display. The picture that came up was of seven men standing before a glass wall with the space shuttle Endeavor in the background. "The first time we went to the Moon there were a lot of conspiracy theories about whether we were actually there or taking the pictures on a secret film set. This picture will probably attract some of the same comments, but it was actually taken this morning in front of the real Endeavor on the Moon."

"It really won't matter what they think. In the next year we will have the university running on the Moon," stated the Vice President.

"True, but I can always play the video footage for the media where the astronauts hold a little jumping contest. It is quite an amazing clip," responded Kevin. "Notice that none of the astronauts are wearing their spacesuits. They have already completed the first compartment of the biosphere. It is a geodesic dome which is one hundred yards in diameter and just barely encompasses the first production facility and the edge of the lake. It actually could not be built any bigger than this right now, because it needs to be up against the crater wall to afford some protection from meteorites.

"The production facilities created the oxygen. Yesterday, they diluted the oxygen and increased the pressure by adding nitrogen from the supply of liquid nitrogen sent there by the elevator. The atmosphere is currently twenty percent oxygen, but it is still very thin air. The astronauts could only stay outside a short time before they would get symptoms of altitude sickness. The plant is still producing oxygen though."

"So they are actually outside the shuttle within the confines of a small biosphere which seven men built using lunar material in less than six months?" asked the Secretary of Treasury. "You are actually pulling this project off without cost to the U.S. budget, just like you said Mr. President."

"I told you it would work that way," stated Stephen. "We borrowed the original assets from NASA and the Navy. We used personnel for the project that were already on NASA's budget. We fired up the imagination and learning curve of thousands of students. Just like the armed forces always advertised, young people can be inspired to do anything. They feel invincible and believe that they can accomplish anything. We have created the best crop of astronauts imaginable."

Kevin added, "These young men and women will be getting the finest scientific education accompanied by the best scientific experience. Their schooling will be invaluable to them. We just happen to be using them to build the actual university."

"So how soon before you get the first batch of cadets up there?" asked the Vice President. "Are you going to wait for the start of the regular college school year?"

"The only timetable I like working by is the project," answered Kevin. "I intend on having them up there by the Fourth of July. We actually have two of the shuttles being retrofitted to carry twenty-four passengers in their modified cargo bays. The last shuttle will be heading back with the astronauts to also be refitted and to exchange the astronaut crew."

"So there won't be anybody up there for a period?" asked Stephen slightly perturbed. "That was not the plan. I stated to the American people that this time we were going to the Moon to stay."

Kevin nodded. "That is true. Only six astronauts are coming home. One is needed to keep the production facility running."

*****

It was nighttime and the only light was from the production facility and stars in the sky. Ethan contemplated how surreal it was that he stood there at the edge of Luck Lake all alone on the Moon. He would be much more up for this if it was daytime, but he would not see sunlight for another week. He might as well get this over with. Wearing a dry suit for warmth, he jumped into the water and began to energetically swim.

That was the one order he had been given, other than to monitor and maintain production. He had to get his exercise. The shuttle had taken off with all of the exercise equipment. To counteract the bone loss associated with low gravity, his only option was swimming. Aside from all of the splashing caused by one-sixth gravity, he found the experience exhilarating. Here he was, the only man on an isolated world, swimming.

Afterwards, Ethan sat on the polished glass bank and daydreamed. He was pretty sure that the water level of the Lake had significantly risen. It was a good sign that the production facility was working. Within the close proximity of the biosphere, he could see the facility churning away. Molten materials slowly poured from rotating tubes. Cats stacked the finished products. He could hear the Mole slowly grinding beyond the crater wall. He wondered where that tunnel would end up leading.

In the distance, he could see the Bulls working the far wall of the crater, grading the floor and lasing the walls. What would this habitat eventually look like? They are planning on a university, but could it actually sustain a large number of people? He hoped so, because right now he could really use the company.

He laid back and looked up at the Earth directly overhead. Suddenly, he felt a slight tremor. Was that a Moonquake? He was told that the Moon had very little seismic activity. He was sure of it. He had felt movement and was concerned. Could the glass biosphere handle a large quake?

*****

Kevin rushed into the Oval Office after barely being announced. "Stephen, the Chinese have attacked our Moon base!"

"How?" asked Stephen.

170

"We were monitoring their rocket launch. On its final approach to the Moon, instead of releasing probes as promised, it rained down bombs. It delivered cluster bombs that scattered all over the near side of the Moon."

"Did the outpost sustain damage?" Stephen asked, angrily.

"Kylie, herself, called up to the astronaut. He responded moments later. He was completely unaware of the attack, though he did note minor seismic activity at the outpost."

"If he is still alive in that fragile biosphere, it must not have been damaged at all," concluded Stephen.

"Since the Moon has no atmosphere to carry the destructive force of a bomb explosion, they would have had to gotten a close hit to do damage. They must have taken this opportunity to attack when the base was not yet populated by students. We survived another of their miscalculations."

"Hopefully it will be their last miscalculation, because I am about to make it abundantly clear what my intentions are if this happens again!"

*****

"We are down," announced the shuttle commander.

Ethan waited patiently and was soon rewarded with the sight of the shuttle taxiing down the road into the crater. It pulled up to what appeared to be a large greenhouse extending from the biosphere dome. Ethan turned on a display and used controls to extend a large tube out toward the shuttle. With a turn of a knob, it was secured to the shuttle's airlock. He pulled a lever and air flooded into the chamber. He was anxious to welcome the new inhabitants to Eden.

The first of the group emerged from the hatch into the connecting chamber. Ethan opened the triangular glass doorway. Leading the parade of young NOTC cadets was Kylie walking confidently toward him. Ethan was astounded.

"What are you doing here?" he asked.

She stopped before him, hands on her hips in a NASA flight suit. "We promised these cadets an extraordinary college education. Universities need educators. I happen to have a PhD in Astrophysics. How do you think I came to work at NASA?"

"I thought that you needed to manage the Phoenix Project." stated Ethan, still flabbergasted. "You're willing to give up that control?"

"My goal has always been to get us back to the Moon. Now that we got to the Moon, my personal goals changed. I decided that I needed to go to the Moon, too. I am a scientist at heart, and this University will be where science is done. You, Ethan Dire, are in charge of this outpost, but I have put myself in charge of the university. Besides, I missed you." With that she closed the distance to Ethan and held him tight.

*****

T.J. exited the airlock. Leading the other cadets, he followed closely behind Professor Kylie Williams. It was nighttime on the Moon, obscuring much of the view he was eager to take in. He could have been in the Grand Canyon for all that he could see. He waited as their professor stopped to talk to the man at the entryway. They appeared to know each other quite well.

The man turned to the cadets and said, "I am Commander Dire. The crater we stand in has been named Eden, because it is the place where man first lives on the Moon. Welcome to your new home. I can tell by your expressions that you're anxious to explore. Not that I want to be a tough work boss, but we are on a tight schedule. We need to get things done to increase the chances of our survival. As you can see, there is no structural university. It will be up to us to build it along with everything else for the place that will be our home.

"You can see it is nighttime. That's not an excuse not to get to work, as it will be night for another six days. But the work you will be doing is outside of this biosphere. I know what it is like to be confined to the shuttle for a period of time, so let's all relax for the next eight hours before getting started. Bedrolls can be found along the crater wall. Good night." Then Commander Dire put his arm around Professor Williams and the two walked off together.

T.J. headed in the direction of the bedrolls. He could see other cadets holding an impromptu jumping contest, testing the low lunar gravity. While he had considered exploring, T.J.'s own intention was to get right to sleep as he was anxious to prove himself tomorrow. Seeing bedrolls lined along the glass wall, he chose one and crawled in. This one was much more comfortable than the one he had used during his basic training. It probably had to do with the fact that he was in one-sixth G. Drifting off to sleep, he wondered again why they had sprung the six weeks of army basic training on the cadets scheduled for the Moon.

T.J was one of the first to awaken to Commander Dire and Professor Williams walking among them while conversing. He helped to rouse the others. They all met in an area where food packets and water were being handed out.

As they ate, Professor Williams held up a manual and called out, "You were all given a game book at the meeting I held on Spaceport Phoenix. I assume that you had sufficient time to review it on the trip here. Today, you will have the opportunity to show how well you comprehend the instructions."

Commander Dire added, "You will be working in five crews. Each will be assigned an essential task that needs to be completed as soon as possible. I need not remind you that the success of these projects correlates to the survival of the university."

Professor Williams stepped forward and continued, "So that we are not foregoing a college orientation meeting, here you go. Welcome to Lunar University. Today will be structured like a typical day at Lunar U, if any day can be called typical. The first part of the day will be allocated to Commander Dire, who is charged with the construction and survival of the outpost. Later in the day, I will have the responsibility to oversee the classroom portion of your education. Each day will end with a period of vigorous swimming in Luck Lake."

Commander Dire stated, "I have been told that each of you is an exceptional swimmer. You had better be. Outpost protocol requires one hour of strenuous swimming daily for keeping the effect of low gravity from shrinking your muscles and bone mass. I personally am not the best swimmer and really had to work at it. The water is still freezing cold and requires a dry suit to survive. That's another reason for us to get to work on the tasks I have in store for us."

Professor Williams stated, "You all are certified scuba dive masters and have been given instruction on the use of a spacesuit. Today, four of the groups will have the opportunity to go out of the biosphere to work on Commander Dire's assignments. Remember that you are in a hostile environment. Just like in scuba, you carry your atmosphere with you. You will be working in the buddy system. Keep track to change out your air supplies. Work safely for yourself and your partner."

T.J. was anxious to don a spacesuit and leave the biosphere. He had made it to the Moon. The low gravity was a constant reminder that he was not on the Earth, but he felt that he had not truly achieved the distinction of astronaut until he was suited up and out on a spacewalk. What he wanted most of all was to get to work with this Commander Dire. The game book gave a good biography of the man. It made him out to be the essential commander of the outpost. All critical decisions would come from this engineer. T.J. wanted to be assigned to his crew.

Commander Dire opened a book that was much larger than the version T.J. had been given. "The first two crews will both contain five cadets under the guidance of one shuttle astronaut each." Commander Dire called out names and the cadets aligned into their crews. "Your crews are responsible for completion of tasks two and three in the game book. Priority task two is the construction of a second airlock from this Biosphere 1 into the soon to exist Biosphere 2. Then task three is to construct the structure of this Biosphere 2. Each crew will build the circumference of the dome in opposite directions. It will be much larger than our current accommodations. It needs to be completed quickly to begin collecting oxygen before our next group of cadets arrives in four weeks."

The Commander turned back a couple pages in the game book. "Crew three will be working under my supervision on task one. We will be constructing the second production plant within the footprint of Biosphere 2. It will create the essential oxygen and heat required to sustain that biosphere. I am also looking forward to its effect on raising the temperature of our Luck Lake."

T.J. closed his eyes and hoped to hear his name in this group. He was disappointed when he was left out.

Commander Dire continued, "Professor Williams will lead crew four out. They will be responsible for task four, which is the construction of the Elephant. Elephant is a catchy name given to the Extra Large Payload Handler, essentially a large crane, which will be needed to complete the top of Biosphere 2, as well as for future work on elevated construction projects."

The anticipation was killing T.J. He needed to be in this last group going out. He could not be left behind to hold down the fort. As the Commander called the names, T.J.'s hope faded. He had been left out of the action.

Commander Dire stated, "Now for your orientation to Eden. Right now it is a sterile landscape with the only chance for life within this small pocket of glass. That will change. That is my primary goal, to create an opportunity for life to thrive on the Moon. At this time we have sufficient food and water that was delivered from the Earth. Our goal is to create a self-sufficient habitat."

Gesturing toward the production facility, the Commander declared, "This production plant, plus the two future plants, will generate water, oxygen, hydrogen, steel, and glass. Along with these essentials, they create all of the energy and heat to sustain Eden. I already mentioned the Elephant. Other rover types include the Horses which are used for human transport, Cats which you see handling material created by the production plant, Dogs which do reconnaissance, and the Mole which excavates tunnels. Teams two and three will need to use the Cats to transport sufficient steel and glass out the air chamber to create the Biosphere's opposite air chamber today. All teams will meet now with their team leaders to discuss their plans. Within the hour, I want teams suited up and moving out through the airlock assisted by team five."

T.J. could not believe his bad luck. He was to be left behind to help the others into spacesuits and monitor the airlock. He made it all the way to the Moon and was still not to be a true astronaut. He watched as Commander Dire directed his team toward the airlock and turned back to T.J., and three other sorry looking cadets.

"You four have a very big responsibility," stated the Commander. "You are responsible for the airlock. I want you to come over by my team now, and I will instruct you on its critical use. While everybody else is outside, you have your own task five described in the game book to handle. You might have noticed that I mentioned all of the essentials for a self-sustaining habitat other than food. For Eden to be an ecosystem, it must have its own food. Your assignment is to initiate that capability. T.J. Gillooley?"

"Yes sir," responded T.J.

"You are in charge," stated Commander Dire before heading off toward the airlock, followed closely by T.J.'s crew.

The first two teams out were Commander Dire's and Professor Williams'. T.J. watched through the glass portal of the airlock as the groups mounted the Horses and drove off to their respective projects. Soon, the first of the Cats arrived loaded with quartz plates and steel. T.J.'s team assisted the others into their spacesuits and started the airlock procedure as the last group arrived. Finally, the last group was gone and T.J. was left alone with three cadets.

T.J. introduced himself to the three. Their names were Liam, Quinn, and Jillian. They headed back over toward the production facility where the lighting was best. All four pulled out their copies of the game book and began reading task five. T.J.'s heart sank. He had been proud to have been selected by Commander Dire to lead the team. Now he knew why.

"Were any of you especially good at the NOTC Master Gardener program?" asked T.J.

Each of the others nodded. Liam bragged about how he had been the best of his class.

"Well, I have a feeling that is why we have been left behind to mind the store," stated T.J. "I really wanted to suit up with the others and embark on an adventure. Because we were so good at gardening, we have been stationed within the safety of the biosphere to start up the garden."

"Great," said Liam in disgust. "We get rewarded for our hard work by being grounded to the base."

"I am sure that they mean to rotate us," replied Jillian optimistically.

"Not likely," disagreed Quinn. "If I were in charge, I would allow the same teams to complete each detail. That would be most efficient. From what I make of our task, it could take us months."

T.J. did not like where his team's negativity was going. "Great. So we're all in agreement. We'd all prefer to seek the adventures of working outside the biosphere, but we have been assigned the important responsibility of creating food on the Moon. I suggest that we accomplish the task in an exceptional fashion. If we do it quickly and correctly, I'm sure it will draw the attention of the Commander."

"Let's do it," agreed Liam.

The team's task was to construct a large bank of tanks that would hold the first plants on the Moon. They were instructed to build Spirulina algae farms. The plans called for each tank to be three feet on each side and twenty feet long. Lighting would run down the sides to illuminate both adjacent tanks.

After studying the design, T.J. saw a flaw in the plan. "I can see where they might want to leave the tops of the tanks accessible, but tanks this large should have light on as much surface area as possible to get the most productivity. The tanks need bottom lighting." T.J. explained to the group how he had built a similar structure for the high school project.

"At least it is obvious why you were chosen for the task," stated Quinn. "Do you think it is OK that we modify the game book design?"

T.J. considered for a moment before answering. "It potentially could increase growth rates by fifty percent having lighting on three sides rather than two. I say we start the first tank on that assumption and inform the Commander of our modification at our first opportunity."

Construction of the first tank went quickly. T.J. urged the group along, intent on making a good impression for his team. After less than three hours, they were called back to the airlock to take in the first of the returning teams from outside. They helped cadet after cadet out of their suits. The last man in was Commander Dire. T.J. assisted him and was asked to show the progress of his team.

T.J. led the Commander over to the completely laid out forms of the first tank, while defensively explaining his modification to the plans. Commander Dire studied the work for a few moments before stating, "They made the right choice in you to lead the team. You passed the test they laid for you to see if you would strictly follow the plans or do what was required. I am also impressed with how much you cadets accomplished in such a short time. Inform your team. Good work."

Everyone congregated once again under the relative brightness of the production plant lighting. Lunch was passed out and eaten from tubes. At least T.J. thought it was lunch, being the second meal since arriving on the Moon. It was difficult to tell by the food rations and the fact that it was still night and the sky being black. A check of his watch showed that it was six a.m. Houston Control time.

Professor Williams was passing out books. T.J. received his and saw that it was a physics book. *"What better classroom to learn about physics?"* he thought to himself. His current environment was about as opposite as could be from the cold, white, distraction free room of his junior high school. There was the lunar landscape obscured by shadows. The production facility rumbled at his back. Looking up gave the bright view of the Earth in daytime. He was to be taught physics on the pinhead of science.

"While it might seem like you missed half a day of class time already, you can trust that you will get more than a fair dose of education up here," began Professor Williams. "You will get two hours of daily instruction from me. Later, as more shuttles of cadets and professors arrive, more classes will be added to your schedule. Today we will begin with physics. By the time I am done with you, you will know astrophysics.

"Most often, the introduction to physics is done by explaining Newton's Laws. While it will be essential to learn them, we need to jump ahead to the second half of the textbook on electricity. As you can see, we are off of the Earth's power grids. We have plenty of power up here, but not currently in a useful form. We need to make it accessible. I will teach you how."

She went on to explain about current, voltage, resistance, and amps. The cadets received instruction on the concepts of electrical transmission. It wasn't until Commander Dire and the two shuttle astronauts arrived that T.J. realized two hours had elapsed.

"It's time for a little exercise," announced Commander Dire. "Everyone get into your dry suit. There is a mandatory one hour swim. Remember that the biosphere protective glass goes down about six feet deep in the water. If you happen to swim under it, you will end up without atmosphere and most likely die. Have fun."

Other than the freezing cold temperature against his exposed face, T.J. relished the exertion. Even though he was a remarkably good swimmer, he was surprised by the amount of water which he was splashing in the low gravity. After being cramped up on the elevator and then the shuttle flight, he welcomed the strain on his muscles. Back and forth the cadets sprinted along the thin strip of water, only occasionally being disturbed by the slower presence of the four adults in the water.

T.J. finally crawled out on the glassy shore. He was tired from the day, but still felt good. He ate another tube of astronaut paste and headed to his bedroll to complete the assigned homework. This became his routine for the next seven days. He worked on the algae farm tanks in the morning, learned about electricity in the afternoon, had a strenuous swim, and then went off to homework and bed. He was at Lunar U.

*****

Ethan was impressed by the cadets. They followed directions superbly. They performed tasks efficiently. Mostly, he admired their fearlessness. All they wanted was adventure. They could not wait to get outside the safety of the biosphere. He had been surprised that all members of crew five had individually asked to be transferred to an outside task. He felt guilty denying them their wish, but their dossiers defined them for their job and they were proving to work excellently together.

Ethan turned to the sound of Kylie approaching their bedrolls. They had become extremely close ever since she surprised him by following him to the Moon. He thought about how she completed his world. Then he started to smile.

"What?" she asked, sitting down against him.

"I was just thinking about how you've completed my world," Ethan answered.

"Well, you had better complete my world, literally!" Kylie joked. "How soon before you are ready to light up the second reactor? I can't wait until it brings up the temperature of Luck Lake. I thought you were laughing at my bright red face from that swim."

"My team completed assembly of Production Facility 2 today. Even though the reactor is ready, I don't want to start it up and waste atmospheric production until the dome is closed. We are going to assist the other two teams until the dome is complete for Biosphere 2."

"Their progress has been very fast ever since they took control of the Elephant,'" stated Kylie. "We spent the last two days converting the Cats over to fuel cell technology rather than the solar cells. Even they are now going faster. Next we are moving on to my special project."

"I still think we need to hurry up and complete the dome so that I can start up the oxygen production before the influx of cadets," replied Ethan.

"Well, just borrow my team," offered Kylie. "Crew 5 is way ahead of their schedule. I'll use them for my project."

*****

T.J. watched the sunrise with the rest of the cadets. It was surreal how the sun was up and yet the rest of the sky was still jet black. He finished his morning meal; then he and his crew headed over to the spot where they were building the algae farm tanks. His eyes continued to wander outside to the construction site of Biosphere 2. He longed to sit behind the controls of the Elephant, placing the heavy plate glass, rather than just watching from afar.

"Another shift of assembling aquariums," grumbled Liam. "Why don't they at least fill up the first few and start the farms?"

"Maybe they will, now that we have twenty-four hours of sunlight for the next two weeks," answered Jillian.

T.J. shook his head. "I asked Commander Dire about powering up the lighting that we put in place. His answer was that he did not know how that was going to work yet. I asked about plugging into the production facility's power. He just told me that I would have to wait and see."

"I bet they forgot to bring up extension cords," quipped Quinn. "We'll probably have to wait for the next shuttle to get them."

T.J. watched wistfully as cadets started to don their spacesuits. He and his team reluctantly headed over to the airlock to let them out. As the last of

180

them left, T.J. was surprised to find Professor Williams unsuited and standing among his crew.

"Excuse me, Professor, but did you forget about your crew?" asked Jillian.

"I lent them to the Commander," answered Professor Williams. "I have another project and I am going to need your assistance."

T.J. was anxious to get started, but lost some of his enthusiasm as Professor Williams headed back toward the production facility rather than putting on her spacesuit.

"I realize that you only had one week of physics on electricity, but today we are going to start building something to put that knowledge to use," began Professor Williams. "I will explain the science of it in detail later in class, but for now you will just have to trust that it will work. We will be making a Tesla coil, which is an air cored resonant transformer."

"Not that I want to sound like I don't know what you are talking about," stated Liam, "but I don't know what you are talking about."

"Not many people have heard of this technology," informed Professor Williams, "even though it was invented well over a hundred years ago. When I describe it to you, it will sound more like science fiction, but we are still building one. It is real."

"OK. You have our interest peaked," offered Jillian.

Professor Williams spread out a large blueprint on the ground, and the cadets crouched down around it. At first, T.J. thought it was the plans for the space elevator, as it looked to be a large tower with a doughnut shaped ring at the top.

"The Tesla coil which we will build will take some of the power generated from the Production Facility. A transformer will step up the lower voltage to high voltage where it will store for a short term to a capacitor. Once charged, the current will flow across a spark gap to a primary coil of large copper pipe at the base of the tower. From there, it will wind its way up the tower around the secondary coil of copper wire. This is where the high voltage moves up into the realm of extremely high voltage. The top ring serves as another capacitor. That's where things really get interesting. The top toroid creates an extremely powerful electric field. When it's on, you will see lightning shooting out and a blue halo from the coronal discharge."

"So this is going to be bright enough to light up the whole biosphere?" asked T.J. "Or will it be just a psychedelic mood light?"

"Oh, it will light up the biosphere all right, but not in the sense that you are thinking," answered Professor Williams. "This Tesla coil will be able to power every light we place within the dome. The interesting thing is that the lights will not require wiring. The Tesla coil will create a powerful enough electric field that every light within its radius will light up, without needing power lines. We are essentially creating a means for wireless transmission of electricity."

The benefits of such a technology immediately fell into place in T.J.'s mind. Of course NASA did not forget the extension cords!

*****

Ethan crawled from the water. Kylie walked out and reclined next to him. She was in much better shape than he was, even with his daily runs on Earth transitioning to long swims on the Moon.

"You can already feel the difference in water temperature," stated Kylie. "Soon, we won't need the dry suits."

"Good," replied Ethan. "Because we don't have enough suits for the cadets that will be arriving. With Biosphere 2 complete and Production Facility 2 operational, I feel safe taking on the additional bodies. There is already a detectable oxygen level within Biosphere 2. I am impressed with the lighting that you have made available in this biosphere."

"I have my original team adding more to the dome each day. You can really appreciate them now that the sun is gone for another two weeks. There is another impressive benefit of the Tesla Coil, even when the sun is out. Astronauts in space always need to be concerned with the amount of radiation they receive from the sun. Solar flares and sun storms would expose us to a deadly amount of radiation. The Earth is mostly protected by its magnetic field. Fortunately, nighttime on the Moon allows us the protection of the body of the Moon between us and the Sun. During daytime, we take some measure of protection being in the tail of the Earth's own magnetic field. The Tesla Coil's field offers us a large amount of additional protection from its strong electric field. Once you put up the superstructure and throw in the Cesium to the glass, we don't even require sunscreen. We'll get just enough UV B rays to keep the body healthy."

"So if we have a major solar flare it should…?"

"It should appear as an aurora being deflected around the electric field."

"I love the way you plan," said Ethan. There was a moment of silence.

"I heard that crew five has already produced a crop," said Kylie.

"Yeah, it is amazing. Only a few days after filling the tanks and lighting them up, they have already made a harvest. This algae powder they made is supposed to be some type of super food. We will start supplementing it into our diet tomorrow. It will be the first official food grown on the Moon."

Kylie smiled and said, "We are doing it. We are becoming a self-sufficient ecosystem here on the Moon."

*****

T.J.'s crew finally had use of one of the Cats. Unfortunately, it was still within the confines of Biosphere 1. He opened a section of tank, screened the Spirulina algae, and scooped it out into a large drum placed on the Cat for transport over to an area along the production facility. There were now ten tanks producing.

Construction of additional tanks had slowed considerably as the crew now needed to maintain the growing tanks. As he added nutrients to the warm water, T.J. marveled at how the fluorescent lighting worked without being wired to anything. He placed a large block of dry ice into a side compartment which fed carbon dioxide to the tanks as the algae voraciously consumed what was available in the water.

Biosphere 2 was complete. T.J. listened patiently as the Commander informed the cadets of their next tasks. Their primary task was to be the guides for the new cadets arriving tonight. There would be twenty four new students. Lunar U would also gain a professor of biology, who happened to be a medical doctor.

Biosphere 3 needed to be started immediately. Crew three was again working under Commander Dire, assigned to building the last production facility, while crews one and two built the dome around them. Professor Williams was to build Tesla Coils for Biosphere 2 and 3 using crew four. When they heard the last of the assignments, T.J.'s crew objected, stating that they had the experience working on the Tesla Coil.

Commander Dire took them aside and told them, "I understand your concerns. You cadets were chosen, not only for your abilities, but for your desire to seek out adventure. Right now, you have a job to do which I deem you best for. We need the algae production maximized. Your crew will be getting an additional twelve cadets from the inbound group. They will require your leadership." That had been enough to settle the issue. They were to be leaders!

The shuttle arrived and T.J. watched the new cadets as they entered the airlock. To his eyes they all looked young and nervous. Commander Dire greeted them and requested their presence at the evening meal. T.J. mingled with the new cadets during dinner. He took pleasure in the commander describing their drinks as containing the first nutrients actually grown at Eden.

The meal ended and the new cadets were introduced to Luck Lake. Some of the cadets tested out the water and suspiciously backed away from its cold temperature. It was still only slightly above sixty degrees. Just then the original cadets stripped down to their swim suits and charged into the water. Soon, all of the cadets were splashing around in Luck Lake.

The captain of the newly arrived shuttle brought over a large box. T.J. was close enough to be one of the first to be tossed a set of short fins and webbed gloves. A quick trial showed him that he could almost fly through the water. He loved the experience. The fun they were having got even better when balls were tossed into the water and an impromptu game of water polo broke out. At one point, T.J. sped deep underwater with the ball, broke for the surface, and fired the ball to a teammate after completely breaking free from the surface of the water. A roar of approval rose from the other cadets. Soon, all of them were soaring from the water like sailfish attempting to throw a hook. They had never had more fun exercising.

The next morning, the new cadets were assigned to their crews. T.J. still envied those heading out, but also felt some pride that he was now in charge of the largest crew.

"Here we are again on our own," stated Liam as he approached T.J.

"The Commander was impressed with our previous work," said T.J. "Let's really impress him and get this going. While we are at it, we need to be sure that we make the new group of cadets self-sufficient at the task. Maybe then, we can get assigned to the Tesla Coil planned for Biosphere 3 and break out of our digs in Biosphere 1."

Progress on the algae farms proceeded very quickly with such a large crew. All the while, T.J. monitored the progress on B3 with an urgency to get there. His team began to produce large quantities of the super algae, much more than could be consumed by even a full university. Each tank produced a half drum of strained algae daily, and new tanks were placed into production each day.

T.J. and Liam drove a Cat loaded with filled drums the short distance to the production plant. They instructed two cadets to inoculate the drums with bacteria to start the decomposition. The cadets each took an end of a drum, carried it up a ramp, and placed it at the top of a long line of drums. Placed along the facilities' slowly rotating main furnace, the drum began its own rotation. From below the drums, radiant heat from the reactors' cooling water warmed them. The single celled plants quickly transformed into vast quantities of compost.

T.J. and Liam watched them work from the Cat. "What do you think of these two cadets?" asked Liam.

"I think they are the best of the batch," responded T.J. "That is why I have been delegating so many of my tasks to them with the hope that they will soon be able to replace me. I really need to expand my horizons and get outside this Biosphere."

Over the next few weeks, T.J. started to get optimistic. He saw that Biosphere 3 was nearing completion and the third Tesla coil was already under construction. Biosphere 2 already had sufficient oxygen and had been pressurized. Where he saw an opportunity was in the fact that Biosphere 1 was running out of room for additional algae tanks. They had already collected a few hundred drums of composted algae. They would need to move onto something else soon.

That afternoon the next shuttle arrived and the outpost gained another two dozen cadets and a professor of mathematics. Each of the five teams was assigned new members. T.J.'s team was assigned another dozen cadets, which brought his team to twenty-eight. Nearly half of Eden was in his group. This fact was confirmed when the Commander made the announcement that everyone other than crew 5 and the new professor would be moving over into Biosphere 2 after the evening swim. T.J. was still stuck in Biosphere 1!

The next morning, T.J. went to see the Commander. He went through the open airlock between Biospheres 1 and 2. He was finally outside of Biospheres 1, but still within the safe confines of the base.

"I am surprised that you did not come to me last night," said the Commander.

"I had the new recruits to get settled in," responded T.J. "I have come to remind you that the original members of crew 5 still request a new assignment. We wish to get out of Biosphere 1 and experience some of the adventure of being outside its confines."

"I understand," replied the Commander. He stood there quiet for a moment. "I have to be honest with you, Cadet Gillooley. I am an engineer and have been given the job of constructing this lunar outpost. I also have the huge responsibility of keeping everyone safe in a potentially hostile place. Everything seems to be coming together remarkably well. I have been able to achieve everything that the planners requested." The Commander was quiet again as he stood looking off toward Biosphere 1 in the distance. "The one thing that I have no confidence in myself to achieve is a food supply for the Moon."

T.J. was astonished. "The game book is pretty clear on the strategy, sir."

"I was hoping that you would say that," replied the Commander. "I have no practical way to gauge whether it is or isn't. I have a brown thumb. I have never been able to keep a house plant alive, no less the most essential part of this project. I received assurances from NASA that you and your crew were more than capable of accomplishing the goal. That is the reason that you have single-mindedly been kept on the task. I need you."

"I understand, sir. I can assure you that the goal is very obtainable. The algae farm production is optimized. In fact, right now we have more than

186

enough cadets for the job. The original crew has even been mentoring other group leaders, in case the opportunity arises for additional duties outside the confines of the base."

"You really want to get outside the safety of the biosphere," stated the Commander, shaking his head nonplussed. "Well, hopefully, the next part of your task gives you some measure of the adventure you seek."

He handed over a new section of the game book. T.J. read the title from the cover, *Biosphere 3 – Terrafarm.* He flipped through a few pages before saying, "I always thought they would have us do hydroponics."

"So you think they are wrong?" asked the Commander sounding slightly concerned.

"No," responded T.J. thoughtfully. "Hydroponics would be required on a space station. It would also work here on the Moon. The algae farms are a great example. Already, they are producing a large amount of oxygen along with the yields that we are harvesting. From everything I have seen so far on this lunar outpost, they do everything on a much grander scale than would initially be dreamed. It is one thing to be able to grow food on the Moon. It is completely another to be able to transform the lunar soil into something that can support life and grow our food for us."

"So you're optimistic about the concept?" questioned Commander Dire.

"Well, we have created enough black gold to initiate the experiment." Seeing the look of confusion on the Commander's face he added, "The compost we created, in sufficient quantity to amend the lunar soil. I can't wait to thoroughly read through the plan to see the recommended plant selection. Where is the seed inventory?"

"I had it retrieved from storage on the other side of the crater, and brought within Biosphere 1, yesterday," replied Commander Dire with a knowing smile.

"You could have left us that small bone of going out to acquire them," said T.J. quietly, while shaking his head.

"That brings me to the silver lining of the task. Your team will be required to wear scuba in order to work within the confines of Biosphere 3," said the Commander.

"I don't understand," responded T.J. "We heard that Production Facility 3 is already producing oxygen."

"It is and in two weeks we should have created and diverted enough to support life. The plan also calls for one percent carbon dioxide composition of the atmosphere. At that level, your team would quickly get headaches and find it difficult to work or perhaps survive."

T.J. tried to hide a smile and attempted to play it off as satisfaction. "Excellent. That should increase photosynthesis efficiency, reduce water loss in the leaves, and allow for better growth in low light conditions. It will significantly increase growth rates of our plants." He noticed that Commander Dire appeared to be relieved at the information.

With the meeting completed, T.J. hurried back to his crew within Biosphere 1. While the others worked, he thoroughly studied the new game book. He then called over the crew leaders and shared with them the token opportunity for adventure that had just arisen.

"Well, at least we bust out of these digs," said Quinn. "I recently overheard a Biosphere 2 cadet refer to us as agoraphobic."

"It is unfortunate that our performance in master gardening is haunting us here on the Moon," replied Jillian. "We need to work on our reputations."

"How about a crew name change?" offered Liam. "We could call ourselves the Green team."

"That's lame," countered Quinn. "We would have a mass defection of cadets. Let's keep it cool and simple. How about calling us the Terraforming Crew?"

T.J. responded, "I like it. The others are known as crews 1 through 4. Add to the mix the fact that we will bring green to the Moon and cadets will want to join the Terraforming Crew."

"Now all we need is to get out of this crew ourselves and on to exploring the Moon," stated Jillian.

"Agreed," the others added as one.

T.J. was anxious to get started, so rather than waiting the two weeks for access to Biosphere 3, he had come up with some modifications to the NASA terrafarm game book. The planning was all based on square foot and companion gardening. Each plot was to be a six foot square filled with a food crop and centered with a tree.

T.J. pointed out, "NASA planning calls for growing the trees in the center of each plot. Eventually, either the trees or the food crop will need to be moved to allow for the space requirement of the trees. The game book shows a supply of 1 gallon containers in the inventory. My thoughts are that we start out the trees here in Biosphere 1. We amend some lunar soil and plant the seeds in the walkways between the algae tanks. They will have plenty of artificial light. We can transplant the saplings to the permanent location when they get a couple of feet tall. Worst case scenario is that it puts their growth ahead by a few weeks."

"Anything to get us done a few weeks earlier," agreed Liam.

T.J. sent Liam off with a group of cadets to open the seed crates and acquire all of the different types of trees and the plastic containers. He sent Quinn off with a group to acquire some lunar soil collected by the Mole before it went into the production facility. The other cadets finished the daily harvest of algae. Drums of algae were brought to the production facility and drums of completed compost were brought back. Then the Terraforming Crew began the tedious process of mixing the lunar regolith with a heavy dose of the compost and filling the pots. They began planting the various types of tree seeds.

Even though it was hard work, T.J. noted the enthusiasm as his crew planted. He mused how NASA must have specifically selected his group for their performance in the master gardening program. They planted oranges, lemons, grapefruit, and bananas. T.J. was pleased to see that there were also apples, pears, plums, peaches, cherries, and even paw-paw. "*What is a paw-paw?*" he wondered.

Scanning through the game book, he saw that Biosphere 3 would have an orchard area for the cool climate, deciduous trees along the crater wall and a glass wall to separate it from the rest. That would allow for the 45 degree season of winter that they required for producing fruit. He assumed that experiments and plant selection would have been done on Spaceport Phoenix in an attempt to find those plants most genetically capable of living under these conditions. Trees most likely could not have been grown to maturity on Phoenix; therefore, the wide variety was probably deemed safest to find the most adaptable candidates.

The next two weeks proceeded with the Terraforming Crew planting hundreds of tree seeds. T.J. could feel their anticipation as they waited to see the first seed sprout. He personally could not wait to begin the work in Biosphere 3. Just as he started to again appreciate the position given to him, he noticed that the other crews of cadets had begun another project outside the Biospheres. They were using the Elephant to lay framework high overhead near the top of the crater.

Another shuttle arrived on the day before they would begin the terraforming of Biosphere 3. T.J. was pleased when he was given another dozen cadets for his crew. He was less pleased when he learned that the new instructor brought up was a professor of botany. Would he still be the leader of the Terraforming Crew?

*****

Ethan stood with Kylie at the airlock, ready to receive the newest group. He wished that he could forego his responsibilities and let someone else handle their welcome and orientation, but he was the Commander. What he really wanted to do was catch up with his good friend Jim Hunter who was just coming through. He vigorously shook hands with him, before turning to the new cadets. He enviously watched from the corner of his eye as Kylie led Jim away.

It was not that he was jealous of the two being together. He and Kylie had grown too close to worry about something like that. He really wanted to be with both of them. Instead, he led the cadets off to be introduced to Luck Lake.

Later, he caught up with them at dinner.

"You made some nice additions since I was here," said Jim. "Kylie showed me Biosphere 2 and I could see Biosphere 3 is complete."

"Well, you finally managed to get back here after three months," joked Ethan, throwing a friendly punch to Jim's shoulder. "Every time we received a shuttle, I was expectantly looking for you."

"Hey! Does that mean that you had wished him to come up on the second shuttle instead of me?" asked Kylie pretending shock.

"Of course not!" defended Ethan so earnestly that the other two broke out laughing, followed by Ethan.

Jim produced a bottle of wine and some plastic cups from the bag he carried. He opened it and shared a toast to good friends with worthy goals.

"Don't let the cadets see that you have a bottle of alcohol," joked Kylie as she savored a sip. "This has to be the first truly dry college campus."

"They have shown an incredible amount of ingenuity. I imagine that it won't be too long before we have to deal with one of them figuring out how to ferment alcohol from the algae," replied Ethan. "Just be on the lookout for the first out of control party. All we need is someone to bust open the airlock."

Jim was taking a drink with one hand and gesturing above with the other. "I imagine it is a pretty good view from up there."

At first, Ethan misunderstood and thought Jim was pointing to the picturesque Earth directly above. Then he realized that he had been talking about the sections of scaffolding coming out from the top of the crater wall. "Yes. We have started the superstructure. We have Elephant 1 lifting the heavy steel grids and glass into place. We assembled Elephant 2 equipped with a microwave crane to laser the whole crater wall into solid glass. It is going to take a long time to complete. Next time you come, you'll have to park the shuttle outside as the whole crater will be enclosed."

"Well it wouldn't take you so long if you had more help," offered Jim. "In fact, the best part about being a shuttle captain now is that you don't have to experience the dangers of liftoff from the ground. After leaving here, we would prefer to dock back at the Spaceport Phoenix, pick up our next crew, and ferry them here without ever stepping back down on the Earth."

Ethan was quiet for a moment. Kylie took his hand. This had been a major point of contention between him and NASA. "I made it perfectly clear to them that the safety of those in my charge was my first concern. We cannot take on any more lives until we become completely self-sufficient. We have some capacity to make nutrients now, but until Biosphere 3 is producing sufficient food crops to support more cadets, Eden is full."

Kylie rubbed Ethan's shoulder and said to Jim, "He has the best interests of the cadets at heart. They will just need to be patient with us at this point. It would be difficult to cram the present group into three shuttles if we needed rescue. Besides, while we do have some safety redundancy by having three different Biospheres to escape to in case of catastrophe, it won't be until the superstructure is complete that we have any measure of real safety."

Jim nodded his agreement and topped off each of their glasses. "I understand where you are coming from. No matter how incredible NASA's vision is, these are just kids after all. Your reluctance to follow their plan has caused some to joke that you consider it your own colony and may declare independence. One engineer had the nerve to call you the Governor, which got him laid flat by Warren Poet."

"Warren felt responsible for the men that used the submarines that he built. I am sure that he knows where I'm coming from. By the way, what's he been up to lately?" asked Ethan.

"He requested to be put back to decommissioning submarines," answered Jim.

"He left NASA?" asked Kylie, shocked.

"Of course not," answered Jim. "Not with you two up here. He is in the process of disassembling another sub to acquire its reactor, electrolysis units, and CO_2 scrubbers to send up to you in case you needed spares."

"He's a good friend," responded Ethan. "It's too bad that he couldn't join us for a visit here some time." He took a long drink of wine and shared a look with Kylie. "Which brings me to a special request, but I don't know if you can do it."

"Anything for you," stated Jim.

"You know how captains of ships can marry people? Do you think that it is possible that a captain of a spaceship can do the same?"

It took Jim just a moment before he understood what was being asked. He quickly split the rest of the wine between their three cups and lifted his in the air. "If I don't have the power now, I sure will before the next time I come back. Of course I will marry the two of you!"

*****

T.J. proudly led the Terraforming Crew through the airlock into Biosphere 3. The airlock had not required pressurization as both sides had atmosphere. They just had to keep the high CO_2 concentration from spilling into Biosphere 2 where cadets lived. Biosphere 3 was a different matter as it was the future home of plants. T.J. even had some swagger in his step, now that he was required to use life support.

T.J. checked a gauge he carried and saw that there was already the necessary twenty-one percent oxygen level. His crew wore half facemask respirators connected to air tanks, because there was also a dangerous two percent of carbon dioxide.

Once inside, everyone stopped and waited for orders. T.J. signaled to Liam and Quinn who each dispatched a scout team to survey the area. They marked with flags the central area that was to be an orchard of warm climate fruit trees. Liam and Quinn followed their teams, giving direction while riding comfortably on the backs of their Bulls. Each Bull burned a swath of solid glass into the soft regolith.

Once the perimeter had been marked, T.J. nodded toward Jillian. She signaled to the two Cats that were waiting at the entryway. They slowly began to roll forward carrying numerous drums of compost. Twenty cadets walked patiently in their wakes carrying shovels. When they reached the far corner of the glass sidewalk encircling the orchard zone, the drums of compost were emptied onto the soil. Jillian jumped aboard a Cat and directed them back toward the airlock and Biosphere 2, where they were to be replenished with more compost.

T.J. followed closely behind the cadets equipped with shovels. They did not need to be told what to do. They immediately began to spread the dropped compost over the soil. They dug and turned the regolith. A half dozen other cadets used hand-held tillers to thoroughly mix the compost into the pulverized lunar soil.

Reaching down, T.J. scooped up a handful of the mixture. Even at approximately thirty percent organic matter, it had a very fine texture. On Earth, water would have drained too quickly away from a plant's roots in such a soil. Here in this lower gravity it was estimated that water would penetrate perfectly.

T.J. kept one eye on the cadets digging before him. The rest of his attention was reserved for Professor Mackin, who stood next to him monitoring their progress. He did not feel his usual jealous tendency to watch the other crew building the superstructure high above. T.J. wondered about his position in relation to the new professor of botany.

"Why do you have them starting on the trees, which theoretically won't produce crops for at least a year?" asked Professor Mackin. "Weren't you instructed that the farm crops were the priority?"

"Efficiency," was T.J.'s only reply. He did not elaborate that the Bull teams were constructing the glass walkways around the rows of square foot garden plots. Once they had an area secured, the shovels would be diverted to work there.

The Bulls slowly roamed back and forth. Cats came and went, dropping precious cargoes of black gold. Shovels turned the soil that would soon sustain life. Before the shift was complete, a clump of young orange saplings was placed into the ground.

Once back in Biosphere 1, T.J. sat with Liam, Quinn, and Jillian. "Did he give any orders?" Liam asked.

"None," answered T.J.

"Did he offer any advice?" asked Jillian.

"Nope. He just watched. I have no idea if he is here to control, assist, or just monitor our progress."

"Did you think about asking him?" chided Quinn. "He might just be a professor of botany."

"I suppose that if he did take over leadership of the Terraforming Crew, we might at least be able to escape our responsibilities and get reassigned to outside the Biospheres," stated T.J. "I will try to talk with him later."

It was after T.J. had climbed out from Luck Lake that he saw Professor Mackin sitting by the production facility working on his laptop. It was as good a time as any to find out where things stood between them. He reluctantly walked over to him.

"I see that you skipped your evening swim," said T.J. as he approached. "You know that it's mandatory to get an hour of strenuous swimming."

Professor Mackin looked up from his computer. "I'm sorry. I was aware, but didn't think it would matter on my first day here. It won't happen again."

T.J. was taken aback by the apology. "What was so important that you risked your health and missed some leisure time to continue working?" asked T.J. curiously.

"You have the internet here," was Professor Mackin's answer.

"Of course we do," responded T.J. "The outpost is equipped with   Wi-Fi, but it is comparable to dial up service as the internet connection needs to cross the distance down to the Earth. I hope you're not a gamer."

"No, sir," answered Professor Mackin, "but being able to communicate so readily is a blessing."

T.J. was gaining information, but he had no idea what to make of it. Did the professor just call him *sir*? "Are you homesick already?"

"No. I volunteered for this and was eager to come," replied Professor Mackin. "It's just incredible to find out that I can stay connected to the web up here. It will be invaluable to my research. I appreciate the opportunity to follow your work."

That was an admission that T.J. had not expected. What did he mean by *follow your work*? "So you are here to research botany. How does the web assist you in that?"

"I am a professor of botany. I am here to research astrobotany. It is a newer field with very little real data. I took this position as a professor here at Lunar U so that I could research in a place that is obviously on the leading edge of science. I made it into this shuttle group, just barely beating out a geologist coming to study astrogeology. You already have your astrobiologist. I came here to study your work terraforming the Moon."

Over the next month, T.J. felt satisfied with their team's progress. Plot after plot of square foot garden had its soil amended and was planted with various vegetables. More of the tree saplings were transplanted to this high CO_2 environment where they would benefit most. The first planted vegetables were exploding with growth. The Bulls where sidelined as extra hands were now required to maintain the crops.

The cadets attentively cared for their dependent plants. Each plot was carefully monitored for moisture and nutrient levels. Because no insects were brought to the Moon, all of the flowering plants needed to be pollinated by hand. For this reason, a paintbrush or vibrating wand was required to transplant the pollen. This gave them the additional opportunity to inspect each and every plant daily. They currently did not have to worry about any pests or disease as the seeds had been irradiated, but they were always on the look-out for potential problems. Any unusual observation was brought to the attention of Professor Mackin who was excited to investigate.

T.J. continued to manage the large algae farm production and composting process. They were still making much more compost than they could use in a day and inventories were building. Every day, more farmable plots were created and planted. Instead of maintaining the plants that had sprouted, most of his Terraforming Crew's energies were now going into harvesting a good supply of food.

T.J. was concerned, so he went to see the Commander at the evening meal. "Everything is going too fast."

Professor Mackin, who sat beside Professor Williams at the table explained, "I estimated that plant growth rates are approximately three times that of Earth. It is probably due to the elevated CO_2 levels and the constant presence of either sunlight or artificial light, but they are still higher than expected."

"The plants are growing so much faster than we anticipated," responded T.J. He turned back to the Commander. "As they mature, they require more energy than we have. Each requires watering, pruning, and pollinating by hand. I am either going to have to stop planting for the future or acquire more people."

"I can't spare anyone from the other crews. The superstructure is too important for our safety," stated Commander Dire.

"There aren't enough hours to maintain all of the interrelated systems we have running," pleaded T.J. "I suggest that the school reduce our class time."

"No," answered Professor Williams. "The university is the reason for the outpost's existence. While Commander Dire owns you for half of each day, the university owns your other half."

"Then we need to bring more cadets up," stated T.J., having already anticipated that response.

"I am sorry," said the Commander. "I cannot allow any more inhabitants into Eden until our food supply allows us to be self-sufficient."

"Well then, bring them on up," said T.J. "As Professor Mackin can attest, we should have enough food for twice our numbers by the end of the week."

*****

"I am still against bringing more cadets up too soon," complained Ethan.

"You told NASA to wait until we had a self-sustaining food supply," chided Kylie. "Apparently, Cadet Gillooley believes we are there already."

"He has done a really good job leading that group, but he is too confident in his prediction that we already will be producing twice our current group's needs."

"Professor Mackin confirmed his estimates," said Kylie, trying to comfort Ethan. She could see he was stressed by the fact that the food production had progressed much quicker than the superstructure construction. "If we bring in more cadets, sooner rather than later, we can expand our class schedule into two shifts. That will give both crews double the manpower and expand the work to a full day of labor. You will be able to finish sooner and make us all safe that much faster. It is for the best."

"I suppose," said Ethan, cautiously.

"Are you trying to get out of marrying me?" teased Kylie.

"Of course not!" replied Ethan. "I love you. I am just looking out for the large number of people in my charge. I want to marry you as soon as possible."

"Then call NASA and order up one Captain Jim Hunter on the next shuttle," requested Kylie. She snuggled in close to him. "Marry me."

After that, daily meals became a vegetarian delight. Ethan realized how much he had missed real food. While he could still go for a piece of meat or some over processed prepared food, he started to feel confident that the outpost could really support itself. He still had butterflies in his stomach, which he played off as nervousness about the scheduled heavy influx of new cadets to the university.

Jim brought the next group of cadets. He arrived wearing his full dress uniform, which sent Ethan's head reeling. He was surrounded by assembled cadets that welcomed the newcomers into their ranks. A large procession, comprised of all female cadets, arrived and parted to reveal Kylie in her NASA dress flight suit.

Jim placed his hand on Ethan's shoulder and asked, "Ready?"

This was not a dream. Ethan was an astronaut on the Moon about to marry this smart and beautiful woman. The adventure was just beginning for him. He nodded yes and the traditional ceremony proceeded while Earth hung majestically overhead.

Dinner that evening started with a fresh spinach salad garnished with the first harvested tomatoes from the outpost. The main course was a surprisingly good stir fry of green beans, pea pods, carrots, baby onions and mushrooms. Dinner concluded with the bride and groom feeding each other fresh strawberries as the assembled university applauded.

"Dinner was incredible," commented Jim to the newly married couple. "Not only am I amazed that it was all grown here, but they managed to concoct something very delicious."

"The meal planning was compliments of our newest addition to the university faculty. She is a professor of nutrition," stated Kylie, "which here is more correctly the new field of astronutrition."

Jim stayed a full week with his friends, until the next shuttle of cadets arrived. "I'll be back in three weeks with your last cadets of this round," he promised as he entered the airlock.

"By then, I should actually have the crater enclosed and a new entryway constructed," assured Ethan.

Ethan did appreciate having the extra workers. He had Kylie immediately split the cadets into two groups, one group scheduled for morning classes and the other afternoon classes. This gave him the ability to keep construction and terraforming underway a full eight hours daily. For all of this, he was rewarded with another visit by Cadet Gillooley.

"I wanted to thank you for assigning the extra cadets to the Terraforming Crew," began Cadet Gillooley.

"You gave us the food harvests we needed, so I was able to honor your request for more manpower," replied Ethan. "Is that all?"

"I also wanted to commend you on your decision to break us into shifts, thus expanding the work hours on the algae farm and in Biosphere 3. I believe that will greatly improve efficiency with harvests spread throughout the day."

"I am glad that you agree with the arrangements," stated Ethan, quite sure the request was still coming.

"It did cause me to break up the leadership group of the Terraforming Crew. That way, I can supervise one shift and attend classes during the other. Don't worry though, we have identified and trained numerous members of our crew to be able to handle supervisory duties. You must have a contingency plan after all."

"I like how you are thinking," said Ethan thoughtfully. "It is probably a good idea for all of the crews to have contingency leaders."

"I even went so far as to make sure the original leadership had been delegating almost all of the decisions to others," continued T.J. confidently. "It is not that we aren't doing anything. We are working the plants while watching that everything is still going smoothly."

"Interesting," replied Ethan. Here it comes.

"So I was wondering if there might be another task for us?" said Cadet Gillooley. "Is there possibly something that might contain a little more adventure or exploring?"

Ethan laughed at his boldness. "Your group's hard work has been recognized. I think that I have something that might keep your interest for a little while. How would you like to take over the Mole Crew?"

"We have a Mole Crew?" asked Cadet Gillooley.

"Not yet. I was hoping that you might be able to pick some good cadets to work with you on creating one."

"Sure," responded Cadet Gillooley. "What would you like us to do?"

Ethan gave over the new game book that he had been holding in his hand. He had to hold back a smile as T.J. realized that the conversation's outcome had been expected.

"First, I need to give you a little background on the project that I am currently overseeing. It is the creation of the superstructure over the crater. The first skin of the structure is almost complete and the outpost will be enclosed. I have two additional layers that will be built to give us additional protection within the crater, but for now we can start creating oxygen for the area outside the Biospheres.

"You are aware of the Mole that is digging out through the side of the crater?" continued Ethan. "It feeds the lunar soil that it displaces into our production facilities. Currently, those three production facilities are all running at a fraction of their capacities. We need them quickly ramped up to full capacity. That will allow for the creation of more water for the electrolysis units to make oxygen. It will also give us the needed iron and quartz plates to continue the superstructure construction. That is where the Mole Crew comes in."

"So you need me to oversee the collection of dirt for the production facility?" asked T.J. in a strained voice.

"That is a complete oversimplification as you will see in the game book I gave you," replied Ethan. "Currently, the Mole has moved at a snail's pace directly out from the crater. We won't allow it to randomly race full speed away from the crater. The Mole is capable of being a manned rover, complete with life support. It will require guidance and maneuvering. There are planned excavations that are needed. As you can see, after enclosing the crater with the superstructure, there will be no way in or out. Your crew's first task is to create a tunnel from the base of the crater up to the surface to an area along the shuttle landing strip outside. At that point we will cap it with an airlock and have a new entrance into Eden."

"I accept the job," announced T.J.

"Good. Now pick two crew shifts of two cadets each to perform the work. Our newest faculty member, Professor McShane, the astrogeologist, will help oversee your progress. We need this done quickly, like everything else." Ethan watched T.J. hurry away. He was not surprised that he did not have time to go over the rest of the plan for the Mole. He had lost T.J.'s attention the moment he had informed him that the crew was to take the Mole to the outside.

*****

"You tricked me into giving you my MP3 player," Liam said after he crawled through the hatch at the back of the Mole.

"I did not," said T.J. proudly clutching Liam's valuable collection of music. "I just said that I could only take one of you with me."

"You didn't mention that the other two would be heading out on the second shift!" complained Liam.

"Well, at least the music will be on board for you to listen to as we bore our way out to a new frontier."

"Yeah! At least you broke us out," acknowledged Liam.

Feeling guilty over the deception, T.J. allowed Liam to take the controls. "Make sure you don't forget to put the Mole in *Habitable Passageway* mode. That way it will laser the walls of the passageway we create. That keeps the Moon dust down and the air from seeping out."

"I read the game book," reminded Liam, "but it said not to do it until we reach the point where we start our ascent. This first area is to be a series of chambers that will serve as dormitories for the cadets and classrooms for the university."

"Right. We are building an intricate series of catacombs on the Moon," agreed T.J. "Well, what are you waiting for? We are in a hurry again. Fire this baby up."

Liam hit a series of buttons and the Mole rumbled to life. T.J. plugged the MP3 player into the Mole's console and David Bowie's *Space Oddity* blared hauntingly over the speaker system.

"Pretty warped choosing the ballad of a lost astronaut to start our maiden voyage," lamented Liam.

"It's your MP3 player and your song list," reminded T.J.

"Yeah, well I thought it might play well with the girls up here," explained Liam.

"I will have to remember that, now that I own it," chided T.J. "I calculated that, if we go a sufficient distance this morning and Quinn and Jillian cut a similar distance later, we will be the ones to break the surface tomorrow. Now, full speed ahead."

It was just over a day later that the guidance system indicated that they should be approaching the surface. T.J. was at the controls. He was dying with anticipation. Suddenly, the steady rumble turned into a violent shaking and T.J. quickly eased back from full speed. He hoped that the Mole was not breaking up. With a slight jolt, the Mole tipped forward and came to rest.

"We broke free!" Liam yelled. "We are on the surface of the Moon!"

"Outside the outpost at last!" added T.J.

The two of them put on their spacesuits and vacated the Mole. They were to leave it at this point for the next crew, who would continue to create a separate passageway back to Biosphere 3. They would have to walk the short distance back down the tunnel to Biosphere 1.

"Care to take a surface Moon walk?" dared T.J.

"We don't have permission but nobody will know," ventured Liam. "Let's go!"

They walked up out of the hole that they had just created. The landscape was beautifully desolate. There was nothing of significance to see, just a powdery gray desert. T.J. considered the vista magnificent. After a short period of exploring the area, they went back down the hole and walked back to Eden. Nobody would be the wiser that they had been outside.

Except when they got back, Professor McShane was there awaiting a status report on the tunnel. He took one look at the Moon dust covering their suits and knew where they had been.

*****

"The fingerlings appear to be doing very well," stated Professor Houser, the astrobiologist.

Ethan sat with the university faculty around a large table of steel and glass. "How soon before they are ready to eat?" Kylie asked. "I think we are all ready to add a little meat to our diets."

"That all depends on growth rates here on the Moon," answered Professor Houser. "Tilapia can have a growth rate of up to 3% daily and can efficiently gain one pound when given one and a half pounds of food. Coincidentally, their natural food source is algae, which makes feeding them our high protein algae in a pelletized form a perfect solution. The catfish fingerlings can grow up to 2% daily and can gain one pound when fed two pounds of food."

"If the tilapia are so much more efficient, then why have the catfish?" asked Kylie.

"Why put all of your eggs in one basket?" he responded. "The tilapia are tropical fish and prefer water temperatures between seventy and eighty-five degrees. The catfish are more adaptable and can handle cooler waters. We are not really sure what temperatures the outpost will be able to maintain. While we have a large first batch of fingerlings to raise, there are no guarantees that they will reproduce to create future generations of food."

"So how long before they become food?" Ethan repeated.

"We could have pound and a half fish within six months," answered Professor Houser. "It all depends on when you give them a home."

At that moment, Professor McShane approached. "Professor," greeted Ethan, "please join us. Your timing is perfect. I was just about to tell the group how I was able to complete the first skin of the superstructure today, so the oxygen being created by the production facilities is being bubbled up from the bottom of Luck Lake and into the main chamber. The lake is now ready to accept the new fish farm. Thanks to the Mole Crew's ability to supply the source material, the production facilities are up to full capacity. Do you have a progress report?"

"I am pleased to report that the Mole Crew broke through to the surface outside the crater near the shuttle landing strip," answered Professor McShane.

"Excellent news," stated Ethan. "I will take a crew there tomorrow and begin construction of the new entryway airlock."

"Unfortunately, I have more to report," continued Professor McShane. "When the two crew members arrived back at the outpost, they did not realize that they were covered in Moon dust. It does not take a rocket scientist to figure out that the two of them had gone on an unapproved Moon walk."

Ethan was quiet for a moment before turning to Kylie. "There has to be some type of disciplinary action."

Kylie responded, "Don't be too rash. You have to remember that one of the attributes they were chosen for is their need to seek adventure. Our whole goal is to create a new generation of scientists and explorers willing to use their imagination and disregard the boundaries limiting discovery."

Ethan felt uncomfortable arguing the point with his new wife. "But they risked their safety for which I am ultimately responsible. If they had been killed, the whole outpost might have been shut down."

"I understand where you are coming from. I will have a stern talk with them. I'll let them know that the Commander is very disappointed," said Kylie understandingly. "It does give me an idea, though. These cadets are fearless. They are constantly trying to escape the mundane tasks and get assigned to anything more adventurous. I can use cadets like these for my project."

"You aren't intending to go off already. Are you?" pleaded Ethan.

"Ethan, you know my work has to be done at the Far Base. The Dogs have completely mapped the best route and scouted out the location. We came to the Moon to explore the new frontier for research. The Far Base is the perfect place for astronomy and astrophysics research. It happens to be the only spot in our solar system that never faces the Earth, which means it does not receive the Earth's radio noise. That makes it the ideal spot for a radio telescope. That is where astronomy and astrophysics need to be taught here on the Moon."

"But you will be thirty four hundred miles away," complained Ethan. "Besides, this outpost here is not done yet. The Mole Crew has at least another month of excavation to create the dormitories and university classrooms. We really need the honeycomb of underground rooms to further protect the outpost. "

"Don't worry, dear. You can have them for another month. I would not dream of leaving you while we're still on our honeymoon," she said as she hugged him.

Eventually, the Mole crew did finish the excavation of the university. The chambers spanned from the entry in the crater wall at Biosphere 1, all the way around Luck Lake, and out again near Biosphere 3. An additional tunnel wound from these two entryways up to the Eden's entryway airlock. The whole subterranean habitat had been designed to accept oxygen pumped from production plants 1 and 3. The outpost inhabitants were now taking shelter in this underground domain with the crater being their daily destination. That applied to everyone but the one person Ethan cared for the most, Kylie.

*****

"You said that we would be setting out to explore the far side of the Moon," Jillian accused T.J.

"I thought that we would be getting out of classes to be on this grand expedition," added Quinn. "It has turned out to be class all day long. Once we get to the destination, it's supposed to get even worse. It will be two weeks hard labor constructing this Far Base, and the Professor only brought the four of us!"

"I hate to add to the complaints," joined Liam, "but we won't see the Sun again for a couple of months."

"That's crazy talk," said T.J. He was starting to think that he might actually have a mutiny on his hands. He could see that Professor Williams was trying to nonchalantly hear their conversation over the rumble of the Convoy All-terrain Mobile Lab, known as the Camel. "The lunar day is twenty-eight Earth days long, which means fourteen days and fourteen nights."

"Liam is correct. People often mistakenly refer to the far side of the Moon as the *dark side of the Moon*. We know that this is incorrect as the sun will eventually rise there," said Professor Williams, putting a book down and coming over to join them. "We are in fact going to the side of the Moon that never faces the Earth, so when it faces the Sun it does not have the protection of being in the tail of the Earth's magnetosphere. The Camel left seven days into the lunar night phase. It will take us seven days to travel half way around the Moon to the Far Base destination. Since we are traveling in the direction of the setting sun, we will arrive just as it sets there. It will then take another fourteen days for the sun to rise over our location again."

"So we will have one month without the sun?" asked Quinn.

"Actually, we will have more," continued Professor Williams. "The whole point in traveling at night is to protect us from solar flares and radiation. We are completely exposed out here, compared to Eden within the crater. That is why, once we get there, we will have two weeks to complete Far Base before the Sun comes up. If we fail, we will have to evacuate prior and race away with the night all the way back to Eden."

"If we fail, that would mean five weeks in the dark. What about if we succeed in constructing the Far Base in time?" asked T.J.

"Then we go underground for two weeks until it becomes night again. That will give us two more weeks to begin my research before we finally chase the night back to Eden. Yes, that makes nine weeks of night. You aren't afraid of the dark, are you?"

"Of course not," replied Jillian. "It is just that we thought the trip would be adventure and scientific research rather than schooling."

"It is the same breakdown as in the crater, half school and half labor. It is just that they will each have to be bundled into week long segments. If all goes well, you will be part of radio telescope history, creating a research station only previously dreamed of."

"You mentioned that we would need to go underground when the sun came up again," stated T.J. "Was that figuratively?"

"No," replied Professor Williams. "We will have to be far underground. That is why I needed the Mole Crew."

"We strive to be the best," stated T.J for his team.

By the time the journey was complete, even T.J. was tired of being cooped up for a week within quarters that had served as a dorm, cafeteria and classroom for the five occupants. It had been one classroom session followed by another. Professor Williams had promised them that they would get a full semester of astronomy before returning to Eden. Classroom study was only broken up by the daily meeting to review the game book. Even that got to be tedious repetition, but Professor Williams did not want to miss the small window of opportunity they had to complete the Far Base in time.

As soon as the Camel stopped at the destination, T.J. and the other cadets donned space suits, and finally escaped their confines. They began disassembling the convoy. The last segment was unloaded first. It held a miniature version of the Mole that had been dubbed the Worm. It was capable of boring a hole just over one meter in diameter.

"You're up first, Liam," said T.J.

Liam walked over to the Regolith Collection Unit where Dogs waited to cart away the regolith. He opened a large panel and found the control console. After pulling a sequence of switches, the Worm began to roll forward off its platform.

"How's it going?" asked T.J. He was dragging the end of a long tube which was uncoiling from another convoy segment.

"I'm ready to go as soon as you hook up the Worm's tether line. I can't do anything without power," answered Liam.

T.J. connected the tether to the rear of the Worm. He signaled to Liam, who began to feed hydrogen and oxygen to the Worm's fuel cells. The Worm surged forward. Its front section began to whirl with numerous blades circling in opposite directions. It dug down through the soft lunar surface dragging the tether behind it.

"It is much easier to control than that huge, cumbersome Mole," replied Liam. He was holding a portable laptop controller that was remotely communicating to the Worm through the tether.

"Much faster, too," said T.J. "I can't believe how quickly it managed to burrow out of sight."

Quinn walked up commenting, "The game book mentioned that it could go four times faster if we had it on a water tether rather than the conveyor tether. It is much more efficient to use a water source to pump out the displaced soil. It is expected to be able to go one mile an hour even after it hits bedrock."

"Well, that's its destination to dig out a chamber," replied Liam.

"You still only have half a mile to work with this bulky conveyor tether," added Quinn. "The water tethers extend out much further and are only limited by the number of them that you link together."

"Not to mention the fact that you need water," responded Liam dryly. "We couldn't bring the lake with us. Remember?"

"Hey!" called Jillian from a distance. "You were supposed to get T.J., not take a break. You look like a bunch of construction workers standing around the guy working the jackhammer, but this guy is only holding a remote control."

"Oh, yeah," said Quinn. "Professor Williams requested help with unloading the radio telescope before we get to the solar panels."

"Good luck with that," said Liam. "My work requires a lot of concentration. I am going to go back within the comfort of the Camel."

T.J. chuckled as he headed off. He knew there was truth to Liam's statement. He had a lot to monitor on the laptop controls for the Worm. There were temperatures, conveyor pressures, and blade resistances for starters. Once the Worm hit the safety layer of bedrock, he would have to navigate a topographical map to carve out the subterranean chamber.

T.J. and the others worked closely with Professor Williams on the construction of the radio telescope, and took turns on other tasks while running the Worm. When the first chamber was complete, the Dogs transported supplies and equipment from the camel into their new underground lair. Time seemed to quickly dwindle for them.

Together they stood watching the sun rise, before crawling down the narrow tunnel into Far Base. "At least we were able to see it," T.J. overheard Jillian whisper to Quinn.

Once inside, Professor Williams announced, "You bought us time. Now we can condense the rest of your general physics into the next two weeks."

A quiet moan ensued from Quinn.

"We will also spend some time calibrating the radio telescope and beginning research," continued Professor Williams. "Unlike optical telescopes that are placed to avoid light pollution, our radio telescope works perfectly fine in day or night. More importantly, Far Base is ideally located where it receives no background radio noise from Earth. Once the sun goes back down, we will have the opportunity to set up a second radio telescope of our array. This is just the start of Lunar U breaking through research barriers. While each of the university's professors came up to investigate some hypothesis or another, I will wager that the most extraordinary discoveries will come from right here. On the next trip, we will embark on an even bigger radio telescope!"

*****

Ethan finished connecting the cooling lines and sat back to inspect his work. He would have worked further on the reactor core, but he knew that he was way too preoccupied to take that on. He had been pushing the envelope lately to keep his mind occupied. Progress on the superstructure had been going very well with the large influx of cadets. He was still limited to using them for only two shifts due to their school schedules, so he had figured out how to make a third four hour shift for himself using the shuttle astronauts that were bringing the new cadets up. He and the shuttle crews were building Production Facility 4 outside the crater along the rim wall.

He could not stop himself from scanning the horizon for what seemed the millionth time since exiting the airlock. It had been more than two months since Kylie had been out of radio contact and he constantly worried about her. Her work required her to travel into radio isolation. There were no communication satellites around the Moon. As soon as the Camel had traveled over the horizon, she had become out of contact with Eden. He had no way of knowing if his wife was even alive.

As if on cue, Kylie's voice called out, "Eden, this is the Camel. Do you copy?"

Ethan answered, "I'm here Kylie."

"Expect us home in a of couple hours," she replied.

"I'll be waiting," Ethan signaled to the other astronauts and they headed toward Eden's entryway airlock. Once inside, they unsuited and Ethan sent the others back down to the dormitories to rest. He anxiously awaited a first sighting of them.

The Camel finally rolled up to the airlock alongside the shuttles. Ethan extended the receiving corridor and locked it in place over their hatch. He was soon rewarded with Kylie rushing into his arms.

"A personal reception by the Commander himself," she said kissing him. With the other cadets emerging from the corridor, she finally pulled away and added, "I take it that you missed me." Looking out through the airlock, Kylie commented, "I see that Warren sent up another production plant."

"It is another critical piece to Eden's safety. The crater is now enclosed in three skins of quartz glass."

"Do the extra layers merely function as a redundant protection of Eden's atmosphere?" asked a female cadet behind Kylie.

"While they do that, there is much more to it." explained Ethan. "Between the inner skins 1 and 2 will be pumped the cooling water for this Production Plant 4. That essentially will create a climatic temperature cap on Eden. It will keep the crater atmosphere from experiencing temperature swings from daytime to nighttime. The couple of feet of water will represent miles of atmosphere around the Earth, giving us additional protection for Eden from the Sun's deadly UV radiation. Between skin 2 and 3 will be an area of vacuum to additionally buffer the temperature zone. Lastly, on top of skin 3 will be placed an additional layer of cooling water sitting open to space."

"Wouldn't it be easier to let it freeze solid to a block of ice, like on the Spaceport Phoenix?" asked the female cadet.

"A frozen layer would be opaque, not allowing us to see either the Sun or Earth from within the crater. Liquid water will be sufficient."

"Won't that just evaporate off into space like the atmosphere of Mars supposedly did?"

Ethan saw that the question had come from Cadet Gillooley, who stood on the other side of Kylie. "It will. This final layer is important as it will act as a security blanket to protect us from micrometeorites, requiring them to travel through a few feet of water before potentially striking our quartz ceiling. Fortunately, Production Facility 4 will be able to create enough water to maintain the water level along with creating enough rocket fuel for the shuttles. We just need to set up a crew out here to maintain production."

Cadet Gillooley eagerly offered, "This crew would be willing to take on the assignment."

Ethan looked to Kylie who responded, "They are a good crew. I'll vouch for them."

Ethan considered for a moment before replying, "I have about another week of work before the facility can go live. We'll talk later about what is required."

"You have been quite busy since we left," said Kylie.

"There is much more for you to see," responded Ethan. Leaning in closer he whispered, "You might find it more difficult to escape me next time." He then led them down the tunnel into the subterranean university.

"I am impressed with how well lit the university appears. The polished glass walls seem like marble. It also looks like there are a lot more students," stated Kylie, while watching large groups of cadets heading off toward their beds.

"And twice as many professors are here working for you since you left," said Ethan. They left the Camel Crew cadets in the dormitory area and continued into the crater.

"I see that you no longer have to walk through airlocks or go through the Biospheres to enter Eden," observed Kylie.

"Yes, the atmosphere of Eden has enough oxygen and pressure. In fact, the just three biospheres now all require scuba to enter them since they still maintain elevated levels of CO2. The plants inside are maintaining their own oxygen, while the production facilities housed within them have their generated oxygen pumped out to Eden and the University."

"Even Biosphere 2?" asked Kylie.

"Biosphere 2 is now a large nursery for young trees. With the elevated CO_2 and luck, we hope to be able to transplant them to the main garden of Eden in a short period of time. There they will be necessary to scrub the CO_2 from the air we breathe."

Ethan noticed that Kylie's eyes were immediately drawn to the center of the crater where a giant tower stood sending out arcs of lightning. "I see you're admiring Eden's new Tesla coil. It powers the entire crater now. Are you hungry? I can fix us a nice fish dinner."

Kylie turned to him and asked with surprise, "Are the fish farms producing already?"

"The fish are still a little small, but we started harvesting them. Professor Houser, our astrobiologist, believes feeding them the high protein algae pellets along with oxygenating Luck Lake has contributed to significantly increasing their growth rate. While we had concerns about future generations of fish, he has confirmed that the nursery tanks have already produced fry. It looks like our fish farms are now self-sufficient."

Suddenly, Kylie wrapped her arms around herself and shivered. She turned to Ethan with a shocked expression and said, "Oh, Ethan, it is cold out here."

Ethan's face soured. He replied, "I know it is. Somebody miscalculated. We lazed the crater walls to keep the pressurized atmosphere from leaking away. Apparently, the planners did not take into account the thermal conductivity of glass, which is leaching away our heat."

*****

T.J. watched the Terraforming Crew through the glass from outside Biosphere 2. He felt a pang of regret seeing several cadets working on his former project. Now they appeared to be running all three biospheres. He could see them tending to hundreds of little saplings.

"Hey! T.J., is that you?"

T.J. turned to see his old high school friend, Billy, exiting the biosphere airlock. "Apparently, they'll let anybody up here," joked T.J.

"I did score just about as well as you in our NOTC program," defended Billy. "I was your partner in crime, after all."

"It's really good to see you," said T.J. "It looks like you're on the

Terraforming Crew?"

"I sure am. It's pretty awesome. We even have to wear scuba within the biospheres due to the elevated CO_2 levels. I still envy those cadets working outside on the crater superstructure. That has to be an adventure. How about you? What's your job?"

"I am currently helping with the fish farms." He could see Billy give him a sympathetic look. "But that's because I just got back from a long expedition to the other side of the Moon where we constructed Far Base."

"No way!" exclaimed Billy. "Any idea on how I can get that assignment?"

"The journey did have its benefits for explorers like us, but the long time in confinement getting there and back was tough. I might have another exciting assignment if you're interested. I am going to be heading up a crew that will be tasked with maintaining Production Facility 4. That's outside Eden on the rim of the crater."

"That would be awesome if you could get me reassigned. What is the name of the crew?" asked Billy.

"It is going to be called the Worm Crew," answered T.J. earning a derisive laugh from Billy. "I agree that it's not too flattering a name, but it describes the responsibility given to me by the Commander. We are going to be running the Worm excavator on the outside."

"Well, count me in," stated Billy. "To return the favor, I will pull some strings to get you on my water polo team. We are in first place, and I seem to remember that you were a pretty good swimmer."

A few days later, T.J. was at the controls of a Cat driving out of the Entryway Airlock. They were heading out for the Worm Crew's first shift.

"The GPS says we need to head back this way," said Liam from behind.

T.J. turned the Cat and headed around the airlock on the side away from the crater. Across the airlock, he could see two shuttles, the Camel, and their final destination, Production Facility 4. First they had to go to a supply depot, which thankfully took them halfway around the crater.

"There it is," called Billy pointing to a large stockpile of crates arranged row by row.

Liam directed them, with help from the GPS, before calling out, "Here it is. This crate states it contains the Water Tether."

"So does the one next to it," added Billy, "and the one next to that."

T.J. drove down the row. "They all say Water Tether. There must be hundreds of them."

"Leave it to the military to order up too many," commented Billy.

"I don't think that the NASA planners made a mistake," responded Liam. "The water tether, after all, is multi-versatile. We need it for the excavator to pump out the regolith and supply it with fuel. They are also used to pump hydrogen and oxygen from the electrolysis units or to refuel rovers and shuttles. They even contain wiring to run electricity and communication lines."

"One thing that it won't be used for is ventilation lines for the university," said T.J. "These were supposed to be positioned all over the subterranean labyrinth. The planners decided to repurpose for the Worm to excavate soil for Production Facility 4. Instead of running the tethers for ventilation, we are going to create a series of ventilation tunnels across future mapped sections of the university. Once we cap off the hole to the surface, the Mole will excavate from the interior across our ventilation tunnels and expand the university."

"Well I guess there will be plenty of tethers for future expansion," replied Billy looking out over the crates.

They loaded a roll of water tether onto the Cat and headed back toward Production Facility 4. From there, they walked to the Camel to acquire the Worm and regolith collection segments.

"I still envy the two of you for being part of the group that went to Far Base," said Ben.

"Chance of a lifetime," responded Liam.

"Do you think you will be going back?" asked Billy.

T.J. exchanged a look with Liam. "It was an incredible opportunity, but probably not one that we need to repeat," was all he said.

They connected a section of water tether between the production facility and the regolith collector. The other segment ran between the collector and the Worm. They had just enough time to power the Worm up and move it to where it would start its excavation when their shift came to an end. Jillian's shift would have the first opportunity to start digging.

They had one of the best gigs at the university. Their four hours outside the crater were envied by all of the cadets. They also had four hours of classroom instruction plus study time. After the mandated time at Luck Lake, it was a daily beach party of a few hundred young men and women. Billy had made good on his promise to get T.J. on his water polo team. T.J.'s ability in the water led him to become the team captain. It was incredibly exciting to be a part of Lunar U, and T.J. constantly relished the fact that he was on the Moon!

One morning, heading out of the entryway airlock, Billy nudged T.J. and said, "It's gone!"

T.J. realized that the Camel was no longer parked between the airlock and Production Facility 4. "They must have gone out on another excursion to Far Base," he replied.

"But we didn't hear anything about it," stated Billy, dejectedly. "You would have thought that they would have at least offered the job back to you guys and I could have tagged along."

"They probably knew that we would not have taken it," responded Liam. "The first trip was hard enough. There was way too much confinement, schooling, and boredom."

"Well, I would have taken the trip," declared Billy, "and I am sure T.J. would have, too!"

"Probably not," said T.J., thoughtfully. "It was a thirty-four hundred mile one way trip around the Moon in complete darkness, but it was much more than that. At Far Base, you have complete radio silence, making you feel about as separated from home as you can get. It was kind of disturbing to be separated from everyone so definitively. At least here at Eden, you can always look up and see Mother Earth."

"But that is the adventure of it," debated Billy.

T.J. turned the Worm's controls on and began excavating deep underground while Liam and Billy connected another water tether in series at the regolith collector. "It is too bad we couldn't just dig a hole directly down to Far Base," he joked.

"Yeah! Like digging straight to China! Good one," said Liam.

T.J. stood there as if in a trance until Billy nudged him. "Are you OK?"

"Why couldn't we dig straight through to Far Base?" he repeated.

"Because we would need over two thousand miles of tether," replied Liam, derisively.

"Of course we would need a lot of them, but remember the stockpile," said T.J, not believing his own words. "We have enough. We could dig directly through the center of the Moon to Far Base!"

*****

"I have some fortuitous news," declared Professor Mackin, the astrobotanist.

Ethan looked up from reading a memo received from NASA planners concerning the low temperature dilemma for Eden. Their prognosis was not good. The potential solutions included the addition of another nuclear reactor, solely for the purpose of supplying heat. Unfortunately, there were no more submarines in the recycle program and it was expected to be at least a year before even a new reactor could be made available. It was suggested that he work with what temperature he had. While it was bad news, it was not the reason for his irritability.

"I think that I have figured out why we are seeing higher than expected plant growth rates and food yields," the professor continued.

"It's because of the elevated CO_2 levels, right?" said Ethan.

"We had already predicted the CO_2 factor from previous research. Eden is still doing better, and I now have a theory. It is the Tesla Coils."

"Is the electromagnetic field they create somehow helping the plants?" asked Ethan.

"No. It is the corona discharge that is seen at the top of the tower that seems to be fertilizing the plants."

"How is that possible?" questioned Ethan.

"In the same way that nitrogen becomes available to plants naturally on Earth," answered Professor Mackin. "It is the process of atmospheric fixation. Plants require nitrogen to create amino acids. Nitrogen which is prevalent in the air is unavailable to plants, because the N2 bond is too strong. On Earth, lightning is strong enough to break that bond, allowing it to react with oxygen and water to form nitrates which are an available nitrogen source for plants. The arcs of electricity from our Tesla coils appear to be performing the same reaction. The installed sprinkler system seems to be washing nitrates out of the biospheres atmosphere to the plants."

"So our ecosystem is self-fertilizing?" asked Ethan as Professor McShane, the astrogeologist, and Cadet Gillooley walked in together.

"It appears to be," replied Professor Mackin.

"Does this help us in any way with the issue that Eden is not warm enough to sustain the tropical vegetation that had been planned to scrub the CO_2 we generate?" asked Ethan, critically.

Perplexed, Professor Mackin responded, "No, it does not."

"Cadet Gillooley, I realize you are no longer on the Terraforming Crew, but I would be interested in knowing what you would do with the current temperature of Eden." Ethan watched as the young man considered the problem.

"It is unfortunate that tropical and deciduous trees won't be able to survive the temperature. The number of Bald Cypress trees that I personally planted in Biosphere 1 will never be able to be transplanted to the main garden of Eden. I suppose I would just change out the planned types of plants. I would suggest Evergreen trees. They would thrive in the cooler temperature and still do well if you figure out how to turn the heat up. "

Ethan looked to Professor Mackin, who responded with a slight nod. "And what can I do for you two?"

Cadet Gillooley hesitated only a moment before stating, "I have an idea that I would like to run past you. It has to do with Far Base."

Ethan's jaw tightened. "Continue."

"I want to use the Worm to dig a tunnel from Eden directly through to Far Base," blurted T.J.

"Why would we want to do that?" asked Ethan.

"My team really enjoyed the opportunity to make the first excursion to Far Base, but it is our consensus that the journey itself was too confining to do again. Unless the shuttle transported us, none of us would be volunteering to go back."

Ethan's eyes glazed over as Cadet Gillooley continued. "My idea is to bore a tunnel directly through the center of the Moon to Far Base. The theory is that when you drop in from one side, you fall accelerating to the center of the Moon. Passing through the center you would begin decelerating. Being that it would be in the vacuum of space, you should have exactly enough energy to end your fall at the far surface of the Moon, at which point you could be plucked from the tunnel by a strong electromagnet."

Cadet Gillooley stood there expectantly. Ethan turned to Professor McShane and asked, "What are your thoughts on this?"

"To be honest, I don't know about the physics of the concept," started Professor McShane, skeptically, "but it would be invaluable for my research to capture core samples of the Moon all the way to the center."

Ethan sat there contemplating for a few moments before stating, "I appreciate your ideas, but the Worm is required to create ventilation tunnels for the university. My responsibility lies first with the safety of all inhabitants of Eden. I cannot authorize your experiment at this time."

"But you're not seeing the advantage of the tunnel. The whole trip will expend no energy and take less than an hour. It will appear instantaneous compared to the seven days it takes to travel the surface to Far Base. Everybody would be eager to go."

"Once again, I deny your request. Your idea is too farfetched," declared Ethan, irritably.

"It would work!" exclaimed Cadet Gillooley. "If Professor Williams were here she would back me!"

"Enough!" demanded Ethan. "Your request is denied!"

"That is just Qwerty!" exclaimed Cadet Gillooley as he stormed from the

Commander's office.

Ethan was taken aback by the comment. "What does qwerty mean?"

Professor Mackin chuckled. "It's actually an expletive that the cadets made up. It's kind of a funny story. Have you ever seen an old fashioned typewriter where you press a key and a hammer slaps into the ribbon onto the paper? If two keys were hit at the same time, the hammers printing the letters would lock together. As a result, the sequence of keys was arranged to slow the typist down to avoid the mechanical problem. That keyboard was called the QWERTY keyboard, named after the sequence of the first six letters. It is the US-International layout still taught in schools today."

Ethan was perplexed. "Do you mean to tell me that the computer keyboards that we use today were designed to keep us typing slow so that antique typewriter hammers, that are no longer in use, won't clash?"

"Maybe the computer keyboard that you use is still the inefficient QWERTY type, but the cadets were all issued new laptops with the American Standard keyboard when they arrived at Spaceport Phoenix. In the American Standard layout, the home keys are the most commonly used letters in the English language. They are pretty much the letters always chosen on the television show, *Wheel of Fortune*. When the cadets realized that they had all been taught on an obsolete keyboard just because that was what everyone else had always used, they were furious. Now they had to learn the new keyboard from scratch. Qwerty became an expletive meaning something that is not as it appears."

Ethan sat back in his chair and gave a half-hearted laugh. "He is right. Things are not as they seem. Everyone up here on the Moon was chosen for their adventurous tendencies. That is what is believed makes good scientists. I, on the other hand, am not what I seem. I am more of an inventor, trusting innovation to deal with problems."

"I know. You're the engineer that makes this outpost possible and keeps us safe," placated Professor Mackin.

"While I may not be the adventurous type, my wife is. Kylie left this morning, heading back to Far Base with another class of cadets in tow. It wasn't Cadet Gillooley's fault that he chose the one topic that would trigger the memory of the fight we had this morning."

"Our research is important to all of us," admitted Professor Mackin.

"She is foremost the scientist, heading out to where I cannot keep her safe."

"I think I understand," said Professor Mackin. "Cadet Gillooley's idea hit a nerve with you because he was offering a way to make it easy for your wife to escape the safety of the home that you are creating here in Eden."

Ethan just shook his head. "Things are Qwerty, Professor. Kylie's pregnant."

*****

"That's just Qwerty!" exclaimed Billy.

"You mentioned how short a trip it would be?" asked Liam.

"Under an hour," replied T.J.

"And you mentioned how the tunnel would allow for air, water, fuel, and electricity to be supplied to Far Base directly from Eden through a tether?" asked Jillian.

T.J. shook his head. "I never got the chance. The Commander appeared to reject the idea outright as absurd. I tried to explain the physics of it as real, but he would not listen and actually seemed to grow angry when I tried."

"Well, I had a hard time believing the idea myself. It's too bad Professor Williams wasn't around to explain that the concept is not science fiction but sound physics," said Billy.

"Qwerty!" interjected Quinn. "Professor Williams, the Commander's WIFE, is on another excursion to Far Base. No wonder the Commander was in a foul mood. Did you explain to him that communication lines could be kept open between Eden and Far Base? I'm sure that he would want to be able to know she is not completely cut off from the rest of humanity!"

"The issue was closed with the Commander," said T.J. "He is not approachable on the subject."

"Then we will have to wait for Professor Williams to return to Eden to talk some sense into him," suggested Liam.

"But we will potentially miss a window of opportunity," replied T.J. "I didn't even get a chance to tell him that the first series of ventilation tunnels was complete, a full month ahead of schedule. Then it will still take another month for the Mole to complete the next section of the University. That gives us two months."

"Qwerty!" said Billy. "I can see that look in your eyes. This is just like being back in eighth grade and discovering that mysterious hallway. You want to disobey orders and dig it anyway."

"I was not ordered *not* to do anything," defended T.J, "and we know where this hallway leads. This is a good idea that is being ignored. With two months and an estimated eight miles excavated each day, we will be almost halfway to the core before we are even given further directions from the Commander. By then we can remake our case. Come on, you guys know that this is the only way that Far Base can really make it."

T.J. could see that he was close, but had not closed the deal with his crew. "Our primary duty is to maintain Production Facility 4 with a supply of lunar soil. We would still be accomplishing that. Professor McShane was initially on board with the idea. We could keep a collection of core samples for him to buy his support when the time comes. And all of us who spent the two months in seclusion learning physics from Professor Williams know that she will support the idea. After all, it's brilliant."

Billy added, "And with her support, we are assured the Commander's support. She is his wife after all." Once again, T.J. was grateful that his longtime friend has come to his aid. The Worm Crew was in agreement. They were going to drill through the center of the Moon.

The next morning, T.J. stood with Liam and Billy surveying around the entryway airlock. "I think we should just put it on the far side of the airlock," said Liam. "You climb out of the tunnel from Eden, exit the Entryway Airlock, and drop into the Far Base Worm Hole."

"Far Base Worm Hole. That is a catchy name. I'm sure that will help us convince them that this is not just science fiction," said Billy sarcastically.

T.J. walked over to the designated spot. From his vantage point, the airlock was no more than a hole in the ground. Across it stood Production

Facility 4, a parked shuttle, and the regolith collector that had been disconnected from the absent camel. "I like this spot, too. If you were entering or exiting the entryway airlock, you would have no view of the site. We are far enough away to be outside the next area of expansion for the University. We will have to run the water tether around the airlock to the regolith collector stationed by the production facility. Let's drill it."

Billy walked back over to the regolith collector and took the controls of the Worm. He steered the Worm to the position between where T.J. and Liam stood. T.J. signaled and the Worm began to bore down into the Moon. Billy then took the controls through the entryway airlock to continue monitoring progress within the safety of the tunnel, while T.J. and Liam took a Cat over to the supply depot to obtain more tethers.

Upon returning, it took them awhile to figure out how to connect the new roll of tether in series with the first at the regolith collector. When they finally finished, they joined Billy in the tunnel. T.J. told him, "It was easier than I thought to connect the tethers. We just have to make sure to return the empty crates back at the supply depot. It would look mighty suspicious having a few hundred empty crates stacked around the production facility. How is progress coming?"

"I am well into bedrock at over a mile deep," answered Billy, "but our shift is up. Hopefully, the second shift can make more progress."

"Let's hope so," replied T.J. "Otherwise, we will never make it through to the other side in the predicted nine months."

That evening, the Worm Crew was gathered on the shore of Luck Lake. "Nice game, Quinn," chided Billy. He and T.J. had just defeated the others in a water polo match. Quinn had played goalie for the defeated team.

"If you two would just join us, then we would be the best team on the Moon," responded Quinn.

"Sorry, but the Tides had already recruited us before you guys even decided to form the Divers." Billy and T.J. were the top scorers in the league. It drove Quinn mad that they would not change their allegiance to join the team composed mainly of the Worm Crew.

"I really like what they have done with the beach," said Jillian, lying back in the white sand. Just a few days before, it had been a shoreline of smooth glass. "The pulverized Moon dust is a complete nuisance. It was a brilliant idea to take the glass made from the lunar soil and grind it to the texture of course sand. If they could only turn up the heat, this beach would be the envy of everyone in our Solar System." As soon as they had left the water, they had to dress in sweat suits to stay warm.

Liam came rushing over holding a tray of drinks. "Anybody care for a cool refreshing watermelon punch?" As he passed them out, he gave a mischievous wink toward T.J.

T.J. took a sip and his eyes widened. "They made it."

"Yuck! This tastes funny," said Jillian, pushing the glass way.

"Don't waste that!" begged Liam. "There's not much to go around."

Billy made a sour face after taking a drink. "What are you talking about? This doesn't taste very good."

"It's a drink concoction that T.J. came up with months back," said Liam, smiling foolishly.

With everyone looking at him, T.J. explained. "When we were on the Terraforming Crew, we planted a batch of watermelons. They were supposed to yield super sweet watermelons with twelve percent sugar content. I proposed an idea to those cadets who ended up taking over the crew. I thought that it would be easy to ferment the melons and make alcohol."

Everyone looked back down at their drinks. "You got it!" slurred Liam. "They call it Moon Juice."

Billy looked upset. "It was your idea, T.J. Now they stole it. We could have started something ourselves with this."

"Sure. It would be the first capitalistic venture on the Moon," said T.J. "The only problem is that we haven't invented lunar currency, yet. We could run our own bootlegging crew." Everybody laughed, but T.J. could see that they were all thinking about how they could make that happen.

They tasted their first alcoholic beverages at the university. It became the Moon's first beach party. Suddenly, everyone became less critical of the cool temperatures and the cadets stayed on the shore of Luck Lake much later than they had previously.

The party was the whispered conversation among the cadets for the next week. Everyone was waiting expectantly for the next one. Unfortunately, their small batch of watermelon Moonshine had been depleted and it would be weeks before an encore party could be held. While T.J. also looked forward to the next event, Billy was still preoccupied with the idea that T.J. should be given credit.

"So if it was your idea and you were the Terraforming Crew leader, couldn't you request a piece of the action?" Billy asked T.J.

"Piece of what action?" responded T.J. "It was free alcohol, so they didn't profit from it. If you haven't noticed, this outpost acts as a communal society. What would there be to gain?"

"There is the prestige to be gained from creating an environment for socializing," debated Billy. "We are living with prohibition here on the Moon. This is an opportunity that we should be taking."

"We are already taking an opportunity that could lead to fame. It could also get us in a lot of trouble if the Commander finds out before we have presented our work to Professor Williams. We can't take the additional chance of getting into trouble as moonshiners."

Later that evening, Quinn approached T.J. "Billy told me about your misgivings about being caught making the melonshine. I think I have a solution. We can set up the melonshine operation out at Production Facility 4. There is unlimited space, no supervision, and no way to be caught. It will be just like creating the Worm Hole outside of Eden where no one would know to ask about it."

T.J. was surprised that Billy and Quinn were working together on the dubious scheme. "I still don't see the benefit. The Worm Hole opens the possibility for Eden to have almost instantaneous access to Far Base. You especially can appreciate that benefit. You went completely stir crazy on our expedition. Show me some benefit in becoming bootleggers."

A few days passed before Billy attempted to win T.J. over again. T.J. was monitoring the controls of the Worm which had just reached thirty miles down from the surface. Billy was just returning from taking a core sample at the regolith collector. "I don't know why you consider it bootlegging. We wouldn't be breaking any laws."

"What about a bunch of nineteen year olds making and consuming alcohol?" asked T.J.

"That is illegal only by state laws. If you haven't noticed, we are far outside any state's jurisdiction. Along those lines, Quinn and I believe this could ultimately be very beneficial for our crew. It could be just like when gangsters ran the economy during prohibition."

"What are you talking about?" demanded T.J., flabbergast. "Are you proposing we strong arm the command of Eden?"

"No," said Billy. "I just think that if we can control production of alcohol on the Moon, we can create the first capitalistic venture on the Moon."

"But there is still no money to be made on the Moon."

Billy looked like he had been waiting for T.J. to make this point. He said confidently, "Why couldn't we come up with our own currency? It could be a credit card or even an I.O.U. Maybe we even hand out Lunar Dollars for free at first to just get the cadets used to the idea and then assign a value to them later when they want more. They will be more than willing to take on some debt to get their hands on our melonshine. Imagine it. Our own night club set along the shore of Luck Lake."

T.J. was impressed with the thought that they had put into their plan. "Keep working on it. If you guys can present your case to our whole crew and get the rest of them on board, then I will see what I can do to talk the Terraforming Crew leaders into joining us."

After that conversation, T.J. did not see Billy or Quinn at all outside of work, school or swimming. They were probably spending all of their time hatching their plans.

Days later, T.J. and Liam were suiting up at the entryway airlock while Billy sat at the controls of the Worm. "Look! The Camel has returned from Far Base," said Liam. Looking over at Billy he asked, "You still want to head out on its next expedition?"

"Nope. I'm good with managing our progress here. Maybe I will go to Far Base via the Worm Hole when we're done."

T.J. could see the Camel parked in the distance over by the shuttles. "They are back already? The Worm is only down fifty miles," he said. "Well, at least we can present our case to Professor Williams. She is sure to see the benefit and defend the physics to the Commander."

T.J. and Liam went out through the entryway airlock and climbed up onto a Cat. Liam drove them toward the supply depot. They loaded up another water tether and headed back to the Regolith Collector where they found Billy.

"What are you still doing outside?" asked T.J.

"I just needed to check out something at the production facility."

"But you can't be outside by yourself!" declared T.J. He could see the Worm's controls set down on the stairway. "You're supposed to be monitoring the Worm! Here you are probably trying to figure out where to set up the moonshine stills, and I bet you didn't even notice that the Worm's temperature is elevated."

"I did too! It's probably cutting though a vein of dense rock. I already reduced its speed to compensate," said Billy "And it's called melonshine. Now that you mention it, maybe you could help me with something. What temperature were you running the composting ovens at back when you were on the Terraforming Crew?"

"One Hundred and twenty-five degrees."

"But these can be adjusted, right?" asked Billy pointing to the unused ovens running the length of the turning regolith furnace. "They could be set to maintain the optimum fermentation temperature of ninety-five degrees Fahrenheit?"

"Sure they could," answered T.J. knowing where this was going.

"And you inoculated the batches with microorganism, right? That is how you got the decomposition started."

"Yes," answered T.J. "As you recall, soil is a living thing. Compost adds the essential nutrients for life. Since the Moon only has sterile soil, the inoculation is critical to making the compost and bringing life to the lunar soil."

"And you inoculated the soil with yeast?" asked Billy brimming with curiosity.

"I suppose there is yeast mixed in with the microbial mix," replied T.J, "but I know where you are trying to lead me. I found it rather by accident. Some of the inoculated algae did not turn into the black gold compost we were expecting. Upon investigation, I found that the drum used to inoculate it was actually identified as yeast. We had mistakenly taken a wrong drum from the supply depot."

T.J. could see that Billy was still confused. "Yeast is the magic ingredient you wanted me to tell you about. Yeast is a fungus that is found in healthy Earth soil. It eats sugar and water and excretes alcohol and CO_2."

"So that is what we need to make alcohol?"

T.J. nodded. "The stuff we found was baking yeast. I did some research on it. It is best for eating sugars quickly and creating the CO_2 gas that cause bread to rise. Brewer's yeast is actually better for making alcohol because it converts the alcohol slower with less byproduct and makes it taste better. We only had baker's yeast."

"But it still works for fermentation," reasoned Billy.

The controls for the Worm started beeping.

"Check this out," said Billy, finally showing some concern. "The Worm's temperature has ramped up again."

"Well, slow it down!" said T.J.

The temperature reading continued to rise until it suddenly blinked and then read nothing.

"What's happening?" asked Liam.

They stood there looking at each other wondering how they were going to explain the Worm breaking down fifty miles below the surface.

T.J. checked the regolith collector's control panel. It too showed no pressure and therefore no soil moving back to the production facility. He was going to be in trouble. He turned back toward the Worm Hole just in time to see the most astonishing sight.

Molten lava was exploding out of the hole and up into the night sky. The lunar landscape was illuminated by an eerie red light. He watched in awe as lava fell back to the Moon and began to pool around the excavation. As the pool grew, it began to flow toward them.

"We have to get out of here!" yelled Billy.

It was too late for that. They watched in horror as the lava flow reached the entryway airlock where the quartz glass exploded into space.

T.J.'s mind raced. "We are trapped outside with the lava approaching."

"It is not getting any closer. Look!" exclaimed Liam pointing over to where the airlock had once been. The lava is flowing down the airlock hole and into Eden."

T.J. found himself saying, "Follow me. The Camel is our only chance for survival."

As they ran, T.J. saw that the eruptive column of magma being ejected from the worm hole that they had created was shooting hundreds of meters from the surface. It created a brilliant red plume against the pitch black sky. It was where the arch ended that made his heart lurch. It was raining the molten magma down over the center of the crater which housed Eden and all of his friends. A billowing gas cloud erupted violently into space. He had just killed everyone on the Moon!

*****

Ethan held Kylie tight in his arms. "I am so glad you're back. I don't want to fight about it anymore."

Kylie squeezed him and replied, "Everything will turn out fine, and you will be a marvelous father."

"I still worry about you and our unborn child. Can a baby even grow to term and be delivered in low gravity? Can we handle a caesarean delivery if it's required?"

Kylie kissed Ethan. "Our professor of astrobiology is a medical doctor. He is an experienced surgeon. That is one of the reasons why he was chosen to be at this remote outpost of humanity. He has been setting up a medical facility here at Eden from the day he arrived. He also has experience delivering babies."

"But how will our baby grow and develop without an Earthly amount of gravity. Will its bones develop? Will it have sufficient muscle tone to ever visit or even survive on Earth? Will it ever know Mother Earth?"

"We will be okay," assured Kylie, kissing Ethan again. "There has been a lot of debate on how infants can develop without gravity. Physically, what I can tell you is that the Moon has some gravity and Luck Lake gives the opportunity for our toddler to get all the exercise needed. Mentally, our baby will be perfectly nurtured by two loving parents."

"But the Moon has such a harsh environment. It's too dangerous a neighborhood to raise a child."

Kylie smiled and kissed her husband once more. "Our child has a most ingenious father who is protecting us all. Here we are on the frontier of space and you have done an amazing job creating a safe environment."

Ethan's phone suddenly started to make a loud siren sound. His face went ashen as he read its display. "Eden's structure has been breached."

Kylie looked around and asked, "Then why aren't we dead already?"

"It was at the entryway airlock, but we have a secondary airlock further down the tunnel which sealed when the massive pressure loss was detected." Ethan scrolled down the information on his phone. "Oh no! We have a crew of cadets working outside! We have to try and save them!"

Ethan rushed out of the room with Kylie at his heels. As he reached the secondary airlock he realized that all of the spacesuits had been stored further up the tunnel at the entryway airlock. He turned and ran all the way back to get suits from storage. He returned with two suits and quickly scanned the faces of the waiting professors and cadets.

"One of those suits had better be for me, because I am coming with you," said Kylie.

Ethan hesitantly handed one over and they suited up. They went through the airlock and headed up the tunnel. They soon came to the place where the white marble-like floor was covered in smoldering molten lava. Peering down the tunnel, they could see that it was completely blocked. They had to turn back.

Ethan saw Professor McShane waiting for them at the beginning of the tunnel. "The tunnel is blocked. It appears to be molten lava."

"That might explain reports that I am getting from some cadets. They report that part of the superstructure over Eden is covered with a black substance which might be lava."

"How can this be?" asked Ethan.

"Maybe there was some kind of lunar volcanic eruption and the lava has found our safe haven. It is strange that we did not encounter any seismic activity that would indicate a moonquake or asteroid strike. We are lucky for the deep layer of water protecting the superstructure, but the entryway airlock apparently was not so lucky."

"There is volcanic activity on the Moon?" asked Ethan.

"Evidence shows that there hasn't been any for perhaps billions of years, but there appears to be lava flowing up outside the crater."

"There are cadets out there!" declared Kylie. "We need to get to them if they are still alive!"

Ethan thought about their options. "When the Worm crew dug the ventilation tunnels for the university expansion, they started from the lunar surface. That original hole was plugged with a miniature airlock, serving more like a bolt hole. If the lava isn't covering it, we can get out to the surface there."

Ethan and Kylie headed to the ventilation tunnel. As they were about to start the crawl up the tunnel, Professor McShane ran up wearing his own spacesuit. They passed through two small airlocks and found themselves on the surface of a now unfamiliar lunar landscape.

Production Facility 4 was still there. The shuttle and Camel could be seen in the distance. It was what stood between them and where the entryway airlock had once been that was surreal. There was a sea of smoldering lava.

"Thank goodness that we stand under the hard freeze of nighttime," said Professor McShane. "If this had been during daylight, it might still be flowing out over Eden."

"I don't see any sign of our missing cadets," stated Kylie.

"There safe!" declared the voice of Professor Mackin over their headset.

"We just got a message from them over the radio. They are taking refuge within the Camel."

"Well, there appears to be only the long way around to them," said Professor McShane, and they started their way around the lava flow.

When they reached the Camel, they found the boys safely residing in the living quarters. Ethan was relieved that nobody was killed in this freak occurrence. He was still bound and determined to never have anyone die in his care again. They gathered the cadets up and headed to the safety of Eden.

Back at the university, Professor McShane asked the boys, "So, what happened?"

Cadet Gillooley stepped forward and declared, "It's my fault. I convinced the Worm Crew to dig the Worm Hole."

"What are you talking about?" asked Kylie. "We know that you lead the Worm Crew and are charged with digging ventilation tunnels for the university."

"Actually, the Worm Hole was a proposal I had previously made to the Commander. We took the Worm and began to excavate a tunnel which was to run directly from Eden, through the center of the Moon, and all the way to Far Base."

Kylie stood there stunned. "Why would you do that?"

"To make travel there nearly instantaneous compared to the long and tedious journey in the Camel," answered Liam, trying to take some of the responsibility.

Kylie was still confused. "How was that going to work exactly?"

"Well, you taught us the physics of it," answered T.J. "The physics of a falling object shows that the potential energy will exactly match the kinetic energy required to get to the other side. An object falling into the hole at Eden will gain speed from gravity until it reached the center of the Moon. Then on the second half of its journey, it would decelerate until it came to a stop exactly at the rim at Far Base. It was our solution for nearly instantaneous travel from here to there."

Hanging his head T.J. added, "Apparently, there is no direct route to Far Base."

"I told you that you did not have permission to make your Worm Hole," said Ethan emphatically. "I specifically told you not to even bring it up again. You still went ahead and risked your crews' lives. By not obeying orders, you jeopardized the survival of everyone on the Moon. There are going to be consequences, Cadet Gillooley. I am going to send you back to Earth on the next shuttle. You are expelled from Lunar U."

CONTINUING EDUCATION

T.J. was hurrying to finish the last section of the chapter before the library closed.

"They told me that you would be the last person in the library," said a familiar voice.

He turned to see Billy walking down the aisle in the familiar NASA flight suit. How he envied him for that flight suit. "What are you doing back down here? Did they finally kick you out, too?"

"No. After a couple years of ferrying up cadets, they hit capacity for the outpost at two thousand. Now they are allowing us to come back to Earth for one month every year. I just got back down and thought that I would look you up on my way to see my family. How have you been?"

"I've been staying on top of my studies, trying to atone for my crime," answered T.J. "When I got back to Earth, I expected NASA to be done with me. I was met by none other than the Secretary of Science, Dr. Kevin Scott. I expected a berating at the minimum but was given a pep talk instead. He told me that while I might have caused havoc at Lunar U, I shouldn't give up the dream of being part of NASA. I still had a full scholarship in the NASA collegiate program here. He told me that my curiosity had brought about the discovery of a resource on the Moon that turned out to be invaluable."

"That's an understatement," replied Billy. "The garden of Eden is now a tropical rainforest because of what we did."

"How did discovering that the Moon still has a molten core give the university a jungle?" asked T.J., skeptically.

"Professor McShane explained it in his astrogeology class. I should also mention that he put up quite a fight for you. He felt that you were only doing what you had been chosen for, seeking adventure. He also pushed the fact that the ends justified the means. Your decision to collect those core samples for him, and ultimately the discovery of a molten lunar core, has made him a fierce ally of yours," said Billy.

Seeing that T.J. was still confused, Billy continued. "The Moon was always considered to be a cold, dry, desolate place. Terraforming it was deemed impossible. NASA showed that you could make water on the Moon. They had us terraforming an area large enough to maintain a small city. Unfortunately, the grand scope of the project was going to fail, because the Moon was too cold. Their resources could not support more than a couple of hundred people. What we found changed that."

"So we discovered the geothermal heat source that warmed up Eden," stated T.J.

"Nobody had even considered that it might be there. They knew that the near side crust was thinner than the far side and that lava had flowed out into the lowlands billions of years ago. We gave them proof that the Moon has a molten core, but also that the near side mantle is still in a molten state. Professor McShane thinks that it has to do with tidal interactions with the Earth."

"Well it must be a jungle up there, because you can literally see the green using a telescope."

"The heat we found allows for more than just a jungle. It has allowed for a literal rain forest," said Billy, emphatically. "We now have rain up there."

"Rain? With a superstructure ceiling less than a few hundred feet up in the air? Impossible."

Billy just nodded. "At timed intervals, similar to the produce section at the supermarket, geysers rain water over the garden of Eden. They pump water deep down to where it is superheated and expelled back up to the surface. It sheds enough heat that it creates a warm rain. That is how we are keeping the garden of Eden warmed and watered. It's a paradise. You might have sacrificed your Lunar U diploma, but you saved the university."

T.J. closed his book and started to pack his bag. "The library is closing. I'm here every night trying to keep up with you guys. Do you realize that, with the Lunar U accelerated schedule, year-round school seven days a week, a cadet will complete the bachelor's degree requirements in two and a half years?"

"So you are taking so many classes in the hope of keeping up with us?"

"I am still holding out hope that they will let me graduate with my class at Lunar U. I make the request every quarter with a copy of my grades. With what I have learned from you, I think it might be time to send my appeal directly to Dr. Kevin Scott."

*****

T.J. Gillooley entered the room. Seeing Dr. Kevin Scott, he immediately walked over and shook his hand. "Thank you very much for agreeing to hear my case," he began. Then he noticed that the man sitting next to the Secretary of Science was not just an assistant. It was the President of the United States. T.J.'s face went ashen and he fell silent.

"Please, Mr. Gillooley, have a seat," said the President. He had wanted to meet this young man for a while. "I hope that I can put you at ease. I know your story and appreciate everything that you have done."

He could see a smile creep to the corners of T.J.'s mouth. "Thank you, Mr. President."

Stephen leaned forward over the table. "I would like to share a little story with you. Back when I was in college, my best friend and I competed fiercely in our academics, but we were also obstinate troublemakers. I say troublemakers, because we were always getting into serious scrapes. In truth, we were curious youths seeking out adventure and avenues for discovery. Sound familiar?"

T.J. leaned forward in kind and said with a smile, "If you are looking to hang out with me, you are welcome."

Stephen laughed. "That friend ended up throwing a large brick of sodium into the school's Olympic swimming pool and almost burned down the building. He was expelled." The smile fell from T.J.'s face.

Stephen continued, "Twenty years later, that same boy became the head of the chemistry department at that same university and is one of the most respected professors in the field."

After a moment of reflection, T.J. said, "Thank you for your encouragement, Mr. President, but I was still hoping to be able to finish what I started and graduate with my class at Lunar U."

"Yes, I know," said Stephen. "Let me ask you something. What do you see as the future of Lunar U?"

"It will be the leading research location for humanity. The boundaries of knowledge will be expanded at an unprecedented rate. Science won't know what hit it."

"That's a good answer," replied Stephen, "but not if Lunar U only offers an undergraduate education. Those best suited to research will want to stay. Those best suited to science won't ever want to leave. Lunar U has to become more than what it currently is. While I still have a year left in office, I want to insure that grand future. I am going to add a graduate education program at Lunar U. What do you think?"

T.J. could hardly sit still. "I think that is an outstanding idea. Sir, I would do anything for an opportunity like that!"

"Well, only if you graduate," remarked Stephen before granting the young man's wish. "Let's say you get back up there in time for the graduation ceremony of the first class. And so we don't waste all that energy getting you back there, afterwards you can just stay and participate in the new graduate program. They are going to need a few good teachers' assistants up there spreading their curiosity around!"

*****

Stephen watched the young man leave the room, before continuing his private conference with Kevin. "We are not out of the woods, yet."

"The paradigm worked like a charm," stated Kevin dismissively. "The space race took the bravado right out of the Chinese and Russians."

"They were brave enough to ignore the whole of the South American Alliance and take the northern part of Tierra del Fuego from Chile."

"But their move was before we could sign on and grow it into the full American Alliance Treaty."

"Which has held them to the peninsula," agreed Stephen, "but politics, plotting, and the game continue."

Kevin smirked. "The United States has become so technologically superior to them that the Chinese won't make a move."

"Maybe you are right," agreed Stephen, "but look at it through the eyes of our opponent. What chess move would you make next?"

Kevin was quiet for a few moments considering. "The attention of the whole world is on the advancements being made at Lunar U. They will likely never catch up as long as we have that and they don't."

"But we know that they are going to set up shop on the Moon soon," added Stephen.

"You were the one that invited them to the neighborhood," chided Kevin. "But they will never be able to settle in as grand a scale as us because they don't have the Phoenix Spaceport."

"So what would be your move?"

"They cannot hit the spaceport as our defenses around the elevator are too strong." Kevin tapped his temple as he thought. "They could try their own elevator at Everest, but it is not at the equator so the geosynchronous anchor in orbit wouldn't work. A space elevator can only be built at the equator, but technology doesn't exist to make a tether strong enough to get all the way to the ground except at Mt. Chimborazo where we are based."

"Currently, no technology exists," agreed Stephen, "so what would be your move."

"I guess I would be limited to going to the Moon on a much smaller scale at a much higher cost. It is not the best option, but it would save face."

A thought dawned on Kevin and he became excited and concerned. "But I wouldn't be going there for research!"

"Of course they aren't," stated Kevin. "We have to be ready for them."

*****

T.J. followed the captain of the shuttle crew through the new entryway airlock. He wanted to rush out ahead, telling them that he knew where he was going, but a group of cadets stood waiting to welcome and give them their introductory tour of the university.

T.J. saw his old accomplice and yelled out, "Liam, I'm back!"

"T.J." Liam came up and slugged him playfully in the shoulder. "Let's break you out of this tour and go down to find your old friends." The two left the group and rushed down the tunnel and through the university. "What took you so long? You told me two months ago that that you were coming right up."

"Can you believe that they made me do another six week round of army basic training?" stated T.J. "The order came down that everyone needed it before being allowed access to Lunar U."

Liam was nodding, knowingly. "Makes sense. We have been doing daily drills and weekly maneuvers outside Eden. It is like they expect an alien invasion or something. I've been given the rank of platoon sergeant, and I've got some bad news for you. You are in my platoon."

He again punched T.J. in the arm. "Dinner's finished and everyone will be at Luck Lake. Let's go."

Entering Eden took T.J.'s breath away. It was a warm, tropical environment. There was green everywhere he looked. Geysers could be seen spouting in the distance. While the trees were still young, he could see that everything was growing voraciously.

Luck Lake was the most incredible sight. Thousands of young adults swam, splashed around the shallows, or lounged on the beach. Numerous tiki huts running along the shore with long lines of cadets before them.

Liam nudged him and nodded toward the huts. "Those are ours. I suppose that you will want a piece of the action now."

T.J.'s attention was caught by the sound of a small child laughing. He turned to see the Commander and Professor Williams each holding the hand of an infant boy and swinging him into the water. Also recognizing T.J., they walked over.

"It is good to have you back, Cadet Gillooley," said the Commander. He reached down and picked up his boy. "I would like for you to meet our son. We thought about giving him the corny name of Adam, but my wife talked me into naming him Tim after you."

Professor Williams smiled broadly and added, "You owe me now. And you work for me, I hear. Let's see if we can harness some of that curiosity."

T.J. could not even talk. He could only smile. Qwerty. He was home.

ABOUT THE AUTHOR

Scott Blakely graduated from the University of Illinois with a Biochemistry degree. He manages a network of laboratories and enjoys the challenge of working with intelligent coworkers. Life is an adventure, science is the paradigm, and his writing is filled with imagination to inspire our future. Scott, his wife Darlene, and their children live just outside Chicago, IL. Visit with him at Philosophersweb.com.

www.ingramcontent.com/pod-product-compliance
Lightning Source LLC
Chambersburg PA
CBHW030136180626
46812CB00002B/707